Kalidasa

K.C. Ajayakumar (b.1964), recipient of Sahitya Akademi Translation Prize (2015) and Vishwa Hindi Samman (2018), has authored four novels in Malayalam and four in Hindi. Widely known as a consummate translator from Hindi into Malayalam, his primer on Malayalam grammar for Hindi readers won the Government of India Award (2000–01) for non-Hindi writers writing in Hindi. His doctoral thesis on Indian nationalist novels in Hindi is a pioneering effort. Apart from this novel, three more— *Tagore: A Novel, Sankaracharya* and *Satyavan Savitry*—have already been published in English translation.

Geetha Nair, the translator of this novel, has been teaching English, editing several books and translating from Malayalam into English for over three decades. Her translated books include *Tagore: A Novel, Sankaracharya* and *Satyavan Savitry*.

Also by the same author

Tagore: A Novel
Sankaracharya

Kalidasa

K.C. AJAYAKUMAR

Translated by
GEETHA NAIR

RUPA

Published by
Rupa Publications India Pvt. Ltd 2021
7/16, Ansari Road, Daryaganj
New Delhi 110002

Sales Centres:
Allahabad Bengaluru Chennai
Hyderabad Jaipur Kathmandu
Kolkata Mumbai

Copyright © K.C. Ajayakumar 2021

This is a work of fiction. All situations, incidents, dialogue and characters, with the exception of well-known historical and public figures mentioned in this novel, are products of the author's imagination and are not to be construed as real. They are not intended to depict actual events or people or to change the entirely fictional nature of the work. In all other respects, any resemblance to persons living or dead is entirely coincidental.

All rights reserved.

No part of this publication may be reproduced, transmitted, or stored in a retrieval system, in any form or by any means, electronic, mechanical, photocopying, recording or otherwise, without the prior permission of the publisher.

ISBN: 978-93-91256-14-2

First impression 2021

10 9 8 7 6 5 4 3 2 1

The moral right of the author has been asserted.

Printed by Nutech Print Services, Faridabad

This book is sold subject to the condition that it shall not, by way of trade or otherwise, be lent, resold, hired out, or otherwise circulated, without the publisher's prior consent, in any form of binding or cover other than that in which it is published.

1

As the fire raged, ready to engulf everything, Shambhu realized that he had to run. He could see the fire spread from tree to tree. The bowers covered by the climbers caught fire. The beasts in the forest fled with pitiful cries. With a confused uproar, the birds rose up from the branches in the hundreds. Some of the birds that had made their nests in the trees circled above, reluctant to leave their little ones in the nests.

At first it seemed to be an attractive sight. They were climbing trees, gathering fruits when the boys first noticed the fire. They watched the fire, spreading from dry grass and leaves to the climbers on the bowers. But soon the heat was too much and they started to retreat. The sight of wild animals running away from the fire frightened them. The heat became unbearable and they realized that the fire would engulf them soon. 'Run...' someone cried. The boys ran and Shambhu couldn't remember when he realized that he was alone. There was no time to stop and look for his friends. The fire was moving fast towards him and he had to run.

After some time he stopped...breathless and exhausted, he looked back. He saw the deer and the rabbits running. The strong wind helped the fire devour the trees in seconds...and the fire from the thickets was climbing up the trees.

No. There was no time to stand and look back. He had to run to save his life. Usually it's the wild animals that invoke fear, but now it was the fire they were fearful of. He saw some deer and two or three tigers running together as if they were in a race. They too knew that in that moment, their life was more precious than the hierarchies of the jungle.

Shambhu turned and started running towards the place where there were not many trees. The animals were also running in that direction. They knew where safety lay. He stopped when he reached a boulder of rocks to look back once again. The animals had not stopped there; they were running on between the rocks.

Shambhu climbed up the tallest boulder. He saw that the trees that grew in the crevices of the rocks had all shed their leaves. The surface of the rock was big and smooth. There was no chance of the fire spreading to that rock.

He looked around him. Below, the fire was still burning in the forest. He was parched. It was Shambhu's first time witnessing the tandava of the fire. He had seen the fire in the kitchen and dry leaves being burned in the compound near his house. He found it to be beautiful and enjoyed adding dry twigs to this fire. The sight around him now was beautiful...but it was a terrifying beauty. The flames that rose high into the sky invoked terror and not pleasure in his mind. He suddenly realized how far away from home he had run. His father and mother must be looking for him.

How would he reach home? It might be possible to reach home if he went back in the same direction. But he couldn't remember where they had gathered fruits, so he couldn't trace his steps back home. The fire continued to rage and destroy everything in its path. He looked around once again. The fire was on one side of the rock; the trees on the other side were safe, for now. The rock on which he was standing might prevent the fire from spreading to that side.

Smoke rose up to join the dark clouds scattered across the sky. The wind carried dry leaves up into the sky...some burnt and some still burning. The air was heavy with the deafening roars of wild animals caught in the fire. Shambhu sat down on the rock.

Had his friends managed to reach the ashram? Or had they also lose their way? Hid some of them gotten caught in the fire? Fear was rising in his mind. His house was very close to the forest... and it was surrounded by trees. Had the fire reached his house? The gurukul was next to his house, would he be able to go in that direction? No. The fire was still burning. He would not be able to go to his father and mother immediately. Tears welled up in his eyes.

He soon realized how exhausted he was from thirst and hunger. The sun was setting; it would soon be dark... How would he remain there all alone at night? Shambhu realized that no one would come and save him no matter how loudly he screamed for help.

Shambhu contemplated climbing down the rock. The sun had set and it was dark but the light from the fire remained. The sight of the flames glowing in the faraway sky terrified him. The embers that rose up seemed to be competing with the stars. It was horrifyingly beautiful. There would be lions and tigers and other wild animals everywhere...and Shambhu was not sure about where he had to go.

Shambhu sat looking at the fire for a long time. The fireflies he saw had a pure white shine. But the fire was different. It bore the colour of the Ashoka flowers as if strewn with vermillion. And the wind made the flames rise higher. He could hear the echo of bamboo bursting in the heat of the fire. Shambhu sat watching the burning leaves fly across the sky like glow worms and disappear into the darkness. They would never be able to compete with the stars...they will perish before they can float high up in the sky.

He lay down on the rock, looking at the stars twinkling in the sky. When one of the stars seemed to be falling, fear gripped him and he closed his eyes and lay face down. The fatigue caused by fear, sorrow, hunger and thirst soon overpowered him and he fell asleep.

The chirping of birds in the morning woke him up. The sun had not yet risen. Shambhu looked around and noticed that the destructive rage of the fire had subsided. Smoke rose from many places spiraling up like snakes. The sky was covered in this dark smoke. Would he be able to go home? He was extremely hungry. The fire had not spread to the other side of the rock where he was lying down. There were trees and plants and he might find some fruits that he could eat but he was afraid that there would also be wild animals in the area.

Shambhu prostrated before Goddess Earth and bowed before the sun.

He came down slowly, holding on to the sides of the rock. The forest on this side was denser than the one that had been destroyed by the fire. He climbed a tree and gathered a few fruits. He came back to the rock and ate them. As his thirst and hunger subsided he felt better, and more confident of facing the crisis.

Shambhu got down from the rock and started walking to the side of the forest that had been destroyed by the fire. Some of the trees were still burning and smoke was rising from the ground. At certain places the ground was too hot for him to walk on. The trunks of the trees that had fallen down were still smouldering. He walked around carefully and felt the heat engulfing him. Will it be dangerous? He could only walk where there had been a few trees. Everywhere else the tree trunks were still burning. The burnt bodies of many animals lay here and there. Many were only partially burnt and their bones were sticking out. The gruesome sight of some of the animals that lay trapped under the fallen trees and the piteous cries of the animals that came from all directions added to the terror in his mind. But he had to move on. The heat of the sun and the smoke made it unbearable for him to walk. He had no idea how long he would have to walk. When running away from the fire the previous day, he had not thought of the distance or the direction. Some tall trees and clumps of smaller trees still stood, resisting the heat. The wind blew and the ashes rose to the sky. It seemed as if he would be blinded by the ashes but fortunately, it was not hot.

By afternoon he had reached the slope of a hill. He felt that it could be the slope that stood on the northern side of his house. But when he looked down, terror gripped his heart. He must have followed the wrong direction. He could only see the deep, thick forest below him. This was not where his house had been. Now how would he reach home? He sat down looking at the endless sky and the row of mountains in the distance.

He managed to reach the correct place soon. The fire had destroyed everything. As all the trees, plants and climbers had been reduced to ashes; it was impossible to guess where his home was. There was a raised ground and some bamboo poles still smouldering. Trembling with fear, Shambhu searched for burnt human remains. He found none and heaved a sigh of relief.

He looked around. One tall tree still stood untouched. That was the saptaparni that stood near the house. The fire had not been able to destroy it. The hermitage had been completely destroyed but the lotus in the small lake near his house had escaped the fire. There was ash on the leaves and in the water. Some of the leaves were completely covered in ash. The wind had swept the ashes in the water to the side of the lake.

Many questions arose in his mind. Could his father and mother have escaped the fire? Where had the guru and the students gone? Who all had escaped? Where were the boys who had gone with him to pluck fruits in the forest?

Shambhu got into the pond. Moving the ashes to one side with his hands, he drank handfuls of water. Oh! It was such a relief! As he was about to turn back, something on the other side of the pond caught his attention. A lotus flower stood blooming there. The flower seemed unmindful of the destruction caused by the fire all around it. The drops of water on the leaves reflected the light of the sun. The flower moved slightly in the wind...beautiful, like hope blooming in the middle of despair!

Shambhu once again went to the place where his house had stood. Everything had been destroyed. Some pots and pans lay here and there. Everything was covered in ash. He thought of how his parents must have cried when they could not find him. Where were they now?

Shambhu examined the floor and the surroundings of his house once again. He could see some footprints there. Someone had been here after the fire had caused destruction. Nothing had escaped from the fire. The earthen cistern with the soaking writing leaves was the only thing left. The branches of the bakul tree had been burnt. The trunk was still smoking. Shambhu held the trunk and stood there for some time. There was nothing left for him here. He had to go. Everyone must have fled and sought safety. Would he be able to find his parents?

Shambhu walked over to the place where the hermitage used to be. Nothing remained anymore. Smoke rose from some places and the thatch and bamboo poles had all succumbed to the fire.

The boy sat on a stone in the courtyard. Hundreds of images went through his mind—him living happily with his parents, his mother attending to the affairs at home while his father got things ready for the hermitage. His father provided the hermitage with writing leaves and milk.

This was where he had played...where he had grown up. Somehow, he had never become a resident of the hermitage, maybe because his house was close by. Now there was no hermitage...and no house. Does he have anybody left? Where had his parents gone? Had the fire caught up to them? Shambhu's mind was in turmoil, riddled with anxiety and sorrow.

Where could he go now? His parents would be looking for him. They might think that he had been caught in the fire when they realize he wasn't with the other boys.

He couldn't decide what he should do and there was nobody to tell him what to do. It was this hermitage that had persuaded his father and mother to stay near it. The hermitage was built some distance away from the village in a beautiful place near the forest and his father had been employed by the hermitage. Now the hermitage was gone, and the thought that his parents might be gone too came as a shock to Shambhu.

Shambhu drank some more water from the lake. He wandered about there, unwilling to leave the place, even though he knew that he had to leave. There was no point in waiting there. So at last, with a heavy heart, he started walking. There was no definite path or direction that he decided to take. The fire could not have consumed the whole world and this forest had to end somewhere. Even if the fire had engulfed the whole forest, there had to be a place beyond... Shambhu started walking, choosing the places where the heat didn't burn his feet. He could see vultures circling in the sky and swooping down to the remains of the animals that had perished in the fire. Fear gripped his heart—he too could become prey to the vultures. He hoped they would leave him be as long as the carcasses were available. Shambhu took a stick that was still burning at one end. He should have something to protect himself!

Shambhu knew that he had to reach someplace where there were other people, before sunset. Will he be able to reach a village or a part of the forest that had escaped the fire before sunset? Because otherwise, he will be in trouble. He could become prey to wild animals or the vultures.

Before sunset, Shambhu reached a place where some greenery was left. As there were very few trees in that place, the fire had not spread. The dry grass had caught fire but it hadn't spread wide as there were no trees to burn. A few shrubs had also escaped the fire.

He could see the fields at a distance. There must be some people living there. Shambhu dug out some tubers that were almost ready to be harvested. He felt better as his hunger subsided. He walked on with the hope that he would soon reach a place where there will be people.

There was nobody in the fields. They must have gone home as the day was about to end. Leaving the fields, he walked along the footpaths. But soon he reached the forest. He should have walked in the opposite direction, but he had walked along the footpath. Shambhu started feeling terrified. Was there no end to this forest? As he walked further, he reached the banks of a river.

He remembered that he had once been here with his father. Yes, it was river Kshipra. His father had told him that people sometimes called it Shipra. When he had seen it for the first time then, the river had been brimming with water. The river had less water now, some parts of the river bank had turned into sandbanks.

Shambhu walked towards the sandbank. He knew that it was a dangerous place. It was near the forest and wild animals would come there to quench their thirst. It was likely that the animals would gather in this place because of the fire.

He had to leave here as soon as possible. He had heard that there were many pilgrim centers on the banks of rivers. If he could travel through this river he'd be able to reach one of those centers or a place where people lived. There could be temples or inns, and he'd be able to take shelter. That was the only way to safety. But how would he travel through the river?

He looked up and down the river bank. There he saw a tethered old raft. Fear was making him lose his mind, but there was no other way. He had to leave the place and go wherever the raft would take him.

He pushed the raft into the water. The sun was setting as he started his journey. He had nothing but a long stick with him, he hoped it would come to his use.

Drinking some water from the river, he sat there watching his raft sail along the current. As it became dark, he lay down. He was tired after walking the whole day and soon fell asleep.

He woke up sometime in the night to a quickened current. The moon had reached the middle of the sky. There was still a long time to go for the sun to rise. He closed his eyes again. He could hear the cries of the night birds and the hooting of owls from the forest. He had to overcome his fear and face whatever happened.

Shambhu woke up in the morning before the light of the sun had spread. The raft was moving fast. This fast flow of the water must have made people call it Kshipra, a shortened version of *Kshipragaami* which meant 'fast moving'. Shambhu sat, watching the trees that enveloped the river from either side. As the sun rose higher, he saw birds flying out in large numbers and a few animals that had come to the river to drink water.

He saw two or three people on the side of the river. The area was flat and some mechanism to draw water from the river to the fields had been set up with poles and boats. A few people were taking a bath in the river. Shambhu sat up, looking anxiously.

Shambhu lowered the stick he had taken with him into the water. It did not touch the bottom; the river was very deep. He tried to row his raft towards the shore but the current was too strong for him to negotiate. His raft was moving faster than he had expected.

He could see people bathing in the river ahead of him. And beyond that, he could also see the dome of a temple. Relief spread over him as he thought he could seek shelter in the temple.

The man bathing in the river seemed to be an ascetic with long hair and a beard. Shambhu raised his stick and called out. He tried to direct the raft towards the shore, but the man did not see him. The ascetic was engaged in dipping his body in the river and offering water to the sun god. Shambhu tried to catch his attention again by calling out, 'Swami...Swami...' but it was in vain. His raft went past the bathing ghat before he could attract the attention of the ascetic or others on the river bank.

The boy sat disillusioned, looking at the receding ghat. Then he started waiting for the next place where he could find someone to help him.

As the sun rose higher, it became unbearably hot. The shores now looked different from the place from where he had started. There were no tall trees; only a few shrubs grew here and there. In some places it was just a few rocks and sand. The river seemed to flow endlessly. No people and no animals were visible. After some time he lay face down; he could bear the heat of the sun for some time. Then he tried pouring some water on his body to beat the heat. When he felt hungry and thirsty, he drank the water from the river.

His raft continued to move ahead between the forests on either side. The flow became faster now and then and the breadth of the river became vast. He saw smaller rivers join Kshipra. When he saw men bathing and washing on the banks, he shouted to attract their attention. Some of them heard him and said some things in reply. He couldn't understand what they were saying. He thought they wanted to save him, but without a boat, they could not come to him. None of them would brave the deep waters of the river to save a boy, after all, they couldn't have known the dire situation he was in.

Shambhu fell into an exhausted sleep that night. In the morning he saw that he was passing through an area where people lived. But the river had become even wider. There were some boats near the banks. Some were moving in the water while others were tethered to the banks.

He was too tired to even sit up on the raft. He just lay there face downwards and passed his third night on the river.

But Shambhu was not fated to drift endlessly on the river or get lost in the waters of the sea. Some men in a boat that were nearby, saw a raft made of three or four pieces of wood with a boy lying on it. The vultures were circling above them. The men could not ignore the misery on the face of a mere boy lost in the middle of the river. They decided that they would rescue him if he was still alive. They brought their boat near the raft and shifted the boy onto their boat.

Shambhu was unconscious and they tried to revive him. They sprinkled some water on his face. As the boy opened his eyes there were two or three anxious faces looking at him. He was not strong enough to talk and closed his eyes again. The men who had saved him moved away to row the boat and a man who looked like an ascetic came and sat near him.

The man looked at him in wonder. His hair, body and head were covered in ash. One of the men told him how they had seen his raft and rescued him.

The ascetic placed his palm on the boy's forehead as if to infuse life and strength into him. Slowly the boy regained consciousness and was able to talk. They fed him milk and some food and soon he was strong enough to sit up and talk.

'Where do you come from, my son?' the ascetic asked him as he ate.

Though he could not follow the language fully, Shambhu understood what the man was asking. It was similar to the language that they spoke at the gurukula.

Shambhu did not know what to say. He could not say which place he belonged to because his village did not have a particular name. The only thing that he could mention was the hermitage of Guru Devasraya and that it was far away from Ujjaini. He knew that his land was known as Malava. Most of the boys in the gurukula came from the villages nearby.

That gurukula was the only landmark he could mention. Shambhu remembered his guru telling them that Sanskrit, the language of the Gods, was known all over this ancient land. This man before him was an ascetic. He would know that language. So Shambhu tried to explain: 'I started off in a raft from someplace in Malava two or three days ago. My house was about 12 miles away from that river, near the hermitage of Guru Devasraya. A devastating fire spread in the forest four days ago. I had gone to the forest with my friends to gather fruits and vegetables. As the fire spread, we ran to escape from it. I got separated from my friends along the way. I could walk back home only after a day. But I couldn't find anybody there. The hermitage and my house had been reduced to ashes. I walked aimlessly from there. I got an old abandoned raft and traversed the river but I could not reach any shore. I do not know how I got on this boat.'

The ascetic was surprised to hear Shambhu talk in Sanskrit. As he questioned him further, it was clear that the boy had learned Sanskrit from Guru Devasraya. The monk held the boy's head in his hands and looked at his face. Then he placed his hands on his head in blessing.

The boat went on its way throughout the day. Just before sunset, it reached a ghat where many things were unloaded from the boat and much was loaded onto it. Shambhu watched all this in wonder. The monk told him that his name was Shalibhadra and that he was going to a place called Champa, near Kashi.

The boat started sailing again after sunset. He was told that they would reach Kashi the next morning.

The boat reached a small ghat in the morning. The ascetic told Shambhu that he was going to the temple in Champa village and that the holy city of Kashi was near it. 'I will stay here for a few days. I have some spiritual matters to discuss with Shivasoma, the pujari at the Kali temple here. Then I also have to see some learned men in Kashi,' he explained.

The boat went on its way after leaving Shambhu and the monk there. It was with great gratitude that Shambhu bid farewell to the men on the boat.

He took a dip in the water and bowed before the Sun God reciting the *Surya Gayatri*.

He felt better when he had washed away the ash that covered his head and body. But he had no cloth except the one he was wearing. He washed the cloth and wore it as he got out of the river. He remembered his mother. She was not with him now to tell him not to wear wet clothes and to remind him to wipe his head carefully after a bath. Tears started flowing from his eyes. The monk held the boy close and comforted him. He could understand what was going on in the boy's mind.

They both walked towards Kali temple.

Shambhu prostrated before Goddess Kali, wearing his wet cloth. He was now an orphan. He did not know where his father and mother were; he did not know whether he would ever meet them again. His mind seemed to tell him that Goddess Kali was his only support now. He submitted to Goddess Kali completely.

As he got up, the ascetic was standing before him with prasad from the temple in his hands. Tears still fell from the boy's eyes.

'Don't cry, my boy, Goddess Kali will look after you,' the monk said.

As he received the prasad from him, Shambhu asked him, 'Is this the place named Champa that you spoke of?'

'Yes,' he said. 'This is a small village named Champa, near Kashi, a part of the state of Kashi. Kashi is a holy place as well as a famous trading centre. It is on the banks of the holy Ganga. Your raft came to the Charmanawati River through the Kshipra. From there it came to the Yamuna and finally reached the Ganga. It was a really long journey, my boy. It was only with the blessings of the Goddess that a small boy like you managed to remain safe on such a raft for so long. You crossed many areas where people lived. But no one came forward to save you. You traversed wild forests and deep waters. No wild animal in the forest or the creatures in the water attacked you. The sailors told me that when they saw you on the raft, vultures were circling the sky above you,' Shalibhadra explained to him.

Shambhu felt relieved. Goddess Kali's blessings had saved him, first from the fire and then from the many dangers that awaited him. Now he had left his Malava and reached a place so far away. If his parents had escaped the fire, they would still be in Malava. Here, he was an orphan.

'Guro, I am all alone now. I cannot decide what to do, I am worried,' Shambhu said.

'We all come to this world alone, my boy and we will be alone when we leave. It is karma, duties that make each one of us bound to a particular life. Pray to the Goddess to relieve you from the bonds of duties. Try to understand this world and the effulgence that illuminates this universe,' Shalibhadra advised him.

'Swami, allow me to be your disciple. I have heard from my guru that the way to salvation is through knowledge.'

'Anyone can acquire knowledge. But it requires a lot of hard work and penance. Real wisdom is certainly the path that leads to salvation.'

'I am ready to undertake any penance. Accept me as your servant and show me the path to wisdom. I desire to study the vedas and the vedangas. My mother and father used to talk about it,' Shambhu said.

'Don't be my servant, be the servant, the dasa, of Goddess Kali. The divine mother will grant you whatever you need. She is the embodiment of mercy and the one who provides wisdom. Try to know the Goddess and all wisdom will come to you.'

The priest in the Kali temple was Shivasoma, and Shalibhadra introduced Shambhu to him. He explained how the boatmen had found Shambhu on the Ganga and told him about the boy's condition.

Shambhu stayed in the temple with Shalibhadra for a few days. He would get up in the morning and help clean the temple and the surroundings. Shivasoma, the priest, came to be impressed by the boy as the days passed.

But the deep look of sorrow on Shivasoma's face troubled Shambhu. One day he asked Shalibhadra about it: 'Guro, I have often seen Swami Shivasoma weep in sorrow. Do you know what is causing him such sorrow?'

Shalibhadra looked at Shambhu. 'Shivasoma stays near the temple. He lived with his wife and two children—his son Jayasoma and daughter Malini. It was Jayasoma who helped his father in the matters of the temple. Then one day, Jayasoma did not return with the sheep that he had taken to graze. The sheep reached home at sunset without the boy. They feared that something might have happened to him as two sheep were also missing from the herd. Did some wild animals attack Jayasoma and the sheep? There had been instances of leopards attacking sheep. The people searched the whole area with torches and drums throughout the night but they could not find Jayasoma. The next day the remains of Jayasoma's body were found in the forest.'

Shalibhadra paused before continuing. 'Jayasoma was your age. The death of his son still causes deep sorrow to Shivasoma. He feels that life is meaningless. But what can he do? His daughter Malini is a small girl. Bringing her up and getting her settled is their responsibility. No one takes the sheep to graze any longer.'

Shambhu listened in silence to what Shalibhadra said. He felt pity and compassion for Shivasoma.

Shambhu was already helping Shivasoma at the temple. But now he felt that it was not enough. Shivasoma did not have the capacity to feed and look after him. He felt that it was wrong to burden Shivasoma so.

One day Shambhu approached Shivasoma and said, 'I can understand your sorrow. No one can replace the son you have lost. But please consider me as your son.'

Shivasoma blessed the boy by keeping his hand on his head and said, 'Shambhu, I can understand what you are thinking. But I do not think that your life should be wasted in a village like this. You are capable and intelligent. And your abilities should benefit the whole world.'

'Swami,' said Shambhu, 'It was only by chance that I came to this temple. Please permit me to stay here as Kalidasa, the servant of Kali. It is also my duty to help you in whatever way I can. Please do not stop me.'

Shalibhadra, who had been listening to the conversation, now came forward. 'Isn't it better for Shambhu to do some work rather than spend his time at the temple? He could do something to help you. It has been a long time since your sheep have been taken out to graze. Don't you have to look after them properly? How long will you keep them in the cages? Don't think of Shambhu as an outsider. You can see it as each helping the other.'

'As you say,' said Shivasoma.

Thus, Shambhu's daily routine was fixed. After worshipping Goddess Kali in the morning, he spent his time with Shalibhadra learning the vedas and the upanishads. Then he took the sheep out for grazing and came back a few hours before sunset. Shivasoma's wife, Arundhati would pack some food for him to eat at lunchtime. By the time he came back, Shalibhadra also would have returned after going to different places. He used to go to the palace of the king of Kashi and the gurukula there. He had to meet the other scholars and hold discussions with them on different philosophical matters. Shambhu would then perform the evening prayers and visit the temple with him and then take rest. But this time of rest was really the time for Shambhu to increase his knowledge. Both Shalibhadra and Shivasoma taught him grammar and the etymology of words.

Shambhu spent his time at the temple of Kali and its surroundings as the servant of the Goddess—Kalidasa.

2

As per usual, Shambhu took the herd of sheep to the side of the hill. The animals walked in a group without straying, eating shoots of grass and shrubs on the way. As they reached a vast open area, Shambhu left the sheep to graze and sat on a rock under a tree.

Scenes from the past passed through his mind. Here he was, grazing sheep in a strange place. He was not sure whether his parents were alive and they didn't know if he was alive. They must have thought that he too had been caught in the fire that had consumed the forest. In a way, he too should have been caught in that fire. He was not sure how he had escaped. If what Swami Shalibhadra said was true, everyone had a destiny that had been decided beforehand. Death claims one only after fulfilling this. Yes, there must be some duties that he was destined to fulfil.

It was just a spark of fire that had fallen in some corner of the forest that led to his escape on the raft. What was the power that brought him to this place? In a way it could be said that it was the water that flowed through the rivers Kshipra, Charmanawati, Yamuna and Ganga that brought him here. The amount of water in those rivers, the depth of the rivers, the bends and curves in the course of the rivers must have controlled the speed of his journey. The amount of water in the river must have been decided by the rainfall somewhere at some time. If the flow of the river had been faster, he would have reached some other land. Then his life would have been different. But that did not happen as he was destined to reach here.

Now he was a help for the family of Shivasoma, the priest. Their son was fated to spend only a short time of his life with his parents. But nature had now sent Shambhu here to fill the vacuum. A boy who had been living with his parents and studying under Rishi Devasraya in a forest far away on the banks of river Kshipra had now come to be a support for them.

But there were moments when Shambhu's mind wavered. Was it his destiny to be a shepherd in this village? Goddess Kali was helping him earn wisdom under Guru Shalibhadra. He gathered knowledge from the pilgrims who frequented the temple. All that knowledge was prompting him to leave the village. There was a treasure of knowledge and sights that awaited him outside the bounds of the village. Cities, hermitages in the forests, huge mountains, rivers, seas, ports and different lifestyles; all this was waiting for him.

The people who came here talked about different countries. Many had talked about Koushambi and Prayag. Shambhu listened carefully when someone talked about the road that started from Prayag and reached Hastinapura after passing through Kanyakubja. He had heard about Hastinapura. Guru Desavsraya had told them about the kings of the Kuru dynasty who ruled there and about the war between the Pandavas and the Kouravas. Hastinapura was the capital of the Kuru dynasty. He had nurtured a desire to visit that city. As he listened to the men talking about the variety of sights that different places offered, he felt a desire to experience it all.

Far away in the north there was a huge, snow-covered mountain, the Himalaya. Snow... At first he had no idea of how the solid form of water would look like. Then when particles of snow also fell with the rain, it was his father who had gathered some of it and showed it to him. Now when he heard of a mountain covered with such snow, he wanted to see it.

He had also heard about the highway that led from Mathura

to the vast river named Sindhu and the city of Patala. This road passed through desert land with not a blade of grass in sight. So many different types of lands! Shambhu failed to understand how there could be so much variety in nature.

He had already noticed that many of the plants and trees that grew here were not seen in the forest near his house. Even the soil was different. The mountains had a different type of beauty. There many trees had red leaves that gave the impression of the forest being on fire. But here most of the leaves were yellow. Many people talked about the mountain ranges and huge rivers of different places. The Ganga joined the ocean at some distance from here, and there stood the famous commercial city of Thamralipti. There, beyond the Gangetic valley and the ranges of mountains, was the city of Pragjyotishpura, the abode of Devi Kamakhya.

By afternoon when the sun had reached the zenith, Shambhu was no longer in the shade of the tree. He looked at the sheep. It was an open area and so wild animals did not usually come there. The sheep also knew that they should not wander far. So they were all within his sight.

Shambhu noticed that the grass had started wilting. It had been many days since it had rained there. And there was no chance of rain for some time to come. Summer had come. The grass that stood drooping now would regain some gloss when the sun went down. But the next day when the heat of the sun increased, they would droop again. They would be able to regain their strength like that for a few more days. Then they would be so weak that the moonlight would fail to restore their life. As days pass, this meadow would consist only of brownish grass. Then it would be useless to bring the sheep here. He would have to gather the thorny plants that grew in the shade or the leaves of some forest trees and give it to them in their hold. Shambhu was thinking ahead. He could see the beginning of the dry season.

He heard somebody shout 'Kalidasa' from far away. He thought it was a cuckoo calling in a sweet voice. In nature, did all the sounds echo in the same way? The tenderness of the voice seemed to mingle with nature as it resounded. If he replied to that call, he felt that it would be a jarring note here, where only the murmur of the wind and cooing of the birds could be heard.

Shambhu was surprised to realize that he had recognized and responded to that name. He had been used to the name Shambhu. When he came here and sought refuge in the temple of Kali, he became a dasa...a servant of Kali. Now that he had become attached to the temple, he got used to being called Kalidasa.

Shambhu could see Shivasoma and his daughter coming up the hillside. They were coming with the food for him. The sheep had eaten their fill of grass and leaves. There was a stream on one side and they drank the clear water from there. But the stream will dry up soon too. The water level had gone down and the flow had become weak.

They reached the shade of the tree and placed the vessels on the ground. Malini went around petting the lambs and talked playfully with him.

Shambhu called out to the herd and started walking to the base of the hill. They all followed him. Shivasoma also went with him. He left them there to drink the water and came back to the shade of the tree after washing his hands.

After he had finished his lunch, he left the herd under the care of Shivasoma and Malini and walked into the forest with an axe. He had to gather some firewood for the temple.

Shambhu walked around looking for dry branches. He spotted a huge tree, covered with climbing plants near the path, with a low withered branch.

As he started cutting, he realized that it was a strong branch. He felt that it would be easier to push it down with the weight of his body.

Shambhu shifted his position to the tip of the branch. He could hold on to the upper branch. The branch would break with his weight along with a few strokes of the axe. Once the dry branch fell down, he could lower himself down as he was holding on to the upper branch.

Shambhu started cutting the branch enthusiastically.

~

Maharaja Govindavarma and his minister Manadeva had tried every means to find a suitable bridegroom for Princess Vidyothama. Everybody had approved of the prince of Koushambi. But the princess declared that he had no knowledge of philosophy and he left humiliated.

The king and queen tried to make their daughter understand that she should not be so adamant. But Vidyothama refused to listen to them. Everyone in the palace admitted defeat before the obstinacy of the princess.

Manadeva, the minister, had long cherished a hope to get the princess married to his son Sonabhadra. But he did not dare speak about it to the king. When the princess kept refusing every suitor with disdain, the king agreed to get her married to anyone she liked, whoever that was. This revived the hopes in the minister's mind. His family had always stood firm with the royal dynasty of Kashi. His own father had also been the chief minister of Kashi. But the close association with the royal family never progressed to any familial relationship. Manadeva now started dreaming of his son getting married to the princess and becoming the king of Kashi after the death of the present maharaja. But Manadeva did not have the courage to reveal his desire to the king. He was quite aware of the deficiencies in his son as well as the abilities of the princess. If anyone challenged his son, the young man would certainly run away without accepting the challenge. He had no inkling of what philosophy was. Compared to the princess, his personality paled.

Hence it was after a lot of consideration that Manadeva placed such a proposal before the king, through the court jester Bahuka. Strangely enough, the king agreed to it. But as soon as the princess declared the conditions in the court, Manadeva started having nightmares about the humiliation that his son was going to face. He coached his son on many subjects before bringing him to the court.

The court announcer read out the conditions before the questions were asked. When it was announced that if the suitor failed to answer the questions satisfactorily, he would be given a 'gift'—his head would be shaved, his face branded and he would be paraded around the town on a donkey—the minister became agitated. He consoled himself with the possibility of the special consideration his son coud get because he was the minister's son. But as soon as the princess started asking questions, the young man went pale. She had asked only two or three questions but all those with some common sense realized that the answers that he gave were all foolish.

There was no way of escape from the 'gift' that had been offered. Though the king asked his daughter to show some leniency as he was the son of the minister, the princess insisted on the conditions being followed.

It was then that the minister decided to teach the princess a lesson. He decided to find a fool and present him as a very learned person. The man would be taught the answers to all the questions that the princess usually asked. The minister decided to get the greatest fool for this. His heart had ached to see Sonabhadra paraded around the town on a donkey with his head shaved and face darkened. So he, along with a few friends, set out to look for the greatest fool in the world.

~

The minister and his companions were intrigued to see Shambhu cutting the branch on which he was seated. Deciding among themselves that he was a real fool, they approached him.

'Hey! What are you doing?' one of them asked and laughed aloud.

Shambhu was surprised. The men appeared to be from the king's palace. Why had they come to this forest? Anyway, Shambhu did not like the way he was questioned. Their expression seemed to suggest that he was doing something foolish. They were trying to ridicule him. Shambhu started getting angry.

He asked, 'Why? Can't you see what I am doing?'

'Yes, we can. That is why we asked. Who does something so foolish?' Manadeva asked.

Shambhu felt that he must be joking. 'Isn't it that the person who cuts the branch should decide how it should be cut? I need some dry wood. So I am cutting,' he said.

'That may be so. But why would anyone cut the branch on which they are seated?' asked one of the men with Manadeva.

'Is that so? I like to do it this way,' Shambhu replied.

'All right, tell me your name,' Manadeva asked.

He said, 'Kalidasa,' and continued with his work.

The men looked at one another and nodded their heads agreeing that this was the man they were looking for.

'You must come with us immediately,' Manadeva said to Kalidasa.

'Where?' he asked.

'To the palace,' he was told.

Shambhu was apprehensive. Why were they taking him to the palace? He'd never had anything to do with the palace. He had not even been near the palace.

'Why should I come to the palace?' he asked. 'Is cutting the dry branch of a tree such a great crime?'

'The princess wants to see you,' said one of the men with a smile.

'Why does the princess want to see me?' asked Shambhu.

'She is going to marry you,' replied the man.

'Why? Have all the other men in this country decided to be ascetics?' asked Kalidasa.

'You need not know all that. You must come with us. You will lack nothing there. Here, take this gold coin as a present in advance,' said the one who looked like the leader and held out a gold coin.

Shambhu looked at the gold coin and the man who was holding it out to him. He had heard that gold coins were given out from the palace. He was seeing one for the first time. But he could not go with them. He had to be back to take the sheep home, otherwise, they would all be worried.

'All right, I will come tomorrow,' he said.

'No, no. You have to come with us now. Here, I will give you one more coin,' he held out two coins. Shambhu noticed that one of the men had his hand on the hilt of the sword. He seemed to say that if Shambhu refused to go with them, he would have to use it.

He was seeing gold coins for the first time, they looked attractive, but Kalidasa did not want to go to the palace just for that. He did not think that there was anything great in possessing gold coins. But their weapons would be sharp. He knew that it was impossible for him to win against those who held power. What he needed to use here was his intelligence. It seemed to him that the men had some secret mission. He would go with them and find out what they wanted.

Shambhu left the axe stuck on the tree and got down.

The men left with Shambhu.

Shambhu changed beyond recognition when he was taken to the palace of Kashi. They had dressed him up in royal clothes and a turban.

Kalidasa had decided to act his part to perfection. He must watch carefully what was going to take place there. He might be able to see the burning embers of pride and ego flowering out in the corridors of power as well as time exercising its brutal power on it. *'If the princess who has grown up in the lap of luxury is full of ego, she should suffer the consequences and come to know what real life is. Or even if I have to play the role of a spectator there, I can take it as a chance to witness some comedy,'* he thought.

Still there was something that troubled his mind. People who were now his own in the village of Champa would think that he too had been attacked and killed by some wild animals as had happened to Shivasoma's son.

Kalidasa was accorded a seat in the assembly as if he were a prince who had come as a guest.

Maharaja Govindavarma arrived in the assembly accompanied by his retinue. Minister Manadeva welcomed everybody.

'Maharaj, a new guest has come to our state today. Kalidasa, who has come from far away Kushavati, is a great scholar. He has heard of the conditions regarding the swayamvara of Princess Vidyothama and has come ready to participate in it. He is the foremost scholar in any branch of philosophy. He has immense knowledge of logic and Vedanta. He is still young, though a vastly learned scholar. He has defeated many great philosophers in arguments. If he wins in this contest, it will be fortunate both for him and our princess.'

Kalidasa got up and bowed before the assembly.

Princess Vidyothama soon arrived.

The minister made the announcement: 'Princess Vidyothama, the daughter of Maharaja Govindavarma will now test the knowledge of this young man. If he fails in the test, his hair will be shaved off, face darkened and he will be paraded on the streets of the city on a donkey and then forced to leave the country.'

The assembly was silent. All of them must have felt sad thinking of the misfortune that was to befall another young man. They had already seen many great scholars admitting defeat before the princess. Many of them felt that this young man, still in his adolescence, should not have come to this country.

The minister continued, 'But if this young man replies to all the questions in an appropriate manner, our princess will wed this man on the seventh day from now.'

The assembly welcomed the announcement with applause.

'The princess has laid out some more conditions. She has decided to ask questions today using only gestures. He has to reply in the same way. The court scholar, Pushpadanta, will decide whether the answers are correct.'

'Let the debate start,' the king announced.

'Do you agree with the conditions?' asked the minister turning to Kalidasa.

'Yes,' he replied.

'If you are defeated, you should be ready to accept the punishment that has been announced. It should not lead to any friction between the countries,' the king warned him.

'Okay,' he agreed.

'Let it begin,' the minister said.

All eyes were on the princess. What would she ask today?

The princess stood up and raised one finger of a hand.

Now everybody turned their attention to Kalidasa. The princess had asked the question...or had said something. Now he had to understand that and give a suitable answer.

Kalidasa thought for a while. The raising of that one finger could mean many things. It could mean that she was planning to ask only one question or it could be something related to the exalted heights of vedantic knowledge. So what he said will not be important; but how he analysed it would be of great significance. He did not have the freedom to explain what his answer meant. It was those who forcibly brought him there who would decide upon the meaning and explanation of his answers. Pushpadanta had told him what the princess would ask in the assembly and had taught him the gestures that he should show as answers. So he did not have to think much.

Kalidasa raised two fingers thinking, '*Let them decide whatever they want*,' pretending, with a smile, that he had given the correct answer and defeated the princess.

There was a look of surprise on the face of the princess. Seeing that, all those who were present in the assembly clapped their hands. Kalidasa was astonished. Even though he himself was not sure what his gesture meant, all the others had understood something or they were pretending that they had understood something great. They had given some significant meaning to the sign of two that he had shown.

As Pushpadanta stood up, the princess and Kalidasa sat down. Kalidasa waited with curiosity to hear what he was going to say.

'Words are inadequate in praising the deep wisdom of the princess,' he began. 'The princess does not bother to speak about worldly pleasures or about anything that provides momentary gratification. She has laid bare before us the spiritual essence of this universe. She said, "The essence of this universe is one. It is a single power that controls the universe and leads it to greater heights. But such an achievement is not easy to gain. Understanding the real essence of the universe and realizing its unity is as difficult a task as climbing a steep mountain at one stretch without taking a break to rest.'

The assembly broke into even louder applause. They shouted for the greater glory of their Princess Vidyothama.

Pushpadanta continued, 'I fail in trying to shower praise on this young man who has come from Kushavati. While our princess raised a perpetual truth before our eyes, Kalidasa went on to show some truth that is equal to it or even greater. He does not refute what the princess has said. But he says, "The power that rules this universe is one but also two. The cosmic power becomes complete only when Shiva and Shakthi come together. Neither Shiva without Shakthi nor Shakthi without Shiva has an existence. The existence of this cosmos is based on the correlation between Shiva and Shakthi or the concept of Ardhanarishwara, the deity in the form of half man and half woman. Still, it is not possible to say that Shiva and Shakthi are definitely two different entities." Hence this young man has explained the essence of the power of the universe by adding to the concept that the princess has presented. This country has never seen two such wise minds before this. Pushpadanta here salutes Kalidasa.'

There was a roar of applause from those who had assembled there.

Kalidasa could not contain his surprise. He remembered what his guru used to say: 'No work in this world is meaningless. No action ever goes in vain. No aspect ever fails to signify something. Everything attains a special significance according to people's logic and intelligence as well as the differences in place and time.'

Pushpadanta continued, 'The princess will ask more questions. If the young man can give suitable answers to these, he will be given the title of *Jnanasarvabhouma* (Omniscient). This is the decision of the king.'

The king nodded his head agreeing with what Pushpadanta

had said. The princess got up. This time she raised her hand with all the five fingers spread out.

This was strange. Kalidasa suspected whether she was asking him to read her palm. But he could not waste any time in thinking. He stood up. She might be saying that the power of the hand lay in all the five fingers together. It was possible that, as Pushpadanta had done earlier, he might find deeper meanings in this also. They could attach whatever meaning they wanted, it didn't matter to Kalidasa. Kalidasa drew a circle in the air.

'Excellent! Well done!' Pushpadanta was on his feet immediately shouting in excitement. 'The princess has said that the one power in the universe remains as the five elements in any body. What a magnificent idea!'

The men in the assembly clapped and they praised the extraordinary intelligence of the princess again and again.

When the uproar subsided, Pushpadanta spoke, 'What the young man has said is even more significant. He has said that all this is only a part of the supreme power that fills this whole cosmos. We have seen so many great scholars who have come from different parts of the world. They take days to think of an answer to the questions that our princess asks. And still their answers were always foolish. But here is a young man who instantly answers the questions that our princess asks only through gestures. There are innumerable wise men in this ancient land. But we are indeed blessed by the good deeds we have performed in previous lives to be able to see such a great man.'

Kalidasa was embarrassed to listen to such words of praise for him. What you see in this world is not as important as how you see it. Those who had found his way of cutting a branch by sitting on it a foolish action were now declaring his foolish gestures as the greatest wisdom in the world. 'Yes, one can pronounce that the shadow on the face of the moon has destroyed the beauty of the moon; it can also be said that it is that shadow that adds to the beauty of the moon,' Shambhu's mind reminded him.

The maharaja got up from his throne and approached Kalidasa. He patted the boy on the shoulder in appreciation. Then he was led to a seat near the throne. Kalidasa noticed that the princess was blushing deeply. This created a sense of fear in his mind. He came with the men as there was no way of escape. It seemed just a joke till now. But now he knew that the situation was becoming serious. Now he might be forced to marry the princess. He had to find a way to escape from there.

The king spoke, 'This young man, Kalidasa, has proved his mettle in the intellectual discussion that he had with the princess. His wisdom has been revealed before me and this assembly. So the marriage between the princess and Kalidasa will take place on the seventh day from today. Till then he will be provided with all the facilities for a comfortable stay in the palace. Our messengers will go to Kushavathi today itself. We wish that his parents will be able to come here for the wedding.'

Soon the assembly dispersed. Kalidasa tried to talk to the minister and Pushpadanta. But they kept themselves away from the young man. Kalidasa was given a room in the palace. He was busy thinking of ways to escape from there. The men who had brought him there, who had promised to send him back by evening, were nowhere to be seen. It was already time for the evening prayers. Guru Shalibhadra and Shivasoma would be looking for him. He had not been able to leave any hint about what had happened to him. If he did not escape now, he might never be able to do so. He would be attached to the palace. He would either be married to the princess or imprisoned when the soldiers who went to Kushavathi came back with the information that there was no such prince in that land. He had to escape from there before either of these happened.

Kalidasa stood looking out of the window. He noticed the princess crossing the garden and coming towards him along with her companions. He knew that he had to reveal the truth to the princess without wasting any time. It would be better to behave like a fool since that had been the impression created in the minds of those who had brought him there.

Kalidasa came out of the room. Vidyothama greeted him bashfully.

'You did not give me the present that you had promised,' said Kalidasa.

'What present?' asked the princess in surprise.

'While we were in the assembly, didn't you say that you will give me one gold coin?' Kalidasa asked.

'No, I didn't say so,' Vidyothama said.

'Then why did you do this?' Kalidasa asked raising his finger as the princess had done in the assembly.

Vidyothama was confused. 'What are you saying?' she asked.

'The men who forcibly brought me here from the forest gave me two gold coins. That is why I told you that I wanted two gold coins,' Kalidasa said, raising two fingers as he had done in the assembly in reply to the gesture of the princess.

Vidyothama sensed that something was amiss. 'Did you say that you were forcibly brought here from the forest? Who did it?'

'I had left the sheep to graze and had climbed a tree to cut some firewood. They made me come down and instructed me to do as they said in the palace. For that they gave me two gold coins. They threatened to kill me if I refused to obey them. They also promised to give me some more when I went back home.'

The princess understood what had happened. As she looked closely at the young man before her, she realized that his body did not look like that of a prince. She realized that she was being cheated.

'When I raised my hand, why did you draw a circle in the air?' she asked him.

'You said you would give this much of money, but I replied that I wanted this much,' Kalidasa explained raising his hand first and then drawing a big circle with both hands.

'Who brought you here from the forest?' Vidyothama asked.

'Her Highness, the minister and the man who explained the meaning of the gestures that you and I showed and there were two or three others also,' Kalidasa tried to open a way of escape from there.

'Where did you get these clothes that you are wearing now?' the princess asked.

'Those who brought me here gave them to me. They are beautiful, I am seeing such clothes for the first time in my life,' Kalidasa perfected the appearance of a fool.

The princess now realized that they had succeeded in presenting a fool as a wise man before her. They were trying to fool her. She knew that it had been caused by her own carelessness. She was angry with herself. She realized that Pushpadanta had trapped her by suggesting that she ask questions through gestures.

If this man remained here any longer, she would have to marry him. It was a punishment cooked up by the ministers to counter her insistence on getting married only to a very wise man. It was fortunate that she had come to know of it on time.

'You must leave the country immediately. If you are seen anywhere in Kashi, you will be punished with death. I will make sure that the same punishment is meted out to those who brought you here, they cannot get away with fooling the king. You can go now,' Vidyothama said.

Kalidasa smiled inwardly. A man can rise to glory and fall

to insignificance within seconds. He had been a shepherd till that afternoon. Then he became a prince. Soon afterwards he became a wise man and the prospective bridegroom for the princess of Kashi. The sun hadn't even set yet and he was going to be the shepherd boy once again. The man who had been the minister in the assembly and the learned scholar of this country may not continue to hold those positions for long. They could get their hair shaved off and be paraded on the streets with darkened faces. Oh! What variety of incidents can happen between sunrise and sunset each day!

As it had become dark, no one noticed the princely clothes that he was wearing. Even if someone noticed them, they would only show him respect thinking he was a member of the royal family. The incidents in the assembly had not become public.

Kalidasa walked fast, looking for the way to the Kali temple in Champa.

3

Kalidasa was very careful finding his way to Champa. He should not fall into the hands of those conspirators. It was only during the last quarter of the night that he reached the temple. Even then Shalibhadra and Shivasoma were weeping, thinking that Kalidasa had met with an untimely end. They were making plans to gather more people and search the forest for him in the morning. How happy and relieved they were to see Kalidasa. Kalidasa showed them the royal clothes that he was wearing and described all that had happened to him.

Kalidasa was happy that he could come back to his own life without getting entangled in the webs of power and wealth. Shivasoma and Shalibhadra embraced him with relief and joy.

But Shalibhadra cautioned Kalidasa that it was now dangerous for him to continue living there. 'The enmity or the close friendship with those in power will always act against the acquisition of knowledge. And travel is the best means of gathering wisdom about the ancient land that stretches from the Himalayas to the ocean in the south. I too am leaving this place shortly,' said Shalibhadra.

'Let it be as you suggest. I have been helping Shivasoma and his family. My only worry is that they will be left without help now,' Kalidasa replied.

'That does not matter. Time has fixed plans and duties for each one of us. Someone will soon come to marry Malini and he will help Shivasoma and his wife. Shivasoma has already started making arrangements for that,' Shalibhadra assured him.

Kalidasa was happy to hear that. He was more interested in travelling than in staying with Shivasoma permanently. He knew that he had to travel in order to know the land and the cities, to understand the people and their culture.

'Guro, I would like to come with you,' he said to Shalibhadra.

'Yes, Kalidasa. You are not destined to spend the rest of your life here. You should see the world. Acquire wisdom and knowledge. But do not forget Goddess Kali of Champa. Do not give up worshipping the Goddess. Goddess Kali will forever remain as the fountainhead of all your knowledge,' said Shalibhadra as he walked towards the door of the temple.

They were ready to start on their journey early in the morning. Shivasoma blessed Kalidasa, placing his palms on Kalidasa's forehead. 'I have seen the purity of your heart. I know how much you love us and this village. Goddess Kali will bless you. She will forever dance on your tongue as the goddess of letters. You have been blessed by divine powers. I have noticed that each word you utter reflects the beauty of nature. You will never be a piece of wood carried along by the current of time, my boy,' he said as he embraced the young man.

Malini too could not control her tears. She had seen Kalidasa as the brother she had lost. Now that care was also to be lost. She asked in a sweet voice, 'Now who will recite the small poems for me? Who will string garlands for me with the bright karnikara flowers? Who will pluck the lotus flowers for me from the lake?'

Kalidasa could see the sorrow of a younger sister on her face. But he had no answers for those questions. Even he was not sure where his wanderings would lead him. He was not sure whether he would ever come back to this village.

Malini's mother also shed tears as she bid farewell to Kalidasa.

As they left, Kalidasa felt more grief than he had felt when he had left Malava. At that time his only aim was to save his life. He had not wanted to be a prey to the wild animals that came to the river banks from the burning forests and the vultures that circled above in the sky. But now it was not such a flight. His guru had introduced him to various things and inculcated the desire for more in his mind. He was excited at the thought of the unlimited vista of knowledge that awaited him. So he was ready to go wherever his master led him.

As he was leaving the village of Champa, along with Shalibhadra and some other ascetics, Kalidasa could not help looking back. After having to leave the hermitage and Malava to escape the forest fire, Shalibhadra and Shivasoma had filled his heart with care and love, leaving very little room for sorrow in his heart. Shivasoma's wife had been a mother to him and his daughter, a little sister. Now he was leaving them. He was not sure whether he would ever be back.

He thought of Malava. He wanted to return to Malava at some point, the thought that his parents had survived the fire was pulling him in the direction of home. But the pull was not strong enough for him to abandon his current decision. He was more inclined to see where destiny takes him.

'If we move along the banks of the Ganga to the west from here, we will reach Prayag. From there, we can go northwest, along the banks of the Ganga, to Kanyakubj and then Hastinapura. We will cross the Ganga there and proceed further in the same direction to reach Shakala and then Thakshashila. That is the storehouse of all knowledge and wisdom. We will stay there for a while,' Guru explained his plan to Kalidasa.

He then continued. 'If, from here, we go by the river, it will only be the waters of the Ganga that we see. It is better to travel on land. We can see and experience the way of life of the people in different places. We can traverse forests and villages on the way.'

Passing through villages, mountain ranges and valleys, they reached the point where the Ganga and the Yamuna merged. After a dip in the holy waters there, they went on their way. They halted at pilgrim centers, inns and hermitages. They held many discussions with pilgrims and ascetics. Crossing the rivers, they passed through forests. There were barren lands as well as verdant mountain ranges. There were innumerable holy places on the way.

At times, the journey was difficult. Many a time they left the main road to take the less trodden ones. The summer was at its zenith. The sun burned during the day. Even after the sun had set, the heat continued to be unbearable. At first, they noticed that the water level in the ponds and lakes had gone down. Later there were only dry basins of the water spots, with solid cakes of mud. They had left the banks of the river and moved to the inner paths.

As they were preparing to move further northwest from Hastinapura, the guru warned Kalidasa that the next stretch of the journey would be even more difficult. There were many tall mountain peaks to be surmounted. He warned him about the cold that made water turn to ice. Food would be scarce in most places. But nothing deterred Kalidasa. There were men in all these places and wherever a man had gone, he too could go; Kalidasa was determined. He had the courage to face any situation and he had the support of his master.

They continued their trek. The nature of the land had changed completely. This was a land of deep valleys and mountain ranges where the clouds came to rest. Kalidasa noticed the beauty of the saffron flowers. The rivers that rushed towards the plains were trying in vain to gather the coldness of the snow-clad mountains. There were highly populated places along their banks and hermitages above the mountain heights. Even the rays of the sun and the moon appeared to be different here. The sunrays drew another picture of beauty. During the winter these areas would also be covered with snow. The people here knew how to adjust to the conditions of life during the changing seasons.

The guru had mentioned that they would have to walk across the snow-covered mountains. But people had learned to travel along those parts and trees and plants grew there.

As they were preparing for this journey, unhappy tidings reached them. The nomadic Mangolian tribes that lived by fighting and looting had become active once again. It was also learned that the powerful kings of this land had decided to join forces and defend the country against such attacks. The people who came from that part of the country said that the journey to Thakshashila would be a journey to the war front. This information stopped them from proceeding in their decided direction.

Guru Shalibhadra said, 'Kalidasa, I think we should give up our journey to Thakshashila. We will go to the Himalayas.'

It was the picture of Shiva and Parvati that rose in his mind when Kalidasa first heard of the Himalayas. Guru Shalibhadra used to tell him the stories of Shiva and Parvati and this had created an indescribable attraction towards the heavenly couple. Kailas, the playground of Shiva and Parvati was in the Himalayas, the abode of the Gods. He felt that it was indeed a fortune to be able to visit that place. His guru had explained to him that nowhere else could one witness the grandeur, the brilliance, of the king among the mountains.

'When will we be able to see the Himalayas?' asked Kalidasa with evident enthusiasm.

Seeing the eagerness on his face, another ascetic said, 'My boy, we have to walk for many more days before we can witness that unearthly beauty. The Himalayas is the abode of indefinable wonders and indescribable beauty. We have not even touched the feet of the Himalayas yet. But, do you know, my boy, that there the cold is so intense that the blood can solidify? The Himalayas is literally the "alaya"—the abode of "himam"—snow. It means the mountain peak is covered with snow. The flakes of snow will be flying about in the wind. There will often be strong winds and heavy rains. Ordinary people cannot withstand or even imagine the cold there. The body will become like a log because of the cold. You have to learn how to keep the cold away, rather than training the body to withstand the intense cold. So during this journey, you will have to learn much, Kalidasa, before you see the Himalayas.'

Kalidasa spent the time in that beautiful valley of the Himalayas enjoying all the special features and qualities of the land devoted to penance. The bath in the Ganga gave his body divine strength. As the ascetics taught him about yoga and all other branches of study, his mind marvelled at the infinite variety of cultures present in this holy land.

After they had spent some time at the hermitage of Maharshi Mahatreta, Guru Shalibhadra informed Kalidasa that it was time to start as the season had turned favourable for further travel. There were many other ascetics ready to travel with them to the hermitages on the Himalayan ranges. Among the venerable old monks, Kalidasa, was the only young man, hardly out of his adolescence. As he stepped forth uttering salutations to the monarch among the mountains, *'nagādhirājāya namāmyaham'* (my greetings to the king of mountains) the old men felt a sense of love form in their hearts towards that boy.

The sight of the tall mountain ranges before him filled Kalidasa's mind with a sense of freshness and joy hitherto unknown. He could see innumerable peaks and flowing through them, the deep waters of the Bhagirathi.

While walking along the narrow footpaths on the sides of mountains, Kalidasa realized the immense diversity of nature in all its beauty as well as its terrifying gravity. He wondered why the great ascetics decided to tread the narrow paths that hardly had any space as a foothold to go to the Himalayas.

Some areas provided the young man with novel experiences. As he was walking forward enjoying the beauty of nature, he was acquainted with a smell that he had never experienced before.

'Guro, what is this indefinable fragrance that seems to have pervaded this place? What flower spreads such a sweet smell?' he asked Guru Shalibhadra.

'This fragrance does not come from any flower,' Shalibhadra said after glancing around. 'Look there, can you see a milk-like liquid oozing out of the tree? Some elephant must have rubbed his body against the trunk of the tree. The bark must have broken by that and the smell comes from that sap.'

Kalidasa marvelled at what he saw. He had heard and experienced the beauty of sweet-smelling flowers and the fragrance that came from them but an experience like this was new to him. He had seen the latex oozing out of many trees. He had noticed that some of them had a slight smell also. But such a relishing experience, an unearthly fragrance that penetrated the depths of his mind, was a novelty.

The monks with them described the special features of many places. They informed Kalidasa that the Pandavas had walked along this path during the mahaprasthana, the long journey towards the end of their life.

Kalidasa was eager to see more and more of the majesty of the Bhagirathi. She flowed down the mountain, splashing drops of water around like snow. The light reflected off the water droplets creating tiny rainbows. Resting droplets on Deodar leaves were a mesmerizing sight to watch.

As they were resting in a cave, one of the ascetics told him the story of Vyasa writing the Mahabharata. Many monks joined them and some among them remained in the caves as they needed more rest.

Kalidasa was struck by another unfamiliar smell as they continued their journey. It was unlike anything that he had experienced before. 'What is this unusual smell, Maharshi? Is this also coming from some tree?' he asked.

'No, Dasa. This is the smell of musk. Look there...that is the herd of musk deer grazing on the slopes of the mountain. The musk is in the navel of those deer.'

Kalidasa tried to compare these wonders of nature with what he had seen in Champa. There were some wonderful and surprising things in that village too. But what he was experiencing here was indescribable.

There were places where the path seemed to have ended. The mountain stood tall in front of the group. The rocks stood in the way. But some of the ascetics went around the rock and found a place to get a foothold. As they scaled each peak it seemed that they had reached the top of the world. The rishis pointed out for Kalidasa the snow on top of the distant peaks, reflecting the rays of the sun. As they climbed one peak after another, Kalidasa felt that he was no longer in this world. The dew drops that hung from the leaves of the Deodar trees seemed reluctant to leave their hold. Kalidasa went near the leaves to examine them as they reflected the rays of the sun. He could see the reflection of the peaks on the drops of water—an indefinable experience.

They had reached a spot where even one step forward seemed impossible. It was then that Rishi Devasena showed them the path called Krouncharandhram. Cold wind lashed through this passage. The Rishi informed them that they were entering a different terrain of the Himalayas with this path.

It indeed was a new world. The tall snow-covered mountains stood around them. The rays of the sun that reflected these peaks created a bluish light. Many trees and plants grew in clusters and he wondered if they had also learned yoga? No, he corrected himself. They didn't need to learn yoga, since this was their natural habitat. But they would never grow in Malava or in Champa and the trees and plants of Malava or Champa would never be able to grow here either. They were also beautiful, attractive areas. But the beauty that he saw around him was new; he had never seen such a place before. He had seen the red lotus flowers and the white ones, but here there were blue lotuses in bloom. Then again, he corrected himself. How could he call this flower a pankaj, one that grows in the dirt? In the lake in the middle of these tall mountain peaks, would there be any dirt? How could there be a lake with water in it, when all around it was snow? Why hadn't the water turn into snow? Even in such lofty peaks, the sun allowed the flowers to blossom forth... They might be the flowers left behind after the Devarshis had taken what they needed for their worship. The sight of those beautiful flowers inspired poetic images and these images would stay within his mind forever.

Even after walking the whole day, they could not leave that beautiful area. The colour of the snow on the mountains changed with the change in the position of the sun...a sight so enchanting that Kalidasa's mind felt that this must be the often-described abode of the Gods.

The sweet notes from the flute greeted them at one place. 'Oh! The notes of flute here! Guro, is it the land of the Kinnaras? Are they practising for their concert?'

'Many such divine notes can be heard here, Kalidasa,' one of the ascetics replied. 'But they are a part of the music of nature. Look there... Can't you see the sky in between the peaks there?' he asked.

'Yes, Swami... It looks as though a hole has been made in the middle of the mountain!'

'Yes! The wind that comes through that space creates this music like the wind that passes through the holes in a flute. The change in the strength of the wind makes the notes rise and fall rhythmically. When it becomes less cold, the snow will melt and the holes will become larger. The sound that is produced will vary with the fall of snow. There are innumerable such holes on these snow-covered mountains that we will never see anywhere else. The wind flows through all of them and produces these sweet notes. And all of them together produce this heavenly music... Just listen carefully.'

Kalidasa stood still and listened. Yes, apart from what he had heard, there were many other notes acting as a background for the symphony of nature. It could be assumed that the Kinnaras were getting ready for a concert. The white snowflakes that floated by looked like Chamari deers jumping from peak to peak, fanning with their white tails. Of course, this was the monarch of the mountain peaks; there had to be royal pomp and ostentation to go with it. Various bulbs of imagination were taking root in Kalidasa's mind.

'Guro, this beauty is unearthly... Is this what you call heaven?' Kalidasa asked.

'This is not heaven... but it is the path that leads there... the path that leads to salvation. If we walk further, we will reach the abode of Shiva beyond the Manasa Lake—Kailas of Lord Mahadeva. But ordinary human beings cannot go there. And if, with the mercy of the retinue of Lord Shiva, anyone reaches there, there will be no return. Many wondrous sights await us as we go in that direction,' one of the ascetics explained for the sake of Kalidasa.

Soon they reached the mouth of a cave. 'Let us rest here,' said one of them.

The sun was about to descend behind the distant mountains. The play of colours around was an enthralling experience for

Kalidasa. The beauty of nature as a whole seemed to have assembled there. There could not be a more beautiful place on the earth.

But the night had even greater surprises in store for Kalidasa. Before the sun had set and darkness had covered the land, a new form of effulgence seemed to pervade there. The rise of the moon brought before him a beauty hitherto unseen. The other members of the group had started their prayers, singing paeans of Lord Shiva.

Another wonder awaited Kalidasa's eyes there and was revealed when the dark clouds covered the face of the moon. Some of the plants seemed to be illuminated. He wondered how they could radiate light in that way. He could not decide whether they were adding to the beauty of the darkness or decorating the moonlight. These plants could be used as lights during the night. There was no need for any oil or wick or fire. But he was not sure whether they would grow anywhere else. This was the wealth of the snow-covered deity of the mountains.

The ascetics with him explained that the greatness of the Himalayas lay in it being the storehouse of wonders. It was clear that it was not any ordinary world. It was the land of unbelievable wonders. Even in its presence, it leaves you wondering whether it's all just a dream.

In the morning, as the rays of the sun started reflecting off of the huge mountain tops, it seemed as though darkness had come to take shelter in the caves like the one in which they were resting. Kalidasa feared that the cave would be destroyed in the piercing cold wind that blew there. All the plants and trees he had seen the previous day were now covered in snow. Instead of the gentle notes of the flute, they heard an echoing and angry roar like that of the king of the forest. The whole area was covered in snow, making it difficult to decide which way they should now travel.

As they walked on the tall mountains, it seemed that the cave of death would any moment open up to swallow them. Their legs were wounded by the sharp edges of the solid snow. If one was careless for a second, what awaited him was eternal rest in the snow. They had gone so high up in the mountains that it created the feeling that they had reached the sky. The clouds were wandering below the mountain peaks. As the clouds poured in the valley below, they could enjoy the sunshine high up, above the clouds. He had reached a height that not even the birds could scale. The only source of strength was the repetition of the mantra... *'Aum namah shivaya...'* At times, he felt that the Shiva tandava was being enacted on some secret stage in the mountains. They could hear the deafening sound as if mountain peaks were crumbling down.

Shalibhadra said, 'Kalidasa, this huge mountain will radiate brightness during the night and create heavenly beauty during the day. This is the repository of precious stones. You can call it the infinite storehouse of nectar provided by nature. Many medicinal plants that can save lives grow here. It is only on certain occasions that they peak out of the snow and face the sun and the moon.'

Kalidasa looked at him with deep curiosity. 'Master, how can we recognize these medicinal plants and their power to cure ailments? There must be some plants that contain powerful poison also.'

'My boy,' he replied, 'There are many learned ascetics who have made this land of the Himalayas their home. They are the people who go beyond this path that we take; those who live in the deepest of gorges and the highest of peaks that are beyond even our imagination. Apart from them, there are the children of the Himalayas! This is a land of penance, Kalidasa—a land of snowflakes that fly about like cotton as well as the huge glaciers. There are many here who have realized the secrets of each atom in nature through eons of penance. They are the men who have been undertaking penance to realize the blessings of the power of Lord Shiva for the welfare of the whole world. They recognize the qualities that are integral to each particle of life in this world. They write down what they have discovered on leaves for posterity, to study and use them for the welfare of the whole universe.'

Thus, passing through days filled with sights and sounds of wonder and unbelievable rarity, they reached the top of a mountain peak. The rishis informed Kalidasa that they had reached near Manasa Lake. His heart was filled with an indescribable elation as they walked and reached the lake. Lotus flowers were in bloom in the blue waters of the lake. Swans in all their majesty were swimming about among the flowers. And far away there stood the tall mountain peaks! Pointing to the peak that stood beyond the Manasa Lake, one of the ascetics said, 'There, far ahead, is the abode of Lord Shiva, Mount Kailas. From now onwards, the retinue of the Lord will be on guard on the path. No one is allowed to go to the Lord's abode.'

A spectacular sight! The sun had set. The mountain peak stood high with the crescent moon above it. It was only the fourth day after the new moon but even that was enough to spread the soothing light of the moon there. Those ascetics told Kalidasa that a sight of the Kailas, bathed in moonlight is a rare sight; something gained by the virtues practised through many births. He was experiencing that. Kalidasa imagined that he was seeing the figure of Lord Shiva. All the members of the group also might have felt the same way. The chanting of the mantra, *'Aum namah shivaayah'*, became louder and more intense in devotion. Kalidasa knew it was the greatest blessing of his life... to stand gazing at the Kailas, the abode of Lord Shiva, which the devotees generally knew of only through the descriptions given by the great rishis! The domicile of the Lord and his retinue!

He felt a heavenly glow fill his whole being. The resonance of the conch shell seemed to spread all over the place, the rhythmic beat of the Lord's drum echoed from the mountain peaks—the rhythm that gave shape to the letters that denoted the world of sound. The sound of 'Aum...' floated all over the region. That sound went deep into the mind and the heart. The atmosphere led the consciousness to a wondrous experience. His mind became concentrated on that, became unaware of the surroundings. The other ascetics with him seemed to disappear from his sight and mind. There was a revelation of the divine base of the existence of life... *'Aum namah shivayah... Aum namah shivayah.'*

As he prostrated before that presence by keeping his forehead on the rocky surface, Kalidasa felt that he could see the divine family before his eyes. The cosmic couple Shiva and Parvati sat blessing us with their hands, with Skanda on the mother's lap.

Kalidasa woke out of that reverie only when someone touched him. 'Dasa, let us move on. No one knows when the echoes of the cosmic dance by Lord Shiva will start here, it will create a tumultuous atmosphere. No power acquired through yogic practices will help one to withstand that. We now have to return with the experience we have got which can only be seen as the result of the virtues we have attained in previous births.'

Seeing the Lord of Kailas and Goddess Parvati in his mind's eye, Kalidasa turned to go back. But he saw that some of the ascetics were not preparing for the return journey. 'Swami, aren't you coming with us?' he asked.

'No, Dasa,' one of them said. 'The three of us have come ready for the last journey. We understand that the duties of our life are over. We will climb these snowy mountains and walk towards the abode of Lord Shiva, hoping that the Lord's soldiers will allow us to do so, forever! We do not wish to return to this earth.'

'What is there in Kailas and beyond that?' Kalidasa asked anxiously.

'There are two worlds beyond the Kailas. One is the world of the Devas, the Gods and the other is Alakapuri, the land of the Yakshas, Kinnaras and the Gandharvas. One can dissolve oneself into oblivion in the divine presence of Lord Padmanabha who lies on Ananta, the ocean of milk, with Lakshmidevi, in the world of the Gods. Alakapuri is reputed to be the abode of all beauty. There exists another level of what man experiences of worldly life on earth. Happiness and joy are what one can enjoy there. Flowers of different colours and shapes, more exotic than what we have seen here, bloom there all the time... lotuses, jasmine, Lodhra.' One of the rishis explained the exotic nature of the land beyond the Kailas.

'Can we go there?' Kalidasa asked.

'No. Human beings are not allowed to enter Alakapuri. It is the land of the Yakshas, Kinnaras and Gandharvas. We are going to the abode of Lord Shiva,' he explained.

'Aren't they afraid of going there?' the thought rose momentarily in Kalidasa's mind.

They seemed to have heard the unspoken query. 'Why? Who should we be afraid of? Once you have realized that life on this earth is over, the journey should be to the domicile of Lord Shiva. What more can we ask for? We have already realized the cosmic truth and its beauty. Now it is to Shiva! May you, my boy, have all the blessings!' Rishi Haridatha put his palms on Kalidasa's head in blessing.

Kalidasa watched with amazement as they walked off towards the endless Himalayan reaches. The Pandavas must have walked the last part of their life in a similar manner. A journey from which there was no return! But all of them did not reach here. Only Yudhishtira could come up to this point. He had heard Rishi Shalibhadra describe the story of Arjuna's visit to the land of the Gandharvas. Is that possible? The rishi had said that none who went there had returned. Arjuna might have come back... He might have possessed the ability for that.

Bowing their heads in reverence towards that path, Kalidasa and the others turned back.

As they reached the banks of the Mahakoushi River, one of the rishis said, 'Look there, my friends! There is a high rock, like a platform, on the river bank. If one controls the mind and attains the yogic stance, he will be able to see all the land between the ocean in the south and the Himalayas in the north as well as the Indusarovara. When the Saptarishis, along with Arundhati went to Oushadhiprastha to request him to allow Goddess Parvati to be Mahadeva's bride, it was here that the Lord with the trident in hand waited, till their return.'

The river fell into an infinite chasm, a rock that jutted into the open space there. The rishis walked forward and stood on the rock surface. Kalidasa followed them and stood looking at the infinite space from there.

Nothing was distinctly visible beyond the Himalayan valley below. It was just an endless space of nothingness. The rishi had said that one should have the yogic practice to be able to see from there to the ocean in the south. No, his penance had not given him that power.

Shalibhadra came to stand near Kalidasa. 'Dasa, that is not something that can be achieved by the ordinary yogis. Below this, stretches the ancient land with rivers, mountains and valleys till the three seas meet washing the feet of Goddess Kumari Devi. You should travel all over this land, crossing the rivers and the mountains, to know it. Travel to the east beyond Pragjyothishapura to Brahmadesha, to the west till the land of Gandhara and to the south till the great ocean and understand this ancient land. For that you have to travel through each of the territories. You can reach those places with the power of yogic practice. But the real knowledge will be that which you gather by direct contact with the people and their way of life, knowing nature closely. When you stand here the only advantage is that you can gaze at the infinite space without the rising mountains blocking your view.'

Maharshi Mahapadma said, 'There are so many different states like Kashi, Magadha, Vidisha, Malava, Suhma, Vamga, Utkal, Kalinga and Pandya. To reach these places you have to cross many rivers like the Ganga, Kapisha, Narmada, Kaveri and Tamraparni! Then you have to climb many mountain peaks! The seasons will change and at certain places you will have to suffer the height of summer while at others it will be torrential rains and floods.'

'You should see and try to understand everything.'

'Yes, Master, I have to continue this journey,' Kalidasa said with conviction.

'Now we are leaving the land of the Himalayas to Kapilavasthu, from there to Pragjyothishpura and then to Kashi,' the master said.

Rishi Shalibhadra, Kalidasa and the others started walking towards Kapilavasthu in the lap of the Himalayan peaks.

4

Kalidasa was drenched from the unexpected rains when he set foot on the soil of Malava. His eyes too were wet with joy. It was after a long journey that he now stepped on the land of Malava.

Ujjaini is the spot where the sun reaches the zenith at noon, at the end of its journey north, a place that was of immense importance in calculating time. He had heard about the greatness of Ujjaini throughout the journey. The land was also known by other names like Avanti, Avantika, Vishala, Padmavati, Bhogavati and Hiranyavati and the land of Maha Kaleshwara! Now the land was at the forefront under the rule of Maharaja Vikramaditya, the valiant king, who was forever vigilant about the welfare of the people. Under his rule, literature and all fine arts received the utmost support and encouragement. The king knew how to give reverence to the wise.

While traversing the diverse regions of the country, the reports about Ujjaini that he had heard were unanimous in classifying it as a great place. Even those who were politically against the ruler of Malava were ready to admit the greatness of Ujjaini. The feeling of 'my Malava' dominated Kalidasa's mind. The king, Vikramaditya, had gained fame by defeating the Shakas with help from Vidisha, Vidarbha and Magadha.

He had the wisdom he had gathered during his travels all over the country. He had visited almost all the areas between the Himalayas and the ocean in the south. He was in possession of some knowledge of Sanskrit, the language of the Gods.

He had heard about the assembly of the learned and wise

men of the king's palace. Generally, the older among the wise men will not be ready to recognize a younger man easily. It is the younger generation that will be ready to accept what is put forward by the younger men. The older generation will always be reluctant about appreciating the youngsters. They always think from their own plane of thought and ability. From that level it is naturally difficult to accept novel ideas unless their magnanimity of thought is as high as the mountain. Kalidasa wondered if there will be such great men in the assembly of Malava.

He had only heard about Ujjaini during his travels. He had an idea about the city even as he crossed the border with the group of merchants. He was stopped at the army post near the border. He told them that he had already travelled all over the country between the Himalayas and the ocean in the south. Kalidasa informed them that he had been travelling alone. He wanted to meet King Vikramaditya and the learned men of his assembly. His knowledge of Sanskrit stood him in good stead. He was permitted to cross the border. That night Kalidasa could hardly sleep as he was lost in thoughts about Ujjaini.

He was on his way early the next morning. Soldiers stopped him again at the entrance to the city. It had not been long since King Vikramaditya had defeated the Shakas completely and established his power in Malava. Ujjaini was an important city for the merchants as it was on the main path leading from the Deccan plateau to Koushambi and Prayag, passing through Vidisha. They were mainly responsible for making the place so famous. They were grateful to Vikramaditya for saving them from the threat posed by the Shakas. The king had made a strong army, capable of withstanding any attack from outside.

The river Kshipra provided water for the city. The river Kshipra flowed towards the north and joined the river Charmanawati while a small river named Gambhira added its water to the Kshipra. It was believed that when the Devas and the Asuras churned the ocean of milk and got nectar, a few drops of it fell into the river. That was why the Kshipra was considered to be a holy river—Ksheerasagaranandini (Daughter of the ocean of milk). The river is mentioned in the Yajur Veda also: 'kṣipre āveḥ payaḥ'.

He walked to its banks. The landing area was beautifully paved with stones. Jamun, Ashoka and bakul trees provided shade there. Keeping his bundle on the stone under one of the trees, Kalidasa got into the river. This was the river that provided life to this state. He touched the water in prayer and took a dip in it. He drank a mouthful of that water. As he got out after the bath, the fatigue caused by the travel seemed to have vanished. He sat on the rock under the tree.

After a while Kalidasa got to the main path. The city seemed to be well developed on the eastern banks of the river though it extended to the western side also. There was a bridge over the river to enter the city. It was not just for the pedestrians...even heavy chariots and carts with luggage could use the bridge. The streets of the city were also paved and well kept. He could see some houses. The people looked happy and content.

As he walked on in search of the Mahakaleshwara temple, after a while the tower of the temple became visible and that gave him direction. Kalidasa went in search of an inn near the temple. The keeper of the inn welcomed him with respect. He introduced himself. Kalidasa was not surprised to see the respectful behaviour of the innkeeper. Even at the city gates, he had noticed how the authorities gathered details about visitors like him and how the officers behaved with equanimity and dignity. This innkeeper also shared the great culture of Ujjaini.

Leaving the bundle in the room, Kalidasa came out. He stood near the huge lake near the temple. He washed his hands and feet in the water and walked to the temple.

Kalidasa stood for a while before the sanctum of the temple. A rishi was describing the greatness of Mahakaleshwara. A group of devotees sat before him.

There was the temple of Avantika Devi, a little behind that of Mahakaleshwara. As he stood with folded hands before the Goddess, the rest of the world faded away and he thought only of the Goddess. Kalidasa prostrated himself before Mahakali. He felt the blessings of the Goddess of the Vindhyas on his bowed head. The blessings of the Goddess Kali at Champa had been with him all this while. Avantika Devi was none other than Kalishwari!

An anxiety that he had not felt before, persuaded Kalidasa to go in search of his parents. He went around making enquiries for two-three days. He traversed all the places where people lived. He asked for them in farming areas and the trading centers. He met many people, but Kalidasa could not find his parents or his Guru Devashraya.

The sun was about to set. Kalidasa had to end his search for the day. One more day had gone. He would spend the night at the inn and continue with his search the next day.

The gurukula at Ujjaini was very famous. The chief master there was Shankuka. He or any of the others there might know something about Guru Devashraya. Kalidasa wanted to see if he could get some employment there also. So to make a last effort, Kalidasa walked towards the gurukula. But the acharya refused to even meet him.

He came back and stood outside the temple. What was he to do now? He could not continue to live at the inn for many more days. So he had to find a place to stay and he had to find a means of livelihood. He doubted whether he would have to go to the king and request some help. But he knew that it was wrong to go straight to the king of a country when you were in need of some help. He had thought about it many a time and had rejected the idea. Now he did not know what to do.

There were many people gathered in front of the temple. They were all looking at an announcement that had been pasted on the platform meant for giving important information to the people. The announcement was written on a piece of silk in golden letters. The title given was for the completion of a puzzle. 'A prize of one thousand gold coins and a place in the assembly for the one who can present a beautiful couplet in the royal assembly! Wait for the royal announcement in the evening.' This was all that was written on the cloth.

The men were waiting anxiously. Kalidasa listened to the conversation of the people. A present of one thousand gold coins and a seat in the royal assembly was no small achievement. But there was nothing mentioned about the puzzle.

Kalidasa also felt anxious about it. More and more people were joining the crowd. Why had the king not announced what the puzzle was, in the notice itself?

Soon the official royal announcers were there. There was a rush of men towards the platform from which the announcement would be made. Two soldiers positioned themselves on either side of the announcers. A man stood ready with the huge kettle drum. Another man was there with the trumpet. One man stood ready to read the announcement. When all the people had gathered near the platform, the drums were sounded and the bugle was blown. When the sound of the bugle subsided, the man read out aloud:

'The King of Kings, Vikramaditya, makes this announcement! A gift of one thousand gold coins and a position in the royal assembly for the one who is proficient at solving this puzzle! *Dhadhaṃ dhadhaṃdhaṃ dhadhadhaṃ dhadhaṃdhā*,' he repeated it three times and the drums were sounded again.

Somebody raised his voice, 'Tell us what the puzzle is!'

But the announcers did not say anything. They kept on

repeating the announcement. Kalidasa listened carefully. The king was inviting one who had the proficiency to solve the puzzle. But the puzzle was not announced. After the announcement, there was a rhythmic beat on the drum. Hey! How could it be so?! There must be a secret behind it. He had to find it. Kalidasa's mind started looking for the secret.

As he was thinking, the rhythm of the drumbeat echoed in his mind. He thought of finding the meaning of that rhythm. There is an eternal link between the idea and the word... Words... What rose from the rhythmic sound of the small drum in the hands of Lord Shiva... Words... Coming together and merging as the soul and the body, as letters, standing together to form words, entering the consciousness as word and its meaning. Those that arose from the rhythmic beating of the Mahadeva's drum!

Kalidasa's mind whispered. There is nothing meaningless in nature. Each emotion and expression has its own meaning, each sound has its own meaning. Even the letters have their own meaning! Words always have their special meaning. Each sound keeps a meaning hidden in itself—some idea hidden in it. Many such ideas passed through Kalidasa's mind.

Whoever was behind the creation of this puzzle must be a person of imagination and abilities. The genius of King Vikramaditya must be behind this. Kalidasa listened once again. They had not changed the rhythm after the announcements. Like their maharaja, they too were proficient in their art.

Kalidasa did not leave the place. He sat under the banyan tree near the temple, fixing his mind on the rhythm. It kept reverberating in his mind and brain. He had a feeling that the rhythm was similar to something he had heard before. That rhythm kept echoing itself somewhere in his memory. As time passed that feeling gained strength.

Kalidasa walked about for long and reached the banks of

the Kshipra. He sat there on a rock looking at the flow of the water. Kshipra had held his hand and sent him safely away from his village on the west of Malava. Then he reached Champa. The picture of Rishi Shalibhadra, the temple of Kali in Champa on the outskirts of Kashi and Shivasoma, the priest there, appeared in his mind. And a beautiful smile seemed to appear before his eyes... Malini...

The rhythm of the drums disappeared from his mind and he felt himself standing before the temple of Kali, the mother who gave him wisdom. The boy who was Shambhu till then became Kalidasa on reaching the abode of Goddess Kali in Champa. Innumerable incidents passed through his mind. He was able to get acquainted with the ascetic, Shalibhadra, Shivasoma, the priest in that temple and Malini, the daughter of the priest... The sound of the rhythmic beat of the drum sounded again in his heart. Yes, he had heard that sound in Champa.

Kalidasa remembered that the festival of Ramleela was being celebrated at Champa at that time. The story of Rama was being enacted in the temple premises. It was time for the coronation scene of Rama to be enacted. Suddenly he remembered that the water for the anointment during the coronation had not been kept ready. He sent Malini to bring the water. As Malini was coming up the steps of the palace with the water, the brass pitcher slipped from her hand and fell on the stone step. *Dham...* The sound reverberated because of the weight of the water in the pot. As the pot was full of water, the sound was something special. Then with rhythmic sounds, the pot started falling down each step. And Kalidasa found that the sound of the drum that had been in his mind since the morning merged with the sound of the pot going down the steps.

Without his being aware of it, the puzzle had been solved. The pot fell down and rolled from step to step. *Dhadham dhadhamdham dhadhadham dhadhamdhaa...* No, there was no need to write it down. That rhythm had been very clearly etched in his mind.

The next morning, he worshipped Mahakaleshwar and walked to the palace.

The main road was lined with trees. At all the main junctions there were sheds where drinking water was provided for the travellers. Elevated places meant to be porters' rest, were also built there. The houses were beautifully maintained. He could see the tower of the palace with the flag fluttering on it. The white towers of the palace with golden flags hoisted on them could be seen from afar. The golden pitchers on them declared royal grandeur. Many horse drawn chariots passed him on the street with the pleasant tinkling of the bells. The highway was paved with black stones and no dust rose from it as the chariots passed. The beauty made it evident that it was a royal pathway. Armed soldiers stood guard at regular intervals.

Even before reaching the gateway, Kalidasa noticed its beauty. The walls of the gateway were made with stones that were smooth and shining so as to reflect everything nearby. The beautiful sculptures added to the beauty of the gateway. Kalidasa stood for a few moments enjoying the beauty and the diversity of the artworks. He had seen attractive architecture at many places. But he felt that the sculptures at Ujjaini were unmatched.

When he reached the gate, the guards stopped him. Here was a man they had not seen before in Ujjaini. But his face had a brilliance and his eyes were penetrating. It was evident from the way he dressed that he was a traveller. Kalidasa informed them that he had come prepared for the completion of the puzzle announced by the royal order. Though slightly apprehensive, they allowed Kalidasa to go in.

He walked forward. The beautiful royal path was flanked by attractive gardens on either side. There was a small lake with a fountain. The water rose up and showered droplets of water. It must be done with the help of some mechanism, he had not seen such a sight anywhere that he had travelled. The rays of the morning sun fell on the drops of water, producing all the colours of the rainbow. There were lotus flowers in bloom in the lake with swans swimming about among them. Pigeons and peacocks were pecking the ground for prey. Parrots made the place resound with their cooing. Tiny birds and butterflies could be seen fluttering about among the plants.

The palace of Ujjaini also was majestic and attractive. There were artistically created sculptures that were more life-like and attractive than those that were placed at the gateway. The number of such sculptures there proved that the art received a lot of support and encouragement in that country. Some of them even made Kalidasa wonder whether they were live men or sculptures. Golden lines were drawn on the walls. The doors were decorated with golden garlands. The floor shone like glass. Silken curtains were hung on the doors and windows. Even the soldiers showed a royal dignity.

Many were walking in a hurry. They must be heading for the assembly. He asked a soldier where the assembly was. The soldier seemed to be slightly suspicious but he politely pointed out the way.

There were a lot of formalities for entering the assembly. When Kalidasa told the doorkeeper that he had come on hearing the announcement about solving the puzzle, he smiled. 'Many great scholars have been trying to figure out what riddle the king had placed before them. So you too must have come to find out what the riddle is,' the doorkeeper ended his explanation with this query.

Kalidasa smiled and replied, 'I have come prepared according to my abilities, my friend.' After a pause, he asked 'Can I go in?'

'Yes. But you should give some details. Your name, please?'
'Kalidasa.'
'Where are you from?'
Kalidasa hesitated for a while. What should he say?
'I cannot mention a place specifically. But I belong to Malava.'
A shadow of doubt appeared on the doorkeeper's face.
'How can that be? I have never seen you before. Where do you stay?'
'I have been travelling all over the Bharatavarsha. I left Malava many years ago. I got here only a few days back,' Kalidasa explained. 'I have heard that Maharaja Vikramaditya is a patron of literature and the arts. That is why I have come here.'
The doorkeeper was not satisfied with Kalidasa's words. But he did not argue any further.
Just then the announcement with drumbeats was heard.
'Victory to the maharaja of Malava, the valiant son of Gardhabhilla Mahendraditya, Maharaja Vikramaditya'
'Please go in and sit on the seats allotted for the visitors. This is the announcement for everyone to be seated in the assembly. The maharaja will arrive very soon,' he said to Kalidasa.
Kalidasa was pleased to see the polite way in which the doorkeeper behaved. He asked many questions and Kalidasa did not have satisfactory answers to give for any of them. Still, he was allowed to go in. It could only be seen as a sign of good governance.
Kalidasa approached the seats assigned to the visitors. Though it was at the back, all the seats faced the Maharaja. It will not be difficult to request a chance to speak.
The drums could again be heard from behind the row of seats, they were announcing the arrival of the king. Some others stood ready with various other musical instruments.
Most of the people had sat down in their seats. The main

part of the royal assembly could be distinguished by the grandeur of the seats as well as the carpets spread on the floor there. There sat a throne studded with gold and precious jewels, it was flanked by the figures of roaring lions. Kalidasa had visited many royal assemblies in this land, but he had not seen such a grand throne anywhere else. There was a shining silk curtain, embroidered with beautiful artistic designs, behind the throne. An ornamental umbrella was seen above the throne. Women stood holding fans made of long white hair of goats. The women looked as if they were sculptures come to life. The royal assembly was a reflection of the grandeur of Ujjaini.

The people who were seated there also appeared to be distinguished from their dressing. Even the expression on the faces of some of them showed their high position in society. They exhibited their importance in the assembly just by their appearance.

Suddenly there was the beating of the drums announcing the arrival of the maharaja.

'Here comes Maharaja Vikramaditya.' As the curtains parted near the elevated throne of the king, everyone stood up.' Victory to the Maharaja! Long live the Maharaja!'—the assembly reverberated with the loud greetings. The king entered, greeting the assembly with raised hands. He glanced around the hall and then seated himself.

Kalidasa observed the king carefully. He looked like a strongly built, valiant soldier with a wide chest and sturdy arms. He walked with steady steps. His face was full of pride and resplendence. He had shining eyes. Though he was still young, his face showed the gravity of being the king of a great country. But there was no sign of haughtiness or arrogance on his face. He exuded the gravity of a king, but was courteous in behaviour. Kalidasa felt proud of him. Kalidasa had travelled through many states and had seen valiant and brave kings ruling over these places. But none of them would stand up to Maharaja Vikramaditya. He was unique! Second to none! And it was evident that he was good at ruling the country.

Amarasimha was the chief among the ministers. In appearance, grandeur and behavior he seemed to be a suitable minister for the king. The official proceedings and the customary practices in a royal assembly were duly completed. The ministers and the other important personalities in the assembly exhibited nobility and sincerity. No one uttered words of praise just to please the king. They were ready with their praise where it was due but were also ready to point out where they had noticed some shortcomings. It almost seemed to be an assembly of men who had been gathered after careful scrutiny from all over the country.

When it was time for discussions on poetry, art and literature, there was an evident eagerness among the people gathered there. The puzzle that the king had placed before them a few days ago still remained a riddle. Many expected that it would be revealed today.

With a smile, the king came to that subject.

'Let those who are ready to complete the riddle and present the couplet in this assembly now come forward,' he ordered.

Everybody remained silent and looked at one another. No one got up from the seat to announce his readiness.

'There are many among our courtiers who are proficient in the art of poetry, those who have gained fame as great poets. We have great expectation that anybody who is ready to challenge the courtiers, will complete the puzzle. We thought there were young men with a spark of poetic genius among the students of the gurukula. But they have all disappointed us,' said King Vikramaditya.

'Maharaj, usually when you present such a riddle, you give some suitable hints also. But this time you have left all of us to grope in the dark. You have not even offered the light that a firefly emits,' said Kshapanaka.

'Kshapanaka, what you say is not true. We told you on that day also that we have given sufficient hints for the riddle. We expect you to understand them. Even at night, if there is even a small spark of light, we should try to use it to see better. Real ability lies in finding that spark. Do you need a lamp to see if there is spark in the darkness? If there is no lamp, what will we do? If the eyes fail us, who will we depend on?' Vikramaditya stopped with this question. After observing everyone in the assembly, he continued. 'The couplet is not to be written down and shown in the assembly for everyone to read; it has to be recited. Do you need light to hear?'

A smile appeared on Kalidasa's lips. The maharaja was giving sufficient hints through his words. He was asking them to keep their ears open. He was making it clear that the hints were in the sound. Kalidasa understood that it was this concentration that they all lacked. The minister said, 'Your Majesty, your announcement has reached all places in Malava. The official announcers have gone to all streets, market places, villages, cities, gurukulas, inns and temples. Now...?'

'We have hope, Amarasimha! There cannot be a dearth of genius in the soil of Malava,' said the king.

'If you had given at least one letter of the last line, we could have heard many beautiful couplets here,' Kalidasa heard the words of Shankuka. He too had not understood the hint that the king had given. He felt that what he had heard about Shankuka, that he was a shrewd expert, was not true.

'This assembly expects more sharpness in the thinking of the masters of our gurukula. No one need expect any more hints on this riddle,' the king indicated that the matter was being closed.

Kalidasa observed that the king was critical of the acharya

of the gurukula also. The king had expected that the acharya would rise up to the dignity of the position that he held. When he saw that no one was coming forward, Kalidasa decided that it was time for him.

He had gone to the gurukula the previous day, hoping to get some employment. But now, if the king likes the lines that he'll present, he would get a seat in the royal assembly of Ujjaini. He felt that it was a puzzle specially meant for him. Kalidasa had complete faith in the quality of the lines that he had prepared.

Kalidasa looked around to see if anyone had got up to say anything. Complete silence prevailed in the assembly. The king appeared to be impatient. The disappointment at the failure of his attempt was evident on his face.

Kalidasa stood up and bowed to the assembly. The maharaja looked at him with a smile as if to give him permission to speak. He had not seen this man in Ujjaini before. But he had got information that such a man was wandering about in Ujjaini the last few days. It was said that this man had travelled all over the country. Let him introduce himself. Vikramaditya remembered the details that he had got from his secret agents and decided to allow Kalidasa to speak.

Suddenly a thought flashed through Kalidasa's mind. He was going to speak something in this grand assembly for the first time. He should not just recite the couplet that he had made. He should first salute Mahadeva, the root cause of sound, word and meaning. Those words of worship should be appropriate for this assembly too.

All eyes turned towards Kalidasa, wondering who this stranger was. Some of them had seen Kalidasa in the city. But nobody had thought that he would come to the royal assembly of Ujjaini with a solution for the riddle.

Kalidasa closed his eyes and visualized the Lord of Kailas, praying for his blessings.

*vēdāntēṣu yamāhurēka puruṣaṃ vāpya sthitaṃ rōdasī
yasminnīśvara ityananya viṣaya śabdō yathārthākṣaraḥ
antaryaśca mumukṣubhirnimita prāṇādibhir mṛgyatē
sa sthāṇu sthirabhayiōgasulabhō niśrēyasāyāstu vaḥ*

(*Vikramorvasheeyam*, Act 1, Stanza 1)

(Let that Mahadeva, who is described as omnipresent in the vedanta, who proves to be the most suitable to be addressed as Ishwara, whom, those who aspire for salvation, try to approach by controlling the senses; let that Mahadeva, bless you.)

There was an expectant silence in the assembly. They all sat looking at Kalidasa. He was a stranger to them. But those who were well versed in literature and the vedic shastra realized that the man who now stood before them was an extraordinary embodiment of radiant wisdom. None had heard this poem. They had read almost all the available works of literature. But in none of them had they seen these lines, praising Sthanu, Lord Shiva, with such meaningful words. No one was heard reciting this in Ujjaini. These were lines that would have become famous if they had appeared in any work before!

'*Each word is loaded with meaning; this is not an ordinary man... There is no doubt about it. He must have completed the riddle,*' Vikramaditya thought. And even if he did not have the right solution to the puzzle, he is certainly a man of great ability. If he has composed these lines that he recited just now, that is enough to show the greatness of his creative genius. The king felt that the poet had also connected the poem to the riddle he had put forth.

Observing the smile on the face of the king, the assembly sat forward, anxious to know if this was the answer to the riddle that he had put forth.

'Introduce yourself to the assembly. You are unknown in Ujjaini,' Vikramaditya said.

'I bow before the king of Malava, Maharaja Vikramaditya, famed as Shakari, the enemy of the Shakas, son of the great Mahendraditya,' started Kalidasa and bowed before the king. He then continued, 'I am Kalidasa. This is the first time that I have come to Ujjaini. For the last few days, I have been wandering about in Ujjaini and even other parts of Malava. It was at the gates of the temple of Mahakaleswara that I heard the announcement. I feel that I have understood the puzzle that you have placed before the thousands of learned men. A stanza has been formed in my mind. That is why I came to this holy arena of grandeur and wisdom.'

Listening to the words of Kalidasa, Vikramaditya clapped his hands instinctively, in appreciation. That spread across the assembly like an echo and became a loud applause. Though the maharaja had defeated the Shakas and established his power in Ujjaini, none had so far thought of addressing him as 'Shakari'—one who conquered the Shakas. The title of 'Shakari' appealed to the people assembled there. Along with that, they were also pleased to hear their assembly being praised by well-chosen, suitable words. 'The holy arena of grandeur and wisdom'—none who loved Ujjaini could fail to applaud at the words of Kalidasa.

'Welcome to the assembly of the learned men of Avanti. If you have deciphered the puzzle that I put forth and if you can create a beautiful stanza according to it, you will be presented with one thousand gold coins and a place in this assembly of learned men,' announced the maharaja, welcoming Kalidasa to the assembly.

'Your Highness, I do not know if my stanza would rise up to your expectation. I have prepared what appeared appropriate as per my ability. Maharaj, I am going to present the lines I have made. Please give appropriate directions to the announcers,'

Kalidasa concluded his words with this request.

Amarasimha interrupted. 'You can recite your lines. What should the announcers do for that?' he asked.

'Amarasimha...!' the maharaja stopped him. 'If Kalidasa wants to give any instructions to the announcers, I hereby give him permission to do so. He has come to our assembly for the first time and we accord him the freedom due to a guest,' said the king with a smile.

Kalidasa had no difficulty in understanding the meaning behind his smile. 'So you have understood the matter,' his face seemed to indicate his happiness at that.

Kalidasa looked at the men who had made the proclamation the previous day. There was no need for a hint. The men bowed their heads indicating that they had understood what was required of them.

All who were assembled there, except the maharaja, were surprised to see all this. What had the announcers got to do with this? What part will the men who beat the drum and play pipes for making royal announcements, have in the presentation of a couplet in the assembly?

Putting an end to their anxious thoughts, Kalidasa started speaking, 'Maharaj, all the arrangements have been completed by morning to anoint Sree Ramachandra, the jewel of the clan of Reghu as Yuvaraj. Without knowing the demands of Kaikeyi to send Ram to the forest, a servant woman has gone to get the water for the ablution of the prince. But as she is coming back, the pot falls from her hands, as if signalling some misfortune. The pot then rolls down the steps before coming to a stop at the bottom.

'rāmābhiṣēkē jalamāharantyā
hastātcyutōhēmaghaṭō yuvatyā
sōpānamārggēṇa karōti śabdam'

After reciting the three lines, Kalidasa looked at the announcers.

They understood what Kalidasa wanted. When they joined on their instruments, the recited lines gained an added perfection.

dhadham dhadhamdham dhadhadham dhadhamdhaa...

As all the musical instruments came together in perfect harmony, the audience felt that they could hear the sound of the pot falling down and going down the steps. Everybody realized that the riddle had been perfectly completed. The assembly reverberated with long applause.

'Welcome the genius Kalidasa, we welcome you to the royal assembly of Ujjaini,' Vikramaditya rose from his throne to welcome Kalidasa.

The musical instruments were played. The soldiers came forward to lead Kalidasa. A new seat had been made ready by then. The maharaja and the minister held him by both hands and made him sit down.

Kalidasa could not help noticing the raised eyebrows and furrowed foreheads of some of the men in the assembly.

As directed by the maharaja, Kalidasa told his life story to those who were assembled there.

'Maharaj, I went all over Malava, searching for my parents. I had a slight hope that they would have escaped from that forest fire. But I could not find them,' Kalidasa said.

'Kalidasa, you need not go anywhere now. You are a citizen of Malava, come back to his land after a long time. Ujjaini needs you. We can search again to find your parents.'

A soldier now approached the throne, bearing a plate heaped with gold coins.

'You are entitled to the prize that had been announced. But, for the sake of all who are assembled here, please tell us how you came to understand the last line of the couplet,' said Vikramaditya.

'Maharaj, each sound in nature has a meaning. Everything has got its own rhythm. I was able to recognize it. When I heard the announcement, I wondered why the last line had not been revealed. I also felt that such an announcement must reveal the last part in some way or the other. It struck me that the rhythm of the drums was different from what is generally used in ordinary announcements. But I knew that what was lacking in the announcement was getting completed by the sound and rhythm of the drums,' Kalidasa explained.

Vikramaditya congratulated Kalidasa again and again. 'Your power of observation is indeed great,' he said.

All the members of the assembly praised Kalidasa referring to different things.

'All arrangements for Kalidasa to stay here in royal comfort will be made. Malava expects a lot from you,' Vikramaditya continued.

As the assembly dispersed and everyone was walking out, one man came forward and stood in front of Kalidasa. He stood there looking into Kalidasa's face and then pointed to his own face. Kalidasa looked at him carefully. The face seemed familiar. Who was this? Yes! Nichula! He used to come to the gurukula of Devasraya from a village nearby. Kalidasa could not control his joy.

'Nichula! You!' he exclaimed.

'Shambhu...!' He uttered the name and embraced Kalidasa.

There was a surge of happiness in Kalidasa's mind. He could hardly believe his eyes. Nichula was with him when the forest fire started. His dear friend! The guru at that gurukula used to love both of them.

'Yes, Nichula, I am Shambhu. I was lucky to escape from the fire then. I became the servant of the Goddess Kali at Champa. I acquired knowledge and education. I was even able to have a glimpse of Mount Kailas. I worshipped the lotus feet of Devi

Kanyakumari. Then I travelled across the country and reached Ujjaini. I searched all over Malava hoping to find someone. Failing in that attempt I came here. Now I have been able to find you at least. Is there anyone else...?' Kalidasa looked with anticipation at Nichula.

'Only Guru Devasraya escaped from the fire. I was able to meet him after so many years. He had come to Ujjaini then. That is how he escaped from the fire,' Nichula explained.

'How did you escape?' Kalidasa asked.

'I was able to reach the hermitage. But the fire had spread there too by that time. I jumped into the water in the lake. I lay there keeping my nose above water to breathe. Though it was difficult even to breathe at times, I was able to escape. I saw the deadly dance of the fire from the middle of it,' Nichula was silent.

Kalidasa could see Nichula's eyes filling with tears. Nichula must have seen the hermitage being reduced to ashes. He would have seen Shambhu's house also being burnt down. Nichula must be keeping silent as he must have seen what happened to Shambhu's parents.

Kalidasa spoke, 'Tell me, Nichula... What happened to my father and mother?'

'No, Shambhu! I do not know if they escaped. I saw the house under fire. I do not know whether they were there in the house or if they had managed to escape,' Nichula explained.

A ray of hope remained in Kalidasa's mind. They might have escaped. He may be able to see them somewhere...sometime.

'Come...' Nichula walked out of the palace with Kalidasa.

5

Kalidasa made efforts to get to know eminent personalities in the assembly of Ujjaini well and acquire knowledge from all of them. But soon it became evident that some of them were only 'frogs in a well'—those who thought that what they knew was the ultimate knowledge.

Nichula helped Kalidasa choose a suitable place to stay. Kalidasa wanted to have a place like a hermitage near the Kshipra River. He could get an order for it from the palace. As he had become a member of the royal assembly, he was made a guru at the Royal Gurukula, as was the custom.

One day, as he was returning from the assembly through the garden, he saw the queen collecting flowers there. On seeing her he had the feeling that he had seen her before. As he turned back to look at her once again, the queen also turned back to look at him. Did it mean that the queen also had felt that his face was familiar or was it just curiosity about the man who had solved the riddle?

Both of them did not want to talk to each other. But there was a meaningful silence between them before they turned away.

Kalidasa searched his memory. He had come to Ujjaini only recently. So he knew that he had not seen her there before. Was it at some other place? He had covered a vast area during his wanderings. Could he have seen her somewhere else? He thought about it till he reached his house. He was sure that the face was familiar. Where had he seen her? Where had he seen this face? His mind travelled back.

Suddenly the picture of the palace at Kashi came up in his mind. The conspirators of that palace had forcibly taken him there. That had happened so many years ago. Yes! The consort of King Vikramaditya was Princess Vidyothama. She had decided to marry him, who had been nothing but a shepherd boy at that time. The princess who had wanted to marry a wise and learned man had now got the most suitable husband. Kalidasa had managed to escape from there by pretending to be a fool. But he had described his story in the assembly on the first day. She must have heard all that from behind the curtain. Or she might have known the details from the maharaja. She had certainly recognized him.

On another occasion, when they came face to face, Vidyothama stood there and looked hard at his face. Kalidasa hesitated for a moment. Had she recognized him? Had she realized that he had been acting a fool to escape from there? When he described his life in the assembly, he had not anticipated such a situation. He had no idea how the queen would behave. Any way he felt that the consort of King Vikramaditya would not be evil minded. She had allowed him to leave the palace at that time; she had not decided to imprison him. Though obstinate, she was wise. That was why she had insisted on getting a wise man as her husband. The queen asked, '*asti kaścit vāgviśeṣā?*'

Kalidasa stood in shocked silence for a while. He didn't know what to say in reply. A question with an implied meaning about the language of signs, raised by the princess then, now the royal consort!

Kalidasa stood looking at the queen without batting an eyelid. After a while, the queen gave him a meaningful look and walked away; either because he had not replied to her query or because she did not expect an answer. Kalidasa felt that there was a hint of a secretive smile on her face.

The next day, the king invited Kalidasa to the garden. Kalidasa felt apprehensive about the unusual summons. He suspected that Vidyothama might have told him about the incident in the past.

When they reached the garden, the king seated himself on the marble platform and asked Kalidasa to sit down.

'Kalidasa, do you know my queen, Vidyothama?' he asked in a grave voice.

'Maharaj! What can I say? At that time, I was only a boy who was looking after the sheep of the priest of the Kali temple in Champa,' Kalidasa started, feeling that the queen must have told the king all about that incident.

'Queen Vidyothama says that you are a fool and that you cheated the assembly by saying something foolish. She says that you are only an ordinary woodcutter in Champa and that you are an imbecile. She therefore insists that you should be made to leave Ujjaini.'

By that time Queen Vidyothama had also reached there. Why should she feel antagonized by him? Why should she be angry with him? He may not have been a fool, but he was not a prince. And the princess had now become the queen of the famous kingdom of Malava. Then why does she want to oust him from there? Many questions passed through Kalidasa's mind.

Seeing Kalidasa remain silent, the king said with a smile, 'You give an answer to Vidyothama's question. The queen has decided that you should be made a prisoner for life for having cheated the grand royal assembly of Ujjaini.'

Kalidasa looked at Vidyothama who had seated herself near the king.

Vidyothama repeated the question, '*asti kaścit vāgviśēṣaḥ*?'

He decided that he was not ready to give a direct answer to the question. If the king and the queen had at least some knowledge, it would be better to counter the question with another one... Kalidasa recited the lines:

'indīvarēṇa nayanaṃ mukhamambujēna
kundēna dantamadharaṃ nava pallavēna
aṃgāni campakadalaiḥ saḥ vidhāya vēdhāḥ
kāntē kathaṃ ghaṭitavānupalēna cētaḥ'

('Śṛṃgāratilakam' by Kalidasa)

(Lord Brahma has created you with eyes that can be compared to the petals of the blue lotus, a face that is like the lotus flower, teeth resembling the jasmine buds and limbs like the petals of the Champa flower. Then why did he create your heart with stone?)

Vidyothama seemed to be too surprised to react for a minute. The next moment both Vikramaditya and Vidyothama clapped their hands.

'Beautiful, beautiful...excellent... Kalidasa,' Vikramaditya said. Turning to his queen he said, 'Vidyothama, now haven't you gotten the answer to your question? Anyone can see the blessings of the goddess of letters in each word that Kalidasa utters. Now give a reply to Kalidasa's question.'

The queen smiled but did not say anything. Just then Princess Mallika arrived and Vikramaditya introduced her to Kalidasa: 'This is Mallika, my little sister. She is interested in poems and plays.'

Kalidasa's mind seemed to tell him that the first three lines of the poem that he had just recited were out of place. They would suit Mallika better. A face that embodied the essence of beauty... An attractive smile... Even an expert with words will have to search for words to describe the beauty of that body; limbs that defied comparison. The radiance of youth seemed to be dancing in those eyes. It looked as though all the ingredients that Lord Brahma had used to create beauty must have been exhausted after he had created her.

'Maharaj, may I go now?' Kalidasa asked when he felt that his thoughts were straying into the garden of the Manmadha, the god of love.

'Kalidasa, you have exhibited your ability in creating excellent poems. There has been a definite change visible at the gurukula after you started working there. You have been explaining so beautifully, the tandava dance of Lord Shiva, the science of performing arts, the *Natya Shastra* by Bharata Muni and the poems and plays for the understanding of the students there,' Vikramaditya spoke of what he had heard about Kalidasa.

'Your Highness, somehow, my interest lies in poems and plays. So, I tried to know what works were available on those subjects in great detail. My travels were for acquiring knowledge. I learned about the literary works that were already well known and those that were becoming famous at each place that I visited. I am now passing it on to the students. Everyone should know about culture, the way of life of the people and the geographical features.'

'That is great. But Ujjaini wishes to see your genius reflected in your works and thereby get some excellent literary creations from you. The lines that you have written have already found a place in the arenas of reciting competitions,' the king commented.

Vidyothama, who had remained silent till then, said, 'You will be provided with all the royal comforts and facilities.'

Kalidasa just smiled.

As he was walking back home, Kalidasa was thinking about Bharata Muni's *Natya Shastra*. Many diverse levels of creative arts were discussed in it. A play should be written keeping the principles and directions given in it. The plays had been written by Bhasa and Soumilla. When a play is presented before a learned audience, who are aware of these details, he must take care to see that it is acceptable to them. There should not be any trace of repetition in it. Even if it is not a creation that excelled the works of these masters, it should at least be equal to them in quality. He felt that he should complete such a play to be presented at the theatre during the spring festival. Kalidasa started giving colours to the characters and emotions in his mind.

On reaching home, Kalidasa sat under the champaka tree, gazing at the Kshipra. The river, as usual, was speeding away, creating uproar as it dashed against the rocks. Lotus flowers were in bloom in a lake that had been formed by the water that came from the river. Swans were swimming about in it.

As he looked at the lotus pond, the figure of Vidyothama came to his mind. His mind made a comparison between Vidyothama and Mallika. Both were blessed with beauty. But if Vidyothama could be compared to a flower in full bloom, Mallika could be considered a bud, yet to bloom. Mallika's posture did not exude the maturity that Vidyothama portrayed; her face was more mischievous...jovial. She had the radiance and simplicity associated with her youth... The beauty of the innocent smile of an infant and a sweet voice. That smile and that sweet voice kept appearing and echoing in his mind.

But Kalidasa forcibly brought his mind under control; it shouldn't be allowed to stray. His mind must be on the play that he was planning to write.

Kalidasa did not attend the assembly for many days after that. Though he went to the gurukula, he did not spend too much time there also.

When Kalidasa had been absent for many days, Vikramaditya sent his men to make enquiries. 'Please inform the king that I am here,' was the only reply that Kalidasa sent with the men.

Kalidas's mind was busy going through the stories and

legends in mythology and ancient texts of history. He searched for a suitable background in the lands he had visited and their history. In the end he came to Agnimitra, who had ruled over Vidisha. He had stayed in Vidisha during his travels and had met Agnimitra.

He had come to Kapilavasthu on the Himalayas with Rishi Shalibhadra. From there he had crossed Vaishali to reach Pataliputra, the capital of the Mourya dynasty.

The country was fully involved in the movement of the army towards the west. But Kalidasa was more interested in seeing the glory of the land of Bharat; so the glory of Magadha and the tumult of the war did not keep him there.

He went to the Rajagruha and Tamralipti. Then through Gaya, he reached Varanasi. He wandered about here and there for a long time, visiting villages and cities, experiencing the diversity of life. He did not forget the village of Champa. Shivasoma and his family were overjoyed to welcome him. Malini had gotten married and life continued there as before. Soon he left for Prayag. The group of merchants that he met there were on their way to the Bhrigukaccha on the northern banks of the Narmada through Vidisha. He came to Vidisha with them and spent a few days there. The place was ruled by Agnimitra, the son of Pushyamitra. It was at that time that Agnimitra got married a second time. Pushyamitra, the ruler of Magadha, had sent his son to rule over Vidisha in order to gather the army to withstand the attack of the Shakas. But Agnimitra was more interested in living as the king than in working as the representative of the king.

It was a beautiful country. It was by pure chance that Kalidasa had been able to meet King Agnimitra who had been giving a lot of support and encouragement to literature and the arts. The circumstances in Vidisha were different from that of Pataliputra. Kalidasa even doubted that the sensuality that had affected Bruhadradha, the last Maurya king, had also affected the son of Pushyamitra. He thought of some stories that he had heard, some matters of royal rule and a king's law and justice. As his thoughts reached this point, he stopped himself. He felt that the germ for the story that he had been searching for had been found. If he used the stories that he had heard at Vidisha and added some details of administration by a king, it would provide him with the background for a play. Yes, for King Vikramaditya, a story of a royal dynasty, a story of royal victories as well as the stories of love associated with palaces, would be certainly attractive. Kalidasa was able to develop a background in which story and poetry could be successfully utilized. Gradually the different scenes took shape in his mind.

He made a start, praying to Mahadeva.

After praying to the lord of the universe to free all from the path of ignorance, a new thought entered his mind. This play will be enacted before an elite audience that has witnessed many other famous plays. There will naturally be a question raised, 'Why are we presenting a play by Kalidasa, a newcomer to the field, at the festival of spring?' He decided to give an answer to that before beginning the play.

At the invocation, during the conversation between the speaker of the prologue and the attendant, he expressed his gratitude for his predecessors, while also hinting that a new playwright should be accepted. Instead of clinging to the old creations, it was essential to provide newer creations according to the taste of the audience. He indicated that he was making an attempt at that. The wise and learned men should examine the new creations and decide whether they were acceptable. No one can say something that lacks quality will be accepted just because it is new.

purāṇamityēva na sādhu sarvaṃ
na cāpi kāvyaṃ navamityavadyam
santa: parīkṣyānyataradbhajantē
mūḍha: parapratyayanēyabuddhi:

(Malavikagnimitram, Act 1, ii)

(Old works need not be of good quality just because they were written long ago. All new works need not be bad. Men of wisdom will examine all works and choose the best. For the foolish, the words of the wise shall be the truth.)

The imagination of the writer found a place on the writing leaves in letters, words, verse and sentences.

The infatuation that Agnimitra felt for Malavika, who had come to the palace as the companion of his wife Dharini, was logically introduced.

Kalidasa immersed himself in writing, almost like a penance. His thoughts and imagination took shape as letters, words and sentences. At places they arranged themselves on the writing leaf as the lines of a verse, as two or four lines in length. He did not go to the gurukula for days together. The senior acharya made enquiries and sent instructions for him to attend to the work in the gurukula many times. But Kalidasa was so immersed in writing that he became aware that the sun had set only when he could not read what he was writing on the leaf.

Malavika's grace as a dancer was revealed by presenting her on stage. The suspicion in the mind of Dharini, Agnimitra's wife, at her husband's behaviour was also presented. A detailed description of the plans made by the king with the help of the court jester to meet Malavika and the realization that she was also in love with him, was written. Next was the scene where Iravati, another wife of Agnimitra, comes to know of the desire in the mind of the king and Malavika. Parts were assigned to the lady companions and other supporting actresses.

Queen Dharini came to know about the love between Malavika and Agnimitra through Iravati. She ordered the imprisonment of Malavika along with her companion, Bakulavali. But Agnimitra managed to get her out of prison using a plan hatched by the jester. Kalidasa took care to join the different scenes together in a manner that would be liked by the audience. Then the secret that Malavika was in reality Madhavasenan's sister, who had escaped from the place and had come to Vidisha when Madhavasen and his wife had been imprisoned, is revealed. Next came the part where the land of Vidarbha is divided between Yajnasenan and Madhavasenan. The story of how Vasumitra, the son of Agnimitra, defeated the Greeks and brought back the horse that had been entrusted to him by Pushyamitra was written. Dharini, elated at the victory of her son, agrees to the marriage between Agnimitra and Malavika.

Three months before the festival of spring was to begin, Kalidasa completed writing the play and kept the pen down with satisfaction.

Now he started looking for actors and actresses suitable for the characters. Who would be good enough to act as Agnimitra? And which actress would be able to enact the part of the queen? But there was no need to search for an actress to take up the part of Malavika... While he was writing, whenever his mind thought about Malavika, only one figure came to mind—that of Mallika. At certain places he had unconsciously written Mallika instead of Malavika. He had to destroy some writing leaves just because of that.

But will the king allow his sister to act on stage with ordinary players? He may, as he did not seem to be a person who would categorize art and recognize artists according to their caste and creed.

Though he had seen Mallika only once, she was always in his memory. Her face was fresh in his memory as if he had met her just yesterday. She had always been there, near him in different forms and moods. The picture of that smile, the beauty of those eyes, the sweet voice, the thick black hair that covered her back—with some flowers on it that seemed reluctant to leave. He felt that the essence of feminine beauty had been infused into her form.

Kalidasa was aware of his inability to control his own mind. But even that misguided wandering of his mind provided some elation. For the first time he felt that there was somebody who could be considered to be meant for him...a sort of solace... an inspiration. The thought of that sweet smile was like gentle moonlight in his mind. But immediately he corrected such thoughts and tried to control his mind.

Kalidasa was ready early the next morning. He had to inform the king that his work was complete. The assembly of the learned men had to approve of the play if it was to be performed during the festival. Still, above all thoughts about the play, stood the thoughts about Mallika. There seemed to be something weighing his mind down.

It was after many days that Kalidasa was coming out of his house. As he looked around, he noticed that the cuckoos had started heralding the arrival of spring. The gentle murmur of the birds could be heard in the wind that blew from afar. The plants and trees were all in bloom and some were about to flower. Innumerable bees and butterflies fluttered about, drinking the honey from the flowers. Kalidasa wanted to go back and add a description of the arrival of spring. But his anxiety to see how the streets and paths that he had not seen for many days were getting ready to welcome spring, led him forward.

Red lotus flowers were in bloom in a pond that was lined with beautiful rocks collected from the Kshipra. Beetles and small birds flitted about among the flowers. Many other flowers had started to bloom. The Ashoka tree was covered with red inflorescence but it had not forgotten to draw a floral carpet on the ground. An unusual show of beauty!

He went near the lotus flowers, inhaled their sweet smell and touched the soft petals. The dewdrops shone like pearls on the lotus leaves. Taking some water in his hands, he sprinkled it over the lotus leaves. These drops joined the dew drops, running around like bubbles of diamonds and some drops fell on the wings of the bees and shone in the sunlight like blue diamonds.

After enjoying this beauty for a while, Kalidasa walked towards the palace. As he walked along, his eyes went to the beautifully attired girls who were walking along the streets. These beauties seemed to add to the beauty of the royal pathways. The flowers that decorated their tresses above the gold ear drops added to their beauty. The garlands of fragrant flowers like champaka on their tresses spread a mixture of different smells as they passed by.

Kalidasa noted in his mind that Kamadeva, the god of love, must have thought spring to be the one best suited to play his tricks on the young girls. Their demeanour seemed to declare to the world that their beauty was now ready to welcome the spring season. Like the flowers that beckoned the beetles, they wanted their beauty to spread the light around.

The men were engaged in their usual activities. They did not feel the necessity to call anyone to enjoy their beauty. Was it the memory of the anger of Mahadeva when he was attacked that prevented the God of Love from trying his tricks on the men?

Kalidasa reached the palace gates without being aware of having covered that much distance. The gatekeepers made friendly yet polite enquiries about his absence from the palace for so many days. It was only then that he felt the weight of the writing leaves that he carried in a bundle on his shoulders. Pointing to the bundle, he said with a smile, 'I too was preparing for the arrival of the spring.'

As he crossed the gateway and went in, he was forced to wonder where to put his foot down. The ground was strewn with the petals of yellow, golden and white flowers so thickly that he was reluctant to stamp the fragrant carpet to go on his way. He walked carefully, causing the least possible damage to the petals. At places he even felt like brushing them aside to make space for his footsteps.

The penetrating fragrance of the jasmine that had climbed up the trees greeted him as he moved on. Beyond that were the Ashoka trees in bloom and the roses and many other sweet-smelling blossoms. Along with the innumerable bees and butterflies that danced and hopped from flower to flower, it seemed to Kalidasa that spring had come to the palace garden of King Vikramaditya to dance. And then a face came into his view—'Does a lotus bloom outside the water body?' he wondered.

Involuntarily his feet paused. What now met his eyes in the garden was a beauty that belied all that he had visualized while writing his play. The drops of perspiration that lined the face like the tender ends of fresh grass were shining like pearls in the morning sunlight. A thousand drums seemed to be beating in his heart. A sensation that went beyond words, of his heart brimming over with an unusual sensation, held him there.

He couldn't move forward. A young lady looking at him without closing her eyelids even for a second! Kalidasa looked at her again. The rose in her hand was yet to leave the fingers as if hesitating to leave the beautiful fingers! What was the expression that remained on the face? What did that expression signify? Kalidasa felt his heart attempting to break free and flee. What was the message in those eyes?

There he stood forgetting that he had set out to go to the assembly. He forgot about the play that he had created through penance of many days. The thought of the assembly left his mind.

'What has happened to the poet?'

But that question did not reach Kalidasa. The voice was lost in the surroundings along with the cooing of the cuckoos.

Mallika raised her head. Seeing the poet looking at her without batting an eyelid, she repeated the question with more confidence, 'Hey! What has happened to the poet?'

Kalidasa's mind experienced a sense of cool and joy. He was listening to a voice that went with the sweet cooing of the cuckoos that came to play the music for welcoming the season of spring. He had never thought of himself as a poet. Though he had composed a few lines of verse, he had never shown his creations to anybody. Still here was Mallika, addressing him as a poet! But if this embodiment of beauty that stood before him sang in this sweet voice, he was sure his pen would create an infinite number of poems. *'Haven't I seen girls before...?'* He wondered. Or was it that there was no other girl like this in this holy land?

Kalidasa smiled. 'Have you seen any of my poems, Princess? I have not composed any poems. How then can I be a poet?' Kalidasa refused to accept that he was a poet.

'It is not the creation of lines that nobody reads, that sleep on the writing leaf or give no enjoyment, that makes a person a poet. Everyone who has learned to read and write in Ujjaini, enjoy reciting the couplets that you have written. These lines are used by young men while addressing the girls they love, husband when speaking to his wife and lovers to their women. Who, in the whole of Ujjaini, does not know the lines, *"indīvarēṇa nayanaṃ..."*.'

Kalidasa was astonished to hear this. 'These were the lines

that I recited before the maharaja when I saw the maharani. How did that reach the young men, the husbands and the romantic men?' he asked.

'My brother recited those lines in the assembly. Everyone was fascinated by those lines. Then they started playing on the lips of all,' she replied.

The mention of the word 'assembly' made Kalidasa remember that he was late in reaching there. 'Princess, the time to reach the assembly is already here. Please let me go.'

He walked with long strides towards the assembly. Did he hear the tinkling of the anklets? He found himself turning back. No, he must have imagined it. Did she take a couple of steps after him? Those black beetles, her eyes seemed to have followed him. They seemed to be desirous of telling him something... like the beetles wanting to be engaged in conversation with the flowers! Those eyes were certainly saying something. But Kalidasa did not have the time to tarry. By the time he reached the assembly, the king had already arrived.

The king clapped his hands in joy on seeing Kalidasa in the assembly, welcoming him after a long absence. This prompted the others also to do the same and offer a warm welcome. Bowing to the assembly, Kalidasa took his seat.

As the routine proceedings of the assembly came to an end, everyone turned their attention to Kalidasa.

The king himself addressed him, 'Kalidasa, it has been some time since you came to this assembly. We heard that you were engaged in writing something. Shall we hope that it has been completed?'

Bowing to the assembly, Kalidasa spoke, 'Yes, Maharaj! I was writing a play that could be presented on stage during the spring festival. Now it has been completed. As I wanted to complete it in time for the festival, I had to keep myself away from many other activities. Because of that I could not attend the assembly and the gurukula.'

Acharya Shankuka intervened immediately, 'Maharaj! The schedule of work in the gurukula was seriously affected because of the absence of Kalidasa. If, in gurukula, the masters themselves are not regular, what lesson will it give to the students?'

The king looked at Kalidasa. Kalidasa was aware that he had not been able to establish himself in Ujjaini by the creation of a masterpiece that would offer a defence against such accusations even though he had been successful in winning the appreciation of a few. Added to that was the fact that Acharya Shankuka and a few others did not seem to approve of Kalidasa. So he felt that his work should be the answer to these accusations. He silently took the leaves from the bundle and placed them before the king.

Then he said, 'Maharaj, these leaves will speak of what I have been doing all these days.'

'What is this? Explain it yourself,' Amarasimha, the minister said.

'This is a play, Maharaj! Named *Malavikagnimitram*. If the group of scholars approve of it, it may be chosen for presentation at the spring festival,' requested Kalidasa.

It was Somabhatta who intervened this time. 'Maharaj! It has been the works of the masters of the past that have been approved by both the players and the audience till now. May I request that no decision be taken that will tarnish the greatness of the festival of spring?'

'Ability should be the basis for recognition. Let the group of learned men examine Kalidasa's work and express their opinion. Then we will take a decision,' Vikramaditya spoke his mind.

Shankuka also agreed with the king. 'Yes, if this work will add to the glory of the festival, we will begin the festivities by presenting this on the stage. Let the experts decide that.'

As the assembly was about to disperse, Kalidasa's eyes wandered to the place where the ladies of the palace usually sat. Had spring come to the assembly?

And for a moment, their eyes met. Kalidasa saw a thousand poems being formed in those eyes!

6

Spring was announcing her arrival in Malava by decorating even the desert land with flowers. The flowering trees showered the waters of the Kshipra with petals. The wind flew around carrying the fragrance of the flowers.

The preparation for the festival of spring was at its height. It had been decided that Kalidas's *Malavikagnimitram* would be enacted during the festival. As Kalidasa had feared, some people tried to prevent it by saying that it was a play by a new playwright. But the forum of learned men could not ignore his work. After *Swapnavasavadattam*, Ujjaini had not seen such a good play. The creative writers of Ujjaini had the feeling that a new full moon was rising in the country, pushing them all to the shade. Some of them welcomed it with pleasure; others found the dark clouds of envy clogging their minds.

The master of dramatics, Devadatta was imaginative and well-versed in the arts. When Kalidasa expressed the opinion that Mallika would be the best person to act the part of Malavika, Vikramaditya was pleased; but it was difficult for him to see his sister as an actress. But when Queen Vidyothama also persuaded him, he agreed to it.

When it was known that the princess was acting as the main character in the play, the efforts to bring the play on stage became a royal matter. That added to the importance of the festival that year; the people were excited.

The celebrations of the festival started at the height of spring. Many special programmes were held in Ujjaini. The people enjoyed themselves with music and dance. Many groups of merchants and travellers had come to Ujjaini to participate in the festivities.

Malavikagnimitram was staged. Mallika became Malavika. It was a day when gratification coloured Kalidasa's mind.

All the learned men of Ujjaini were full of praise for Kalidasa's creative skill. Even among the ordinary people, characters like Agnimitra, Malavika and Dharani remained a topic of discussion for many days. Among the learned men, among those who had artistic interests and those who were well versed in literature, *Malavikagnimitram* was discussed on different planes.

Some took up the introductory verse of prayer and analysed it word by word, praising it for the different shades of meaning that it portrayed. Others argued about the relative merits of Bhasa's *Swapnavasavadattam* and Kalidasa's *Malavikagnimitram*.

Some of the courtiers watched Kalidasa's rise with envy. Kalidasa had become a close friend of Maharaja Vikramaditya. The king invited Kalidasa for literary discussions very frequently. Even the minister, Amarasimha doubted whether Kalidasa was gaining precedence over him. The king had started discussing state matters with Kalidasa before asking Amarasimha for his opinion. Kalidasa's opinion seemed to carry more weight than that of the minister. Queen Vidyothama had also become attracted to Kalidasa's poems. The situation soon became such that whatever was discussed in Ujjaini, the name of Kalidasa would come up in some context or the other.

The poets who had held an important position in the assembly before the arrival of Kalidasa now lost their brilliance like the stars on a full moon night.

Once the festivities of spring had ended, Vikramaditya placed another puzzle before the assembly: '*ka kha ga gha.*'

The learned men of the assembly were surprised. They all felt that this was even more difficult than the previous one where he had not given any word or line as a clue. They had complained about the king not providing at least the last line. They had cited that as a reason for their inability to solve the riddle. But now, this was more complicated. Vowels joined the consonants like the soul joining the body and produced letters; letters came together to form meaningful words; words could be brought together to form lines and these lines joined with other lines with particular meanings to form a couplet. But the consonants like *ka kha ga gha* would not form a word when placed together. The body and the soul were there, but they were only a line of lifeless letters! This line of letters was not a word. And it was impossible to make a line out of a non-existent word.

Days passed. At first, Kalidasa did not attach much importance to the riddle. He had gained entry to the assembly by solving a riddle. He did not want to be known as the one who was engaged in solving riddles. He had realized that his area of specialization was something else.

But one day the letters *ka kha ga gha* came up as a serious matter in the assembly. 'Isn't there anyone in this royal assembly of Ujjaini, capable of composing four lines?' There was a touch of anger in the king's question. 'Or should I announce a gift or even offer the throne for this? Or is it that a poet has to come from some other land for this?'

The words of the king reverberated from the walls of the assembly adorned with artistic decorations. Kalidasa felt that he had never before realized the gravity of King Vikramaditya's voice. Along with that he felt that there was an insinuation that Kalidasa was still 'a poet from some other land'. Did it mean that his own land of Malava had not been able to embrace him as her own? He was surprised to notice that his inability to establish his roots in Ujjaini could have such deep meaning. Waves of pain rose in his mind. He was still an outsider in Ujjaini!

The words of the king made Kalidasa think. Did he consider himself much above the level of completing puzzles after he had gained fame and appreciation for the creation of *Malavikagnimitram*? Did he become so arrogant just because one of his plays was staged and that won the applause of all sorts of people, as to think that he should now write only plays and long poems and not short verses? Did he feel that solving puzzles was a childish occupation?

Kalidasa now remembered his hands, forgetting the leaves for writing, had been engaged in creating new dimensions of beauty with colours on the canvas. The figure of Mallika appeared on the canvas as if all colours were created only to portray the enchantment of the features of that embodiment of beauty. Mallika...who forgot to put the flower that she had plucked into her basket on seeing him, looking at him bashfully through the corner of her eyes!

When Kalidasa realized that nothing more beautiful could ever be created on a canvas, he kept the brushes aside. He stood away from the canvas and looked at what he had created. If anyone came in, they would think that Mallika was there in Kalidasa's bower and only on coming closer would they realize that it's a portrait. It was a life-like representation. The eyes held the same expression. The same grace on the face, the same smile on the lips. For a few days, the portrait remained in Kalidasa's house. Then he realized that he would lose control over his mind if it remained there any longer.

But newer ones took its place. The figure of Mallika as she danced as Malavika when the play was staged had gotten imprinted on his mind. Once he had portrayed the beauty of the romantic movements in dance on the canvas, he wrote the lines from the play under it...

aṅgairantarnihitavacanai sūcita samyagarthaḥ
pādanyāsō layamanugatastanmayatvaṃ rasēṣu
śākhāyōnirmṛdurabhinayasta-kilpānuvṛttau
bhāvō bhāvaṃ nudati viṣayādrāgabandhaḥ sa ēva

(*Malavikagnimitram*, Act 2, Verse 8)

(The gestures reflected the words and their meaning. The steps were seeking the appropriate place. Sentimental emotions seemed to have gained structural form. The slender hands expressed the sentiments to perfection. While depicting different sentiments the expression changed but love, the main emotion, remained prominent at all times.)

The scenes with Malavika and Agnimitra dancing together came to his mind very often. They enjoyed themselves in Gandhamadana or Hemakoota or Kailas as Parvati and Parameswara. During such times the assembly of Ujjaini and the solution for the puzzle that the king had wanted were not on Kalidasa's mind.

After the assembly, Kalidasa walked about, deep in thought. The words of the king remained as tiny barbs in his heart. He had not yet been accepted in Ujjaini. He was still an outsider here. Gradually his mind came back to the new puzzle. He too felt that it was difficult to create a couplet ending with *ka kha ga gha*.

The puzzle became a topic of discussion the next day in the assembly. Many recited what they had written but the king rejected all, saying that they lacked sense. They had brought the letters *ka, kha, ga* and *gha* in verse; but they had not formed a meaningful last line of the verse. Some of them had added deep thoughts before the simple letters. The king mercilessly rejected some others saying that they were only imitations of the grammatical formulae by Panini. The king's comment was that wild jasmine and lotus flowers cannot be strung together in the same garland.

'Has the poetic ability of Kalidasa gone dry?' someone was heard murmuring in the assembly. He did not feel like raising his head to see who had made that remark. But one thing seemed clear, the owner of that voice believed Kalidasa to be the last hope, '*Will I be able to rise to that expectation?*' he wondered.

~

Kalidasa was sitting in the shade of a banyan tree on the side of a road. Many came up to him to make conversation, but Kalidasa replied in as few words as possible and returned to his thoughts. He had decided that he would not go back to the assembly without a good couplet ending in *ka kha ga gha*.

A little girl was coming towards him from a distance, jumping and frolicking as she ran forward. Kalidasa watched her running after the butterflies. She must have known that she would not be able to catch them, or she did not want to trouble them by catching them. But she still ran behind them as if she too wanted to enjoy flying around like them. The butterflies too were fluttering close to her as if they too were enjoying playing with her. She had a writing leaf in her hand. She must be coming back from school. Her friends must have left her as they reached their houses. When she was alone, she made the butterflies her companions. She did not seem to think that there was no one with her.

As she came near, Kalidasa smiled at her. Seeing a stranger smile at her she hesitated for a moment. Her joy and enthusiasm seemed to falter. Kalidasa asked her: '*kā tvaṃ bālē?*' (Who are you, little girl?)

The girl stopped. She was still looking at the butterflies. But she was wondering whether she should follow the butterflies or answer the question. She looked at them and then at the stranger's face. Kalidasa too looked in wonder at the butterflies. They were hovering around a little away as if waiting for the girl to come. Were they also enjoying playing with the girl? A sense of love for the girl came to his heart along with wonder. The girl stood there not sure of what she should do. She had been taught in school that children should respect elders and answer when they asked a question.

'*kā tvaṃ bālē?*'

Kalidasa repeated the question.

'kāñcanamālā,' she told him her name.

'*kasyāḥ putrī?*' Kalidasa expressed his desire to know whose daughter she was.

'kanakalatayāḥ,' she said with a smile, that she is the daughter of Kanakalata.

'*kiṃ vā hastē?*' (What is in your hand?) asked Kalidasa idly.

'tālīpatram.'

The girl raised her writing leaf—tālīpatram—as if proudly declaring that she was studying in school and that she was old enough to write on the leaf.

'*kā vā rēkhā?*' (What have you written on it?) asked Kalidasa pointing to what she held in her hand.

The girl remained quiet for a few seconds and then said, '*ka kha ga gha,*' before running away. 'Don't ask me anything more. Don't you see that my companions have all left?' she seemed to say as she ran away laughing.

With a happy smile on his face, Kalidasa kept looking at the girl as she danced away on her way.

The questions that he asked the girl and the answers she gave with a smile showing her jasmine-like teeth seemed to remove some weight from his mind. The smile remained on the face that had been grave for so long. The memory of the jasmine buds once again took his thoughts to the words of

Vikramaditya. Jasmine and lotus do not go well in a garland. After a while he remembered that the king had uttered the same letters that the girl had said... *ka kha ga gha* as a part of the new riddle.

Kalidasa's mind started working fast. What did the girl say in the end...? *ka kha ga gha...* His mind went back.

kā tvaṃ bālē? kāñcanamālā
kasyāḥ putrī? kanakalatayāḥ
kiṃ vā hastē? tālīpatram
kā vā rēkhā? ka kha ga gha

Kalidasa realized with surprise that the riddle that had been troubling him was getting solved without any special effort on his part. His questions and the girl's answers had made themselves into a beautiful couplet. Each line seemed to be shining with the sweet smile of the innocent girl.

Kalidasa recited the lines in the assembly the next day. The assembly reverberated with applause. King Vikramaditya got up from the throne and approached Kalidasa. Taking the emerald chain from his neck, he put it round Kalidasa's neck. Even Shankuka and Ghatakarpara who were always critical of Kalidasa had to applaud him.

'You are the real poet. Whatever be the riddle placed before you, it is solved in the most beautiful way,' said Vikramaditya, congratulating Kalidasa. Kalidasa got up from his seat and bowed before the king.

'No, Maharaj, this is not a poem that I composed. This was what I got on my way home,' said Kalidasa.

'What! You say you got it from the road? Have the trees and plants in Ujjaini started shedding poems along with flowers and fruits? Or is it that the flowers now turn into poems instead of fruits? Have the cuckoos and other birds of our country started singing poems? Do you now hear lines of poems along with the gurgling sound of the little waves of the Kshipra?' asked the king.

Kalidasa explained the incident. Immediately Shankuka was on his feet. 'Maharaj! I do not think this is a poem. Isn't it just a few questions and some answers?'

Seeing Shankuka so excited, Vikramaditya smiled. 'Oh! How wonderful! It is only a real poetic mind that can convert such mundane questions and answers into a poem. All the letters and words have always been there. The one who can string them together in the most beautiful and systematic way becomes a poet,' Vikramaditya said.

The assembly accepted Vikramaditya's words with loud applause.

A different train of thought was making its way into Kalidasa's mind. He wanted to go to Champa and see the family of Shivasoma. Little Malini must be grown up now.

He knew that the journey would not be very difficult. If he could get a boat to sail on the Kshipra, he would be in Champa in three or four days. Kalidasa decided on a date to start his journey.

Vikramaditya wanted to send someone with him but Kalidasa did not think that it was necessary. That night long ago, it had been a lonely flight through Kshipra to save his life and Kshipra had saved him. Other rivers like Charmanawati, Yamuna and Ganga had guided him. Goddess Kali on the banks of Champa had given him shelter. So even now he could sail on the Kshipra. The Goddess would protect him.

Many people were there to bid him goodbye. Kalidasa felt that there was a hint of tears in Mallika's eyes. What did Mallika feel towards him, love? Or just an admiration for a poet?

Nichula's observant eyes were gauging the emotion in Mallika's eyes. Maharaja Vikramaditya was a connoisseur of arts and literature. He was also broad-minded. But it was not possible that he would agree to his own sister's admiration for a poet, breaking the boundaries of such feelings to fall in love with the man. It would be dangerous for Kalidasa. The king's friendship with Kalidasa would not influence his decision on such matters.

Vidyothama instructed them to visit the king's palace at Kashi and enquire about her father's welfare.

Vikramaditya too noticed the change in Mallika's expression. This made him think deeply. As he was returning to the palace after bidding goodbye to Kalidasa, a sort of apprehension started growing in his mind. He looked at Mallika every now and then. The change in her countenance was quite clear and evident. The ever-smiling face now bore a shadow of sorrow. Why was she unhappy about Kalidasa's absence? Was their relationship breaking all bounds and growing into love? As a poet Kalidasa was supreme. And in a short span of time, he had become one of his closest friends. But Vikramaditya could not even think of him as a suitable husband for his sister. The king could like and respect the poet who walked around with long hair and a beard, carrying a sheaf of writing leaves in a bundle slung across his shoulders, he could give him a lot of wealth, he could honour the poet by bestowing positions and privileges on him. But considering him his sister's husband? No. He could not allow this relationship to develop any further. It was impossible to assume that the threat from the Shakas and the Greeks had been contained forever. The western border was always under the threat of an attack. What Ujjaini and even the whole of the sub-continent needed was a diplomatically and politically strong alliance to save the country from the threat posed by the uncivilized hordes. That has to be gained through Mallika's marriage alliance. Vikramaditya felt relieved that Kalidasa had left the place. Emotions have little relevance in politics.

Kalidasa was reminded of his first journey as he sailed on

the Kshipra. He was just a boy then. It was a journey without a definite destination on a raft made by tying some logs together. He was saddened by the thought that he had lost his parents somewhere in the forest or that they had been killed in the wildfire. He had been running away from the terrifying wild animals. Finally, he came to Malava after a long journey, lasting many years. Though he wandered all over the country, he had not been able to find his parents. Will they be alive now? He had only been able to find Nichula, an old friend. Will his parents be waiting for him here?

Trees stood on either side of the river. At the beginning of the journey there were trees in bloom. That must be the special feature of Ujjaini. As they moved farther away, the trees were huge and growing thickly together. The banks were high. Even if one managed to steer the boat to the side it would be impossible to get onshore. Though he had been watching the banks very carefully, Kalidasa could not find the place from where he had started his life's journey. More than 15 years had passed since then!

For some time, they talked. He had never seen such powerful flow in any other river. Since they had started in the afternoon to reach Charmanwati by morning, dusk fell soon. The sunset in Kshipra seemed special. The river had turned golden in the light of the setting sun.

Time and nature execute their creations with so much beauty, images that never repeat themselves, rhetorical embellishments and poetic flights of fancy, all coming together to create exquisite pictures of nature according to the time and the place. The stars appeared across the sky and the moon in its eighth day rose up. The face of the Lord who adorns himself with the crescent moon on his matted hair seemed to be faintly visible in the light of the moon. White clouds could be seen floating about. He had travelled a lot and seen many beautiful places. But what was before him now, seemed to be so enchanting, it gave him pleasure to see a different and new picture of nature.

Nichula had gone to sleep. Gradually Kalidasa also fell into a slumber, lulled by the soothing sound of the waves on the Kshipra. When he was awakened it felt soothing to lie awake, lost in the music of nature.

Soon after the sun was up, they reached Charmanawati. As he saw the turbulent flow of the river at certain places, Kalidasa wondered how he had passed these places when he was on that small raft as a little boy. The Ganga, as they entered it, was an entirely different experience. It was a huge expanse of water with innumerable boats of different sizes on it. They had a holy dip at the confluence of the rivers and continued on their way.

It was on the fourth morning that the flag post of the Kali temple in Champa became visible. It was here that the boy Shambhu had become Kalidasa.

After a bath in the river, they went to the temple and prayed. Many changes were visible in the temple—improvements that showed that it had royal patronage. After his prayers, as Kalidasa turned around and introduced himself, Shivasoma could see the boy Shambhu and came running and embraced him.

'Come, let us go home. Malini also talks about you all the time. She has learnt some of the lines that you have composed, by heart. She keeps humming them. Her husband, Somadatta, also loves your poems,' said Shivasoma.

'My poems? How did they reach here?' Kalidasa enquired in surprise.

'It was your couplets that reached here first. Soon some of the poems that the travelling merchants brought here also became very popular. They are the people who take all the news and spread the fame all over the country,' said Shivasoma, as they were walking to the house.

Shivasoma immediately called his wife and daughter.

'Shambhu...' he said.

'After he married Malini, Somadatta was there to help us with everything,' Shivasoma started explaining what had happened in their lives after Kalidasa had left Champa. 'Most of the difficulties that we were facing in our life were reduced. Years passed after you had left with Rishi Shalibhadra. You came here once but did not stay for long. With the passage of years, we had almost forgotten you. After Vikramaditya married the daughter of the king of Kashi, Vidyothama, prosperity came to the village of Champa also. A gurukula was established here. Very soon Kalidasa's couplets started reaching the gurukula here through the merchants and other travellers. Soon we heard about the fame that Kalidasa had achieved. We all felt an unspeakable emotion on hearing about the position achieved by the helpless boy, Shambhu, who had come to our village. As both Somadatta and Malini love your poems, we hear them humming those lines in this house also,' Shivasoma could not stop talking about all that happened after Kalidasa had left their house.

Kalidasa was happy to see the love and happiness shown by Malini and her mother. It was like meeting one's own parents and sister. Nichula was introduced to all of them and he too shared their joy.

Kalidasa did not return to Ujjaini immediately. Nichula, who had accompanied him, became his constant companion. Kalidasa found a warm welcome at the gurukula in Champa and the palace in Kashi.

As days passed, poetic images filled Kalidasa's mind. The atmosphere there was suitable for such pursuits. He wandered about on the river banks, hills and mountain slopes of Champa.

Kalidasa experienced the changes brought about by the passage of time. As the intoxicating fragrance of the Saptaparni, the milk-wood pine tree, that came with the soft wind, it seemed to announce the advent of the autumn season. All the plants on the mountaintops had also started putting forth buds. In two or three days they would also burst into flowers, spreading their fragrance everywhere.

The seasons seemed to give life to couplets in Kalidasa's mind. He thought of his childhood spent with his parents. The summer was at its zenith. What a spectacular scene had been created in the forest by the summer heat! The summer was the same in Champa. How was it in Ujjaini? What did the beautiful ladies and the wanton women of Ujjaini do in the summer? Kalidasa took out the writing leaves and a quill. Imagination took shape as letters, words and lines:

*pracaṇḍasūryaḥ spṛhaṇīya candramāḥ
sadāvagāhakṣamavārisañcayaḥ
dināntaramyō'bhyupaśāntamanmathō
nidāghakālō/yamupāgataḥ priyē!*

(*Ritusamharam*-1)

(When the sun is extremely hot during the summer, one wishes for the rise of the moon that brings coolness, as per the imagination of the poet. As the people bathe themselves many times a day, the water in the lakes gets reduced. Oh! My beloved! Now it is that summer when even Manmadha, the God of love, takes rest.)

As he wrote 'my beloved' a question resounded in Kalidasa's mind. Who? To which beloved lady was he addressing these lines? He felt that he should change those words...but his mind was not willing to do so. In those lines, no other word would provide the charm that those words lent.

At times the lines poured forth from his mind with ease; other times Kalidasa had to carry in his mind all that he had observed of the vagaries of time and how nature and different living beings reacted to that. Sometimes he sat for hours absorbed in writing. He also spent hours gazing at the mountains beyond Champa. His mind saw the beautiful as well as the frightening changes in nature. The change of colours associated with the changing seasons transformed themselves into words and couplets.

What would Mallika be doing at this time? Would she be on the palace terrace, enjoying the beauty of the sunset? Would she have gone to the garden to gather flowers for the worship of the Gods? Would she be thinking about him? The picture of the lotus with the tiny birds seated on the flower came to his mind... Or was it the full moon without the mark on its face? That full moon would spread moonlight all over Ujjaini. But... the full moon? No, what if the Rahu, the invisible evil planet shadowed it? A couplet formed itself in Kalidasa's mind:

jhaṭiti praviśa gēhē mā bahistiṣṭha kāntē
grahaṇasamayavēlā varttatē śītaraśmēḥ
tava mukhamakalaṅkaṃ vīkṣya nūnaṃ na rāhu-
rgrasati tava mukhēnduṃ pūrṇṇacandraṃ vihāya

(Lines from 'Shringarathilakam')

(My beloved! Do not stay outside any longer; go inside the house. This is the time when Rahu, the evil planet, covers up the moon. Seeing your face which is without any blemish, Rahu may mistake you for the full moon and hide it.)

Kalidasa was shocked to think that such a set of lines had formed themselves in his mind. Was Mallika his beloved? Was he her lover? Why did he think that her face, beautiful like the full moon, would be hidden by the evil planet? An anxiety, that some danger was about to befall Mallika, created apprehension in his mind. If she went back to her room, would the evil that was to fall on her be averted? What would affect her, time or the evil planet? Or was the evil planet representative of time? Were the thoughts that formed in his mind a warning about what was to happen?

Slowly thoughts about Mallika filled his mind. He felt an urge to return immediately to Ujjaini. The cool breeze from the Kshipra must be wafting through Ujjaini, carrying fragrance. Carpets of flowers must have been formed on the palace streets. The enchanting banks of the Kshipra! The different flowering trees that grew on either side of the river must be offering worship with flowers to the Kshipra that provided the water for their life. His bower stood on the banks of that river! Was Mallika visiting to talk and play with the peacocks, the swans and the pigeons at his house even in his absence? Was she gathering flowers from the plants in the courtyard to make a garland for Mahakaleshwara? Were the birds that had made their nests in the Ashoka tree still there? Was Mallika going there regularly to feed the pigeons?

As the days passed, the different seasons passed through Kalidasa's mind. One after the other couplets were formed on the leaves. And the new work was completed. *Ritusamharam* reflected the sounds and sights of the different seasons.

Nichula was with him but realizing the intensity of his efforts, he stayed away. He spent his time wandering about near the temple or at the house of Shivasoma. Sometimes he went to the gurukula and read the books there. His own poetic genius flowered forth in small couplets at times.

Nichula and Shivasoma helped Kalidasa in preparing copies of *Ritusamharam*. Kalidasa sent a copy of his new work to Vikramaditya through the group of merchants who were going to Ujjaini.

Those who could appreciate good literary works showered

their praise for the new work. Many gatherings of poets were held in the palace of Kashi. Copies of *Ritusamharam* reached many distant lands through the merchants and other travellers. The lines from it reverberated in the halls where literary discussions were held in different parts of Aryavarta. Those who loved poetry found it easy to remember the lines.

Kalidasa could feel the irresistible urge to return to Ujjaini. But at all such times he was also aware of the feeling that it was the thought of Mallika that was pulling him back to Ujjaini. He knew that he should not allow such thoughts to form in his mind. Mallika was a princess. She should be married to a handsome, courageous prince from an illustrious royal family. The love and trust that King Vikramaditya had for him should not influence him to take any advantage. Still, Mallika gave him sleepless nights.

Shivasoma and his family were sad on bidding goodbye to Kalidasa. But they realized that it was impossible to expect that Kalidasa would be with them at all times.

7

On the way he wanted to visit Vidisha. When Kalidasa reached Vidisha and met King Agnimitra, he was surprised by the change in him. The king was living like a monk. Years ago, when he had passed that way, Agnimitra was leading a life of indulgence.

Kalidasa had treated the relationship between Agnimitra and Malavika in his play. The dramatist had allowed his imagination to run riot in describing the circumstances that led to their marriage. It was, indeed, an artistically enticing play.

Kalidasa became acquainted with many of the learned men of Vidisha.

Kalidasa was delighted at getting a chance to meet Agnimitra again. When he came to this land as a traveller long ago, nobody had known him and he had had nothing that would distinguish him. Still he was able to get acquainted with Agnimitra. He based his play on the stories that he had heard here. Still, he was happy that no one could find fault with him for writing something that was untrue in his play.

But Kalidasa was sad that he did not get a chance to meet the maharani, Malavika. She had passed away three years ago. Agnimitra was still mourning the death of his beloved wife.

Kalidasa soon found it difficult to bear the weight that he seemed to feel in his heart while staying in Vidisha. He felt that he would not be able to stay there any longer. Before coming to Vidisha, Malavika had been a woman whom he knew only as a character in his play but when he came to know that she was no more, he felt as if someone closely related to him had passed away. And he could imagine Malavika only as Mallika. That could be the reason why he found it hard to accept the fact that Maharani Malavika was no more on this earth. A vague sort of pain seemed to be smouldering in his mind.

Many messages came from Ujjaini through the travelling merchants, urging Kalidasa to return... And he replied as often, saying that he would go back soon. He had stayed there only because Maharaja Agnimitra insisted on it. Still there was an unperceivable fear which troubled his mind. The fear of how his friendship with Mallika would develop followed him like a dark shadow. He did not want to go anywhere other than Ujjaini, but his mind was filled with a feeling that he would lose his peace of mind in Ujjaini.

As Kalidasa's works got fame and name, some criticism also started appearing. Many expressed their opinion that some of Kalidasa's lines were not fit to be recited in public; that they contained an unacceptable amount of description of feminine beauty. It was even heard that the young men were going in search of Kalidasa's couplets.

When the maharaja came to worship at the temple of Mahakaleshwara, the priest, Hemabhadra, spoke to him in private. 'Your Majesty! Please bear with me! I have seen many plays and poems. But I have never seen anyone write such vulgar lines and go about singing them.'

Vikramaditya looked closely at Hemabhadra. He wondered how anyone who had learned Sanskrit, the language of the Gods, could talk so disparagingly about someone's composition. If such words had come from a common man who was not well educated, it could be understood as arising out of his ignorance. But this man! He was the priest in the temple of Mahakaleshwara. He had an honourable position among the people. Now he was calling Kalidasa a depraved, vulgar man!

'Swami, the learned men have found Kalidasa's writings as

exalted literary creations. Tell me what fault you see in them. If you point them out, I will bring them to Kalidasa's attention. I will also ask him not to repeat them,' said Vikramaditya.

'Maharaj! There is a predominance of erotic sentiments in what he writes. As one who has some knowledge of the language and its literature, I feel that it is my duty to bring this to Your Majesty's notice,' said Hemabhadra after listening to Vikramaditya.

'Kalidasa will soon be back in Ujjaini. I will talk to him as soon as he is here,' though Vikramaditya gave this assurance to the priest, he did not know what he could ask Kalidasa to do. All literary creations belong to the writer in all ways. Many may read the work, write critical appreciations and explanations on it; but the sentiments and imaginative flights of fancy will always belong to the author. Those words are his own. Who has the right to ask him to change it or instruct him not to write like that? Those who do not agree with the author can criticize him and they need not read the work if they don't like it. Vikramaditya's mind was not ready to accept the idea of approaching it in a way that was not related to its literary quality. Even romantic love was a sentiment. Vikramaditya found it impossible to agree with what Hemabhadra had said. Still, it was not possible to brush aside an opinion expressed by the priest in the temple of Mahakaleshwara.

Vikramaditya could not reach a decision on what to do. He then decided to discuss the matter after Kalidasa was back.

Whenever somebody entered the palace courtyard, Mallika would look out in eagerness. Has the person come with tidings about Kalidasa's arrival? Will the man be carrying copies of any new work by Kalidasa? Will he have some news of the poet? Will the visitor be one who enjoys poems and would talk unendingly on what he had listened to at a discussion on those writings?

Once she heard that Kalidasa was coming, thereby putting an end to the long days of waiting, Mallika felt some unusual tremors in her mind. There was a special joy in enjoying the beauty of his lines. His absence had made her days uninteresting, but she enjoyed listening to the news of his fame spreading. She felt as elated and happy on hearing of Kalidasa's arrival as she had felt when copies of *Ritusamharam* had first reached her. How long had it been since she listened to the couplets from his own lips?

But Vikramaditya was thoughtful. He was not sure whether he should congratulate Kalidasa when he returned after a long absence on his new work, *Ritusamharam,* or talk about what Hemabhadra had mentioned. Neither Kalidasa as a poet nor Vikramaditya as a reader could find any lapses in those works. No one had seen creations so rich in poetry in Sanskrit, not just in Ujjaini but in the entire land stretching between the Himalayas and the ocean. That was why his writings were getting so much fame. It was his poetic genius that made the people of Vidisha and Kashi keep him there for so long. There were many other kings who wanted to invite Kalidasa to their royal assemblies. If here, a priest could see only eroticism in his writings, it could only be considered as an error in his point of view. But Vikramaditya felt that he was helpless in this matter.

Kalidasa was back in Ujjaini. People came in large numbers to the literary discussions that the king convened. They were eager to listen to the poet himself reciting the lines of the new work that he had written. People of Ujjaini were talking only about Kalidasa.

But the fame and the popularity that Kalidasa was getting caused the fire of envy to burn in the minds of many. 'Ho! A new poet, it seems! We have all now become mere spectators in the assembly. Only one name is heard—Kalidasa, Kalidasa, Kalidasa! Even in the gurukulas, the students want only

Kalidasa. He explains the poems and plays in a simple manner. And the couplets! When he wants to say something about anyone, the words pour forth as couplets, whether it is criticism or appreciation. There is no doubt that anyone would want to keep on listening to him. It has to be admitted that none can give each word such a rhythmic and mellifluous note. But no one need be great by casting us into obscurity. We shall not allow such a situation to develop where there is only Kalidasa in Ujjaini,' they felt.

The great poets in the royal assembly of Vikramaditya now existed only within the assembly. Outside the assembly, there was only Kalidasa. Wherever discussions were held on literature, only the name of Kalidasa could be heard. All were interested only in his works!

Conspiracies were hatched; the conspirators decided that they would not rest until the maharaja expelled Kalidasa from the royal assembly.

Kalidasa's mind was focused on something different. For many days he had been thinking of writing a new play. He remembered what Rishi Shalibhadra had told him about an enormous composition named the Mahabharata. He had seen a copy of that work in the gurukula in Ujjaini. The eminent poet and dramatist Bhasa had created a play based on one of the incidents in that great work. Kalidasa had gone through the many stories in Mahabharata many times. His mind was hooked to the story of Pururavas and Urvashi. He had seen the same story described in many other works with slight changes. He started writing, confident that he would be able to present it in an attractive manner.

The first act showed Urvashi, an apsara, being abducted by an asura named Keshi and being rescued from the asura by Pururavas. Kalidasa went on to describe how Pururavas and Urvashi fell in love with each other and how their relationship culminated in marriage, in spite of the objection by his wife who was the daughter of the king of Kashi. Kalidasa brought in an occasion for the separation of the two lovers. With utmost dramatic perfection, he was able to describe how the two of them went to Gandhamadana near Mount Kailas to indulge in love and how Urvashi was offended on seeing Pururavas looking at a maiden from the Vidyadharas. Urvashi left Pururavas but a curse fell on her as she had entered a forbidden territory and was turned into a vine. Kalidasa gave a brilliant depiction of the sorrow that Pururavas felt on being separated from Urvashi and the difficulties that he had to suffer while looking for her. In the end they were united and came back to the palace. Time passed. Urvashi would have to return to the land of the devas if Pururavas happened to see her son Aayush. So Urvashi kept the birth of her son a secret from Pururavas and the boy was left in the hermitage of Rishi Chyavana. Circumstances were created for the meeting between the father and son. Pururavas then decided to take up the life of an ascetic in a hermitage and made arrangements for anointing son Aayush as the yuvaraja. The play ended with Devendra being pleased with Urvashi and allowing her to remain on earth till the end of her life.

Kalidasa succeeded in adapting the original story to suit the presentation on stage and added suitable couplets at appropriate places. He had brought in the grandeur and the beauty of the Himalayas into his writings. The different sentiments presented themselves on the leaves through letters and words making it impossible to say whether art had infused the mind or the mind had conquered the art. The play was named *Pururavorvasheeyam*.

But something that Kalidasa had never intended happened when he wrote this play. Both the maharaja and Vidyothama were worried that they had not been blessed with a child. Vikramaditya even asked Kalidasa whether he was drawing their attention to that fact through the play. Kalidasa had no answers for such questions. When he got an opportunity, he made it clear that he had nothing more to say except remind people that those who enjoyed art should have the maturity of mind to be able to see art as art and life as life.

The king gave permission to set up the scenes in an attractive manner and present the play on stage. The play was enthusiastically welcomed by all lovers of art.

Kalidasa felt satisfied that he could finish a task that he had undertaken; rather than being elated at winning renown. The aim of literature was fulfilled by works that brought joy to the minds of those who loved it. He now had the self-confidence that his works had not failed at accomplishing that aim and this was what encouraged him to write more.

Once Kalidasa had gained fame as the writer of *Pururavorvashee*yam as well as *Ritusamharam*, Shankuka and his companions knew that they were now nothing compared to Kalidasa.

It was purely by chance that Shankuka got an opportunity to make a move against Kalidasa. Shankuka had gone for a walk in the garden on the banks of the Kshipra when he heard someone singing some lines from *Ritusamharam* in a melodious voice. His attention was drawn to the area from where the voice was heard. There in the shade of a bower of jasmine, he saw Kalidasa looking intently at Mallika who was reciting the lines from *Ritusamharam* and in an instant all the base instincts that had accumulated in Shankuka's mind started working. This was not a relationship between a poet and a girl who loved his poems. Signs of love, which went far beyond that, were clearly visible on their faces. It was clear on Mallika's face. It was impossible to define the look on Kalidasa's face. It might be the rapture that a poet felt on hearing his lines sung to a beautiful tune by a mellifluous voice. But they could not have reached the bower in an isolated corner in the garden on the banks of the Kshipra, purely by accident. Kalidasa was not a suitable man to wed Princess Mallika. This had to be stopped. This should be enough to bring Kalidasa's presence in Ujjaini to an end.

Shankuka started moving his pawns with utmost care. He knew that it was better to make secret moves than open ones.

Gossip started spreading soon. Though he spread the news here and there and made sure that it reached the ears of Vikramaditya, he did not get the desired result. Then he directly asked Vikramaditya whether he did not feel that the romance between Kalidasa and Mallika was going beyond the limits of propriety. Some of the lines from *Ritusamharam* aided him in that. They were enough to show that Kalidasa's lines showed a tendency to lean too much towards the description of a woman's beauty. Hence Shankuka decided that he could use immorality in behaviour as his weapon against Kalidasa.

'Maharaj! I have been a member of the royal assembly of Ujjaini for so many years. It was your father, Mahendraditya Yajnasena, who made me a member of this assembly. I have always watched with pleasure, the prosperity attained by this dynasty. But now, when I see certain things, I feel sad...and fearful,' Shankuka began.

'What does Acharya Shankuka mean by that? What causes sorrow and fear in your mind?' asked Vikramaditya.

'That... Maharaj... Some thing related to Kalidasa,' Shankuka pretended to be hesitant in speaking about it.

'What is it? I have always felt that one should worship the talent that he possesses. There is news that his writings have become famous even in faraway places like the land of the Cholas and the Pandyas. Now, after *Ritusamharam*, he has written a play, *Pururavorvasheeyam* . How beautiful is that! Many have come forward with enthusiasm to make copies of the work. And there is nothing to be said about the popularity of *Ritusamharam*,' Vikramaditya went on praising Kalidasa's poetic genius.

Though Shankuka was not happy to hear Kalidasa being praised like that, he did not dare to show disrespect to Kalidasa as a poet in front of the maharaja. 'I too have no doubt about that, Maharaj! But even when his genius is to be appreciated, I feel that he should be kept away from the palace. I am speaking from my own experience of life,' Shankuka raised his doubt.

'Why? What makes you say so?' Vikramaditya asked in surprise.

'Maharaj, Kalidasa is very friendly with Princess Mallika,' Shankuka said.

'Yes, his lines are always on her lips. Though we knew that she had the ability to enjoy literature, it was Kalidasa who revealed the fact that she was good at acting also. In fact, I was apprehensive about Mallika dancing as Malavika in *Malavikagnimitram*. It was only upon Kalidasa's insistence that I allowed it,' explained Vikramaditya.

'But I fear that the friendship is going beyond limits. They are seen together in the garden, in the theatre, in the lonely bowers on the banks of the Kshipra and at many other places. The bowers and the gardens seem to be their favourite places,' Shankuka said.

'Kalidasa has got the experience of travelling all over our Bharatavarsha; he also had the fortune to go to the peak that is the abode of Gouri-Shankara, in the company of the rishis. He has been describing to Mallika all the important places from the Himalayas to the ocean in the south. Whenever she is with me, she has nothing else to talk about except for the descriptions of Kalidasa's travels. Now I too desire to travel over all the places from the Himalayas to the south. I too want to hear it directly from Kalidasa,' Vikramaditya said.

'Please pardon me when I say this, Maharaj. I wonder if Kalidasa is speaking about his travels or about the *Kamasutra*, the science of love. I cannot bear to see this dynasty that has arisen from the famous Surya Vamsha to be discredited in this manner,' Shankuka used the most powerful weapon in his hand.

'Enough!' Vikramaditya said in anger, 'You seem to have forgotten that I am the king and more than that, Mallika's elder brother.' Trying to control his anger he continued, 'You are older than I am in age and experience. I did not expect such words from you. You seem to have forgotten that you are speaking like this about my sister,' Vikramaditya said.

'Please pardon me again, Maharaj! The princess is like a daughter to me. She has played in my lap and slept on my shoulders. That is why I was ready to speak to you about this. I only request you to be more careful,' Shankuka replied.

Vikramaditya was silent as he sat looking at Shankuka. When he knew that his arrow had found its mark, Shankuka continued, 'Maharaj, I do not say that Kalidasa is attracted to Mallika alone. I even doubt if all the prostitutes of Ujjaini are not learning Kamashastra from Kalidasa. I doubt if there are any prostitutes in Ujjaini, whom Kalidasa has not met,' Shankuka sent the next arrow.

For a moment Vikramaditya felt that there was some truth in what the acharya was saying. He knew that the acharya was jealous of Kalidasa, yet there may be some truth to his words. There are certain implied meanings, beyond the literary, in Kalidasa's writings. He too had wondered how Kalidasa could describe feminine beauty in such detail.

'All right, you may go now. I will be careful. I will ask the maharani also to keep an eye on the princess,' Vikramaditya bid goodbye to Shankuka.

Now there was doubt in Vikramaditya's mind as to whether it could happen. He too had seen them interact in a friendly manner and he too had doubted whether there was anything more to it. But when it came as an imputation from someone else, he could not bear it. He must be careful. Kalidasa was a young man and a bachelor. There were clear indications in his lines of how he worshipped beauty. Mallika too was in the prime of her youth. The interest in poetry may turn into an interest in the poet and soon transform itself into romance and desire at this age. He must ask Vidyothama to be more careful about Mallika, Vikramaditya decided.

Another day it was Ghatakarpara who repeated some similar accusations about Kalidasa before the king.

If, in fact, Mallika had found a place in the heart of Kalidasa or Kalidasa had found a place in her heart, Vikramaditya would not accept it as the king. If the princess were married to a prince from a strong country, it would add to the power of Ujjaini; it would be a gain for Malava! And that of Kashi! This was necessary for the safety of this ancient land. Kalidasa, as a poet, may be an asset to Ujjaini. The fame of the poet is the fame of Ujjaini and adds to the glory of Malava. It brings glory to the world of poetry. But countries grow through political alliances. The marriage between the princess and the poet will not add to the strength of Avanti. More than all that, if what Ghatakarpara said was true—that he should not be allowed to use the king's sister for the satisfaction of his sexual desires—still Vikramaditya's mind could not agree with what Ghatakarpara had said. His mind told him that Kalidasa could never be like that.

What Maharani Vidyothama had mentioned also pointed to some dalliance in Mallika's mind. She loved to draw Kalidasa's portrait on canvas. She was eager to go to Kalidasa in the morning. Once she started talking with Kalidasa on the banks of the Kshipra in the morning, she would forget to come back till evening. It was especially noticed that she did not come for lunch as she had eaten some fruits with Kalidasa. Mallika, who used to insist on having her meals with her brother, had now forgotten him and remained with Kalidasa! Vikramaditya too feared whether things had gone out of control.

Vikramaditya summoned Chief Minister Amarasimha and discussed the matter. When Amarasimha too expressed the same opinion as that of Shankuka and Ghatakarpara, Vikramaditya felt worried. He had led great battles and strengthened the country. He had made Malava strong with good administration, giving stringent punishment to the guilty and working hard for the welfare of his people. Avanti had become famous for scientific, artistic and literary works. Above all those achievements, Kalidasa had become the jewel of Ujjaini. The glory that Kalidasa's literary works gained, added to the glory of Ujjaini. But a jewel can only be an ornament; rather it should only be an ornament. It should not be a part of the body. Vikramaditya had to take a suitable decision.

Amarasimha made a suggestion. 'For the time being we should keep Kalidasa away from Ujjaini. Persuade him to go somewhere far away from Ujjaini. Thereby preventing him from seeing the princess and thus preventing any further development of love between them.'

'How can that be done? Will Kalidasa be ready to leave Ujjaini? We don't want to force him by using our royal power. If we did so it would hurt Mallika also,' Vikramaditya was still doubtful.

'Let Kalidasa go to Pataliputra. There is no dearth of encouragement to literary and artistic endeavours there. The people of Pataliputra should also know about the greatness of Kalidasa or we could direct him to a place of great scenic beauty. For example, talk to him about the beauty of Ramagiri and persuade him to go there. If he is unwilling to go you should ask him to go and if even that fails you must order him to go,' Amarasimha expressed his opinion.

'But if Kalidasa asks me why he should go to Ramagiri or Pataliputra, what do I tell him?' Vikramaditya could not fully agree with his minister's suggestion.

Amarasimha thought for a while. 'We should not reveal the real reason. If it becomes known that his friendship with Mallika is the real reason behind this persuasion to leave Ujjaini, it will have a favourable effect on their relationship. We should not allow that to happen. We should tell him that we expect a masterpiece from him like *Malavikagnimitram* and *Pururavorvasheey*am and for that it would be helpful if he were in a quiet place of great natural beauty. Suggest Ramagiri for that. Or we may tell him that we expect another work of poetry like *Ritusamharam*.'

'Kalidasa does not seem to be a person who would write poetry under persuasion,' said Vikramaditya.

'Maharaj! Tell him that you think that he would be able to do it in a year's time. If Kalidasa writes something during that time, it will be good. Otherwise, we can just think that our plan to keep him away for a year was successful,' suggested Amarasimha.

'Yes, I don't see any other way. During that time, we should try to get the princess married to a prince.' There was no confidence in the words that Vikramaditya spoke. His mind went on advising him that what he was planning to do was not right.

The next day Vikramaditya invited Kalidasa for a friendly conversation. They sat on the marble platform in the garden and talked about dramatics and poetics. He directed Kalidasa's attention to the need for more great works.

'Many among the assembly of learned men are writing. Many young men are also producing some works. But nothing great is being created,' Vikramaditya expressed his opinion.

'Yes, Maharaj,' Kalidasa agreed with him. 'The gurukula here gives much importance to the study of poetics. But we do not see much progress in the creation of great literary works. I feel that the acharyas are concentrating their attention on providing knowledge. Many of them are interested in writing explanatory works like what Patanjali wrote explaining Panini's *Astadhyayi*. But it is a fact that they have not succeeded in creating anything so great. They do not seem to realize that there should be more independent creation than explanations,' Kalidasa agreed with what Vikramaditya said.

'You must try to make amends for that. You wrote *Malavikagnimitram* and *Pururavorvasheeyam*. They are both plays. But as poetry there is nothing other than *Ritusamharam* except for some small poems and couplets.'

Kalidasa said, 'Your Majesty! There should be a suitable atmosphere to help in the creation of great works and a suitable state of mind. The persuasion for the creation should come from deep within the mind.'

'I can suggest a suitable place for Kalidasa to create his poetic work. Ramagiri! It is a quiet and beautiful place with enchanting mountains and valleys. An environment that would make a poet of anybody,' said Vikramaditya immediately.

'Nature is beautiful all over this ancient land of ours. But it must be said that some places are more beautiful. But great writings need not come just because the environment is changed. Maharaj! The beauty of nature is not the cause for creation. The banks of the Kshipra and the rural areas of Malava are not behind any place in natural beauty. I do not move about here without seeing all this. But the impetus for a new creation has not yet entered my mind. Some occasions, some experiences or some such circumstances that take me to a special mental state...these are the things that lead me to a new creation. When I see certain things, words naturally take a poetic turn in my mind. For that I need not go to Ramagiri or any such place. The circumstances will come naturally,' Kalidasa explained.

Vikramaditya sat silent for a while, not knowing how to

proceed. What could he now say to make Kalidasa go away from Ujjaini? But he had started the conversation; now he could not go back.

'No, Kalidasa, you must go to Ramagiri. You must create a great poetic writing from there. I am sure you will be able to do it,' Vikramaditya forced Kalidasa without giving any reason.

Immediately Kalidasa's mind became clouded. The king was saying that he wanted Kalidasa to go away from Ujjaini. Otherwise he would not suggest a place so far from here, so specifically, without even thinking for a minute. He understood what the king meant. The expression on the king's face revealed the distress that he was feeling. There was no doubt that what he was saying was not what was in his mind. Kalidasa sat for a while looking at Vikramaditya. The king lowered his face. Kalidasa did not need any more explanations to understand what the king wanted.

'Maharaj! What is on your mind? Do you want me to go away from Ujjaini?' Kalidasa asked without revealing the agitation in his mind.

Vikramaditya looked at Kalidasa. He immediately understood that he would never be able to ask Kalidasa to be away from Ujjaini. They both had become so close to each other. Or there was not so much deceit in his mind. He was not good at play-acting. He might try acting on the stage but not in life. Vikramaditya submitted himself to what his conscience dictated.

'Kalidasa, you have been in Ujjaini only for a short while but our relationship is not one of king and a member of the assembly,' Vikramaditya began. 'I see you as my friend. Taking that freedom allowed by friendship, I have to ask you to keep away from Ujjaini for some time. Please don't ask why,' Vikramaditya said.

'I am not going to ask you for any explanation,' Kalidasa replied.

Vikramaditya had no answer to give. He knew he could not act... It was better to tell him the truth. It became clear to him that he would not be able to hide the truth from his friend Kalidasa, even if he could do so from the poet Kalidasa.

Vikramaditya started explaining in detail. 'Many of the members of the royal assembly have been imputing your friendship with Mallika in a bad light. I had to listen to much that was said against you. Many of them wish to see you go away from this palace. I cannot take a decision completely ignoring their opinion. They all love the princess but there is no escape from self-interest. I have come to realize that they do not hesitate to speak scandalously even about a girl they consider as dear as their own daughter. There must be an end to such talk.'

'Do you also, personally, desire my absence from here?' Kalidasa asked.

Vikramaditya searched the innermost depths of his heart. At last he spoke. 'I am happy to see you as the husband of my little sister. The ability to enjoy good poetry that Mallika has and your creative ability go well together; I have felt many a time that no one else can sing your lines so beautifully. I feel you both go together like tune and rhythm. My mind whispers that it is not wrong to say that you both merge as well as a word and its meaning. But all this is what the lover of poetry in me says. The king in me, the ruler in me, cannot accept that. I have also noticed that there is some strong conspiracy being hatched against you. Let them get some satisfaction. I feel that it is better that I take an arbitrary decision now rather than allow the matter to come up for discussion in the assembly and pave the way for some stringent action to be taken. Everyone need only know that you have gone to Ramagiri as per your own decision. I cannot bear to see my sister's love being a topic of discussion in the assembly and listen to whatever the members have to say about it while I sit on the throne.'

Kalidasa understood the situation. Many were there who could not stand Kalidasa being so famous as well as his friendship with the king. More than that, they felt that his friendship with Princess Mallika was going beyond the accepted limits. So his ouster was a royal need, an administrative necessity. To a certain extent it was a good decision.

'Please do not worry, Maharaj. The real nature of our relationship has not become clear so far. This separation will make it clear. Then we will leave everything in the hands of time. Mahakaleshwara has decided certain things. They cannot be changed,' said Kalidasa.

What Kalidasa said brought some comfort to Vikramaditya. He was truthful and straightforward enough to approach problems with an open mind. He was ready to accept changes with an open heart rather than fight against the circumstances. He was ready to move with the times; not compete with it.

'You may get ready for your journey. I will issue instructions to Amarasimha to make all the arrangements,' Vikramaditya said.

'What preparation do I have to make, Maharaj? When I came to Ujjaini, I did not bring any money or other property with me. So there is nothing that I need to carry with me when I go except for the writing leaves. They will always be there in my bundle. Then there are a lot of experiences and memories. Isn't the weight of these on my mind enough, Maharaj? Neither servants nor horses can carry them.'

Even though he had accepted the situation, pain took root in his heart. The weight on his mind was reflected in his words.

After remaining silent for a while, Kalidasa continued. 'I will be on my way early in the morning tomorrow. There is no meaning in continuing to stay here now. If the beauty of Ramagiri attracts me, I will stay there. Otherwise I will move from there too. Doesn't this ancient land stretch from the peaks of the Himalayan ranges to the Indian ocean?'

'Kalidasa, you should not go anywhere else under any circumstances. If you feel tired of being in Ramagiri, come back here. Ujjaini will always be waiting for you. There is for ever a place for Kalidasa in Vikramaditya's heart. So do not even think of going anywhere else,' Vikramaditya did not wish to lose Kalidasa.

8

Kalidasa was not aware of the passage of time. At first life at Ramagiri did not seem uninteresting. There were copies of many ancient and modern works available at the hermitage. The rishis there were masters who had delved deep into the study of philosophy and Kalidasa could open new windows to knowledge by engaging in discussions with them. Life there gave him an opportunity to study art, literature and astronomy in depth.

Nature was not only a gallery of pictures, it was a stage for music too. The sweet music of the streams added rhythm to the silence of the short hours of the dawn, to be followed by the cooing of the cuckoos soon after. The chirping of the tiny birds in groups, the call of the peacocks, the echoing sound of some birds that can be heard coming from afar, the tunes and the rhythm played on the bamboo poles and the branches of trees by the mountain wind, the sun that paints the horizon red both at dawn and at dusk—an enchanting stage!

As days passed, Kalidasa started feeling tired of living in Ramagiri. He started feeling that the pictures of nature that he saw around him were all the same. He seemed to hear the music of nature with the same tune, the same slow pitch and the repetition of the same lines. There seemed to be something lacking in all that was around him. He lost interest in the philosophical discussions of the rishis of the hermitage at Ramagiri. Though there were many people at the hermitage, he felt lonely; Kalidasa's mind was submitting itself to the pain of separation.

What was Mallika doing now in the palace of Ujjaini? Was she also lonely? Or was she laughing and playing with her companions there? Was she wandering about on the banks of the Kshipra and in the gardens, humming the lines from his poems?

Vikramaditya loved him. But there was apprehension in the king's mind also. He could not fully accept Kalidasa's relationship with Mallika. Immediately his mind posed the question: 'what relationship?' but he pretended not to have heard it. Political alliances are the strength of any country. A good ruler should try to make strong alliances. A king has to give more importance to the administrative experts in the assembly than to a poet who has no importance in the political arena. Most of those in the assembly were political strategists, apart from being artists or writers. They know the political game for securing their position. He was thrown out as he was not proficient in that. Though it was a warm and friendly send-off, it was nothing but an expulsion. Still Ujjaini would not allow him to leave.

In Ujjaini, Kalidasa had begun his journey as a poet. There was the bond of friendship with King Vikramaditya. That was the only thing that connected him to Ujjaini. Then there was Nichula and some other friends. There were many who loved his writings and respected him for that. Then there was Mallika... The nature of his relationship with Mallika was not yet clear. Was he just an idol for worship for Mallika? Was her attachment to him just an admiration and adoration for a poet? No...and it did not require any supernatural ability to understand that it was not just admiration, there was no need to think much to understand that. The king must have understood the nature of their relationship. He had given a clear indication of that during their conversation. But Kalidasa felt sure that during his absence, the other members of the assembly would raise more accusations against him. Would the king be able to meet all that? What would Mallika do?

Kalidasa could imagine the intensity of the sorrow that Rama felt on being separated from Sita. He too was suffering the pangs of separation. But his suffering was on a different plane. Mallika was not his wife. Except for the fact that he had a special feeling for Mallika, their relationship could not be defined. But Rama had lost his dear wife. A rakshasa, a terrible monster, had abducted her. But for Kalidasa, the lady whom he missed, was safe in her palace. So he did not have to worry about the safety of his beloved. Still, separation created a unique emotion in the mind. There was something sweet about this separation.

Gradually, a feeling that he was a yaksha, living in exile on being ousted from some country, entered his mind. Then he remembered the story of Sthoonaakarna, the yaksha, who had been thrown out of the palace of the Yaksha king. Like that yaksha, he too had been expelled from Ujjaini. His beloved was waiting for him in that palace far away.

Mallika may be in love with him. But she was a princess... the princess of famous Ujjaini. Did he desire a marriage with a princess? Was being a princess a drawback for Mallika?

Anyone else would be sure that Kalidasa, the poet, was not a suitable partner for the princess of Ujjaini. Princes should wed princesses. But he would never be able to get Mallika out of his mind.

Days and then months passed. The rainy season was approaching. The sky was covered with dark clouds. The pangs of separation, that lay thick in the innermost recesses of the mind, gradually became intense.

Was he a dream in the heart of Mallika? Would she think of him whenever she heard the pigeons cooing and the mountain wind passed through Ujjaini? Would the parrots, cooing in love, remind her of him? Would his alienation from there create a unique emotion in her mind? Would she forget to gather the flowers for worship in the evening? As she plucked the roses from the garden, would their first meeting appear in her mind as a sweet, enchanting picture?

Kalidasa sat with his eyes on the dark clouds that came floating in the sky. Some birds were flying past in a hurry to reach their nests before the rains fell. The hornbills sat on the branches of the trees waiting for the rains to fall, to drink the water to their heart's content. The peacocks had spread their wings and started dancing. No one had to tell them about the change of season.

The raindrops had started falling far away on the mountain tops. The hornbills were flying in the air, eagerly trying to gather raindrops in their beaks. The music of nature changed once the rain started falling. How could the hornbills not cry out in joy? The peacocks had to express their exhilaration by cooing. Accompanying the flashes of lightning were the drum beats of thunder. An enchanting scene!

The branches of the trees bowed, unable to bear the force of the rain. The drops gathered to flow as a tiny channel, many joined to form a stream and many such were seen coming down the mountains.

Gradually the rain started falling over all the mountain tops and falling on the roof of the bower. The mountains in the distance started fading away from sight. A curtain had been raised. Kalidasa leaned forward and gathered a handful of water. He drank that water of the first rain of the season and gathered one more handful, and then again and again. He felt that the rain clouds were raining nectar.

If Mallika had been with him at this time, she would have sung the lines from *Ritusamharam* in a mellifluous voice. The raindrops that fell would have added rhythm to that. She would have cried out in wonder pointing afar at the changing scenes.

These clouds would soon travel away, towards some far away place. A little towards the north from there were the high mountain peaks. The wind would help the clouds to rise high and cross over the mountain peaks. Beyond the mountain was the valley. The clouds would rain in abundance there. As the first rain stopped falling, the people would start preparing the soil that lay in ecstasy after receiving the raindrops, for sowing. As one went westwards from there, the Amrakuta Mountain rose into view. The beauty of Amrakuta Mountain was worth mentioning. Anyone would want to remain there for a while. Kalidasa had stayed there for a day on his way to Ramagiri. The place was full of delicious mangoes; mangoes that had gathered all the sweetness of nature in them. Streams that started from the mountain tops joined together to go around the Reva mountain ranges in a strong frothing flow. A scene of beauty with the fragrance of the Kadamba flowers—the forest and mountain ranges full of different flowering trees. Beyond that lay Vidisha. Vidisha, the capital city of the land of Dasharna, blessed with the waters of the Vetravati. From there, as one takes a slight turn and goes towards the west, it is Ujjaini. Are these clouds familiar with these paths? Will they be passing through Ujjaini on their way?

Kalidasa's mind once again found itself in Ujjaini, wandering about in the streets, gardens and beautiful houses. Nowhere else could one see such beauty as in Ujjaini. Ujjaini was the holy place sanctified by the presence of Mahakaleshwara. During the rainy season, Kshipra would overflow; as the rain came lashing, the people from the market places and the streets would hurry back to their houses. Some people would seek shelter from the rains under the trees, the awning of the houses or at the inns. Drops of water would keep slipping off the leaves of the trees.

Some would get wet, not finding a place to take shelter in; but it was a pleasant experience to get wet in the rain. Children would be running around, laughing loudly, enjoying themselves in the rain. Sometimes ladies, all dressed up, could be seen walking in the rain. Kalidasa felt that it was enchanting to watch the water flow down their cheeks, and drops of water fall from the tip of their nose, lips and chin.

Many would be at the windows and doors of their houses, enjoying the rain. The cows and the horses would gather under the trees to escape from the rain. Some of them would stand in the rain, their heads lowered. Kalidasa imagined himself walking along the streets of Ujjaini in the rain.

As one went further north from Ujjaini, it was Devagiri, the land of Sharavanabhava Karthikeya. Bowing before Karthikeya, as one proceeded further north, passing through Dashapura, Kurukshetra and Kanaghala, one could touch the Himalayan ranges. Then enjoying the beauty of the Himalayas, you could reach the Manasarovar lake. The rain clouds enjoy all this from above, the scenes that Kalidasa had seen as he had wandered on the Himalayan ranges.

If he too could move about like the rain clouds, he would have travelled with them. If he travelled with them, would he stay at Ujjaini, enjoying its beauty or because Mallika was there, or would he proceed further to the abode of Kailaseshwara? No, if he went there again, there would be no return. It was not yet time to go to the Kailas. His mind was fixed on Mallika. He felt that as she expressed her respect and affection for the poet in him, he had seen a good friend in her. What would happen to the friendship now? They could still be friends but marriage would break such friendship. A husband and a wife would seek to establish new frontiers of friendship and that would make any other friendship pale in comparison. Any relationship depended on the unity of the minds. The unity of the mind and the body always grew to the plane of the union of Purusha and Prakruti—man and nature.

A sense of permanence was given to friendship through marriage—like between Shiva and Parvati, Prakruti and Purusha. To be his Parvati, to be his power, to be the Nature to his Manliness, he could find only Mallika. And Mallika's stance was not any different. He had seen the little blackbirds of love flitting about in her eyes that resembled the lotus petals. King Vikramaditya had also observed that. That was why he was making this futile attempt to keep them away from each other. When Shiva woke up from his meditation, he was enraged to see the God of Love aiming his arrow at him and disappeared from there immediately. But that made no change in the heart of Parvati. She undertook penance to be with Shiva. It won't be easy to change Mallika's feelings for Kalidasa. The picture of Mallika as the daughter of Mount Himavan, offering worship to Mahadeva with flowers, arose in Kalidasa's mind.

He could picture Mallika as she came to the garden to pluck flowers, he could hear her asking him again and again, why he was still silent. He could hear her reciting the lines from his *Ritusamharam* as she sat looking at the flow of water in the Kshipra.

Kalidasa felt compelled to say all that he wanted to Mallika. His heart seemed to be full to the brim. They had spent many hours talking on the banks of the Kshipra. Much that he had not spoken at that time now seemed to be rising up in waves in his mind. Kalidasa realized that his mind was revealing the true nature of his emotions for Mallika. Could he reveal the truth to these trees and climbers? What would he gain by speaking about it to these peacocks and pigeons? How could he let Mallika know his feelings?

The groups of merchants no longer passed that way. During the rainy season, they do not travel. Everyone wants to stay in their own homes, with their loved ones. There would be none to go to Ujjaini during the rains with his message. No messengers from the king were likely to come...and he would not be able to send a message to his beloved in the hands of the royal servants.

The dark, rain clouds woke up the poet in Kalidasa. These dark clouds arrive to save the wayfarers from the sweltering heat of summer. But wasn't the presence of these dark clouds responsible for awakening thoughts of separation from one's beloved? Hence, they had the duty to carry the messages of alienated lovers, to provide some comfort.

His mind was once again in Ujjaini—a city as beautiful as Alakapuri, the city of the God of wealth—a perfect stage for art, literature and beauty in all forms. He had been exiled because of a conspiracy hatched by some; a feeling that he was the yaksha, ousted from Alakapuri, rose up again in Kalidasa's mind.

His pen started moving on the leaves, giving form to letters; a garland of beautiful couplets was soon formed. His beloved was far away, at a place where he could not reach, suffering pangs of separation. Who, except for these dark rain clouds, could he depend upon, for conveying his pain and distress to his beloved? These dark clouds will certainly help him. Kalidasa's pen was busy seeking out the most beautiful words, arranging them artistically in appropriate places.

Couplets appeared on the writing leaves, all meant for Mallika. But Kalidasa felt that he was being unjust to Vikramaditya. Betrayal was written large on those lines. But Kalidasa could no longer control himself.

Avanti... Malava... The place that attracted him the most. Was it because it was the land of his birth or because of the prosperity of the place under the rule of Vikramaditya? What made the people look so happy and contented? Kalidasa thought that he could hear the cooing of the swans that were swimming about in the ponds in Ujjaini. The smell of the Kadamba flowers seemed to permeate everywhere. The gentle wind that came from the Kshipra made Ujjaini cool. Kalidasa felt as if he were resting under the shade of the trees in Ujjaini.

Even when he first came to Ujjaini, people had many stories to tell. They proudly spoke of their ancestors. The story of how Udayana, the king of Valsa, abducted Vasavadatta, the daughter of Chandamahasena; the story of Nadagiri, the famous elephant that belonged to Pradyota; the story of how the Jyotirlinga came to be consecrated there; of the temple of Mahakaleshwara, Mahadeva with the trident in hand; of Hemambika, the Goddess of the Vindhyas.

Kalidasa sat for a few moments, lost in the tunes and rhythm of the orchestra played in the temple of Mahakaleshwara. The devotees were offering flowers in worship, chanting the prayers. He could hear the chiming of bells, the tinkling of the bells on the anklets of Mahakaleshwara as he danced in ecstasy, the rhythmic beating of the drums in his hand. Kalidasa felt as if he were in a dream world.

Soon his thoughts left Ujjaini and reached the Manasarovar lake on the slopes of Mount Kailas—the beauty and the luxuriance of the Himalayas! The city of Alakapuri, of Kubera, the lord of wealth! The enchanting garden built by Chitraratha, the chief of the Gandharvas. The gardens full of heavenly flowers! The beauty of the moonlight from the crescent moon adorning the tuft of Mahadeva on Kailas—couplets kept forming on the leaves in front of Kalidasa.

For days on end, Kalidasa was in a unique state of mind and its effect reflected on the leaves in front of him. It was only after he had completed that he noticed, the yaksha was sending the clouds to Alakapuri with his message. Will it reach Alakapuri? No. Let it go at least till Ujjaini. *Meghadutam*—Kalidasa named his new work.

In the palace of Ujjaini, Mallika waited, counting the days. There had been no news of Kalidasa since he had left for

Ramagiri. In the first few days she harboured the hope that someone would bring some news, but it seemed that everyone in Ujjaini had forgotten Kalidasa. There was no need for Kalidasa to be a topic of discussion in the assembly. Her brother had not put forth any riddles before the assembly, and so no one awaited Kalidasa to appear with a brilliant solution to it. No one praised Kalidasa on seeing the beauty of the lines he had made to complete the riddle. The members of the assembly felt their importance once again as Kalidasa was no longer there. Those who had been pushed to insignificance because of the glory attained by Kalidasa's works were once again coming into prominence. They were busy planning some programme to re-establish their own individual glory—gatherings of poets, discussion of poems, explanations! What a deep gulf there lay, between the lines written by Kalidasa, resplendent with poetic beauty and the joyless utterances of these men! What a crowd would gather if Kalidasa was present at these meetings! His lines contained a beauty that was unparalleled! Vikramaditya too felt tired of these uninteresting literary meetings.

Accusations against Kalidasa continued to surface. In the gurukula, there was a ban on reciting and teaching some of the lines from *Ritusamharam*. They were declared to be unfit for students to recite!

It was with shock that Nichula listened to a discussion that took place in the assembly one day.

Shankuka was saying, 'Your Majesty! We cannot ignore the possibility that the lines of *Ritusamharam* are not inspired by the beauty of the prostitutes of Ujjaini. Most of the lines in it are meant to lead young men astray. For example, Your Highness! Have we ever seen any description of women in any of our ancient works as we see in this?'

'What do you mean, Shankuka? Which lines of Kalidasa are you referring to?' asked the king.

'Maharaj, I will recite just one as an example:

"*nitambabimbai sadukūla mēkhalaiḥ
stanaiḥ sahārābharaṇaiḥ sacandanaiḥ
śirōruhaiḥ snānakāṣāyavāsitaiḥ
striyō nidāghō śamayanti kāminām*"

(Ritusamhara 1–4)

(The women wearing silken garments and gold girdle around their waists, their breasts adorned with ornaments and sandalwood paste, their hair scented after a bath, went to their beloveds and reduce the summer heat.)

Isn't this equal to putting all the women of Ujjaini to shame, Maharaj? Isn't it equal to saying that all the women of Ujjaini are like these women of ill repute? There are some lines that are worse than this!' Shankuka said.

Somashekhara now took it up. 'Yes, Your Majesty! He has written lines even worse than these. Most of it cannot be mentioned here. I had to instruct many not to keep the copies of *Ritusamharam* at home.'

'Shankuka, do you know more such lines from the *Ritusamharam*?' asked the king.

'Yes, Your Highness! But most of them, as Somashekhara has mentioned, have to be considered immoral. It will be a disgrace to this learned assembly to recite such lines here,' said Shankuka excitedly.

'But I see that you all have managed to study them by heart!' commented the king.

'That...Your Majesty...that...' Somashekhara had to search for words to answer the king.

'That is all right. We can enjoy them. We can commit them to our memory. We can whisper them in the ears of our beloved ladies. Isn't it so? You must have got all the erotic lines written by Kalidasa committed to your memory, haven't you?' It was evident that Vikramaditya wanted to expose their duplicity.

Many lowered their faces in shame.

'Maharaj! It is true that somehow Kalidasa's lines remain in our minds without much effort. You need to hear it only once and you will be able to recite them from memory. They seem to have some magical quality,' Shashivarma, another member of the sabha said.

'Yes, everyone likes to enjoy Kalidasa's couplets and they become entrenched in their minds effortlessly. Isn't that why those lines remain in our minds even without our being aware of it—because of its artistic beauty, its poetic nature and musical quality?' Jinadeva the dramatist posed the question.

'What Jinadeva says is so true. Who can excel Kalidasa in the excellence of his writings?' Vikramaditya agreed with what Jinadeva had said.

'But is it moral, suitable to our culture, to describe the body of a woman like this?' Shankuka was not ready to give up.

'Isn't everything in nature beautiful? Describing beauty cannot be a crime. We should be able to see what is true in Kalidasa's works as auspicious and beautiful. It is just our view that makes something moral or immoral. Just as beauty is related to what is in the viewers' mind, all artistic creations are related to individual views... But we have not seen any new work from Kalidasa lately. We had hoped that he would create a great work during his stay at Ramagiri.'

Once Vikramaditya had made the final remark, nobody said anything more.

It was at this time that some students from the hermitage at Ramagiri came to Ujjaini. They gave a copy of Kalidasa's new work, *Meghadutam* to Vikramaditya.

Immediately the king issued orders for copies to be made

and distributed among the members of the assembly.

Soon copies of *Meghadutam* reached the lovers of literature. Shankuka and his coterie were envious on seeing this exquisite beauty of the work. They felt sure that Kalidasa will win a permanent place in the hearts of his readers with this one book itself. Now nobody would be able to challenge Kalidasa.

For many days *Meghadutam* came up for discussion in the assembly. People expressed their opinion again and again that it was a literary masterpiece. Now they demanded that since the aim of his ouster from Ujjaini had been successfully accomplished, Kalidasa should be brought back to the city.

But there was strong opposition too. Many tried to establish, with examples taken from the latest work, that in *Meghadutam* also Kalidasa had violated the tenets of morality. It was suggested that Kalidasa was able to make such detailed descriptions of the feminine body because of his close association with prostitutes. Many raised the question of what Kalidasa meant by requesting the dark clouds to allow streaks of lightning to form, and speculated that it was to provide light for the prostitutes to go for their work at night.

Gomedaka, the chief of the library, was given the charge of preparing copies of *Meghadutam*. Shankuka had met him in secret. He gave some writing leaves to Gomedaka saying that they were also part of the work and that they had slipped from the bundle when the king had taken it up to read. Thus some lines, that were not written by Kalidasa, found a place in the copies of *Meghadutam*.

Words were inadequate to describe the emotions that lashed through Mallika's mind. She had to hold her breath as her eyes passed over each word. As she read some lines, she could not control her tears. It was evident that it was Kalidasa's mind that was reflected in the poem. She realized that Kalidasa had understood what was on her mind. Though she was not

Kalidasa's wife, it could not be denied that she was his beloved. Though she was not living in Alakapuri, this separation made her equal to the wife of the yaksha. Mallika was surprised to realize that Kalidasa had clearly understood the different emotions created in her mind by this separation. Each word seemed to proclaim the pain that Kalidasa was suffering on being away from Ujjaini.

She thought of the complaints against Kalidasa. There was no need for the respectable ladies living with their families to feel bad, as the description of the woman's body was being connected only with the prostitutes and not with them. Otherwise these ladies would have had to complain that the poet was describing the beauty of their bodies and limbs to an unacceptable level. The prostitutes will have no such complaints. They would only be happy to see a poet describing their beauty so well. Hence Kalidasa had become famous among the prostitutes and through them Kalidasa's lines were becoming popular among the laity. Mallika was not pleased with such popularity of Kalidasa, but found comfort in the thought that he was not responsible for that.

Vikramaditya and Nichula too recognized *Meghadutam* as Kalidasa's message as well as that of the yaksha's.

This added to the worry in Vikramaditya's mind. Emotions that had been hidden till now were laid bare through this work. What was portrayed as the emotions of the yaksha was, in fact, Kalidasa's own. Were the thoughts in Mallika's mind similar to those of the yaksha's wife? Her expression and behaviour made it appear to be so. It seemed that Mallika already knew *Meghadutam* by heart; its lines were always on her lips. They had gone deep into her heart. Vikramaditya felt that it was now impossible to remove Kalidasa from her mind.

Vikramaditya talked about it with Vidyothama. It was clear that nothing had been gained by sending Kalidasa to Ramagiri and separating them. As he had been forced to be away from her, he had grown even fonder of her. Now even if he decreed that Mallika should not be allowed to see any of Kalidasa's works, it will be of no use. What he had now written, revealed how they could see each other without seeing with their eyes and hear each other without their ears. This separation had, in fact, made them closer to each other.

As days passed, the fame of *Meghadutam* spread all over Ujjaini. People competed with one another in making more copies of that work. It soon reached Koushambi and Vidisha overshadowing the fame gained by *Malavikagnimitram, Pururavorvasheey*am and *Ritusamharam*. Mellifluous presentation of the lines from *Meghadutam* was soon heard at all the gatherings of poets and lovers of poetry. Discussions were held on the different planes of its poetic quality.

As its poetic grandeur was being praised, the cynics, ready to see only the evil, were ready with the accusation that some of the lines in the work showed Kalidasa to be one who led an immoral life. This criticism helped to make the work more popular but the accusers succeeded in creating a bad impression of the poet in the minds of the common people.

Nichula was extremely pleased with the poetic genius of his friend. This work alone was enough to ensure a place for Kalidasa as the greatest among the poets in Sanskrit. A new approach was evident in the work, something unseen in poetry hitherto. It could be seen as the first in the genre of poems sent as messages to the beloved. There was no mention of such a type in the descriptions of the different types of poems. But the emotions revealed in *Meghadutam* made Nichula thoughtful. The poem made clear the nature of Shambhu's feelings for Mallika. Will the king agree to such a relationship? Political diplomacy would never bow before sentiments. Those in power will decree that emotions do not aid administration.

Will the attitude of Vikramaditya, that generally supported poetic sentiments, help Kalidasa? How long will he be able to continue ignoring all this criticism? As her brother, Vikramaditya had the responsibility of arranging Mallika's marriage. Will he be ready to accept Kalidasa as his sister's husband? A tide of questions seemed to invade Nichula's mind.

9

Vikramaditya felt that he had chosen the best available method. He had no other options. So he did not send his soldiers to bring Kalidasa back to Ujjaini. He sent a message with high praise for his latest work informing the poet that Ujjaini was waiting for him.

Vikramaditya decided to conduct the swayamvara, before Kalidas returned, the function at which the princess would choose a husband from among the eligible men gathered. This was done on the advice of the royal assembly. Vikramaditya knew what was on his sister's mind. Vidyothama also had understood Mallika's mind and had informed Vikramaditya about it. They knew the futility of persuading Mallika to get married to someone else. But King Vikramaditya knew that the swayamvara for his sister was a political need. He could not brush aside the opinion of the ministers and the members of the assembly. Malava was a powerful state in Aryavarta. But it was necessary to increase the strength. There were constant threats of invasions at the western borders. So it was important to establish a coalition with another strong state.

Amarasimha held discussions about Kalidasa with Vikramaditya. They decided that they would not publicise what they were planning to do. They made all the plans in secret. They sent invitations to all the royal houses of the different states and made an official proclamation for the swayamvara, only seven days before the event.

Mallika was surprised, hurt and angry at what was happening. She had not expected her brother to make such a move against her wishes. Now the invitations had all been sent. Only princes could take part in a swayamvara; ordinary men would never be allowed to be present there. And Kalidasa was at Ramagiri. She did not think that her brother had informed him about it. She would not get her brother's help in sending someone to Ramagiri. Nichula was the most trustworthy friend of Kalidasa. But whatever Nichula might try, he will not be able to inform Kalidasa about this and make him come to Ujjaini in time for the swayamvara. Even if Nichula decided to go immediately and bring Kalidasa with him, nothing could happen in Ujjaini against the wishes of King Vikramaditya. If he decided that Kalidasa could not set foot in Ujjaini before the swayamvara, that is what would happen. The king had established strict and impeccable administrative methods. Everybody seemed to enjoy all the freedom they needed; but no one was allowed to do anything that went against the royal wishes.

Vikramaditya tried to reason with Mallika—the inevitability of political alliances, the helplessness of even a king before the decisions of the royal assembly, Kalidasa's position as just a poet, the belief that a poet becoming the husband of a princess would tarnish the tradition and esteem of the royal family. He tried his best to make Mallika understand all this, but she was not ready to accept any of those arguments. She made it clear that if she lived, it would only be with Kalidasa. She reiterated her stand that if she were to put the garland around any man's neck, it would only be that of Kalidasa's. Vikramaditya saw a strength and courage that he had not seen in her before. Vikramaditya did not have any more discussions with her, he did not make any further enquiries about her welfare. Vidyothama continued to assure Mallika that nothing but the best would happen to her and that her brother would not have it any other way.

Mallika had also taken a firm decision. Just as Vikramaditya had taken a firm stand, she too did what was within her capacity.

She sent for Nichula. She revealed to Nichula the truth that she had not told even Kalidasa. It was her firm decision that she would not marry anyone other than Kalidasa and Nichula had no difficulty in understanding that. Mallika opened her heart to him. He understood what was on Kalidasa's mind directly from his words and through the lines of *Meghadutam*.

Nichula gave his word to Mallika—Kalidasa would attend the swayamvara. Mallika would place the garland around Kalidasa's neck, ignoring everyone else, not considering the arguments about the pride of the dynasty, unmindful of the reactions of the others who had come to take part in the swayamvara. How that would be achieved, should remain a secret. Nichula had only one request to make: trust him and do not wed anyone else.

Nichula comforted Mallika. 'Vikramaditya would never break the customs or go against tradition. So when you place the garland on a man's neck at the swayamvara, he will accept him as your husband, whoever he may be. But he will also make sure that you do not get a chance to choose a man that he does not like. It cannot be said that Vikramaditya does not like Kalidasa. He accepts Kalidasa's position as a poet and an individual, he loves him too. So you may get ready for your swayamvara with no worries.'

Nichula made some preparations in secret. But he did not send any messengers to Ramagiri; nor did he go there himself. He thought that it would be of no use. He felt that he would be able to manage with a small trick. He knew that no one would be able to oppose what happened afterwards. He was sure that it would all be in Mallika's favour.

The people of Ujjaini were ecstatic on hearing about the swayamvara of their beloved Princess Mallika. Preparations were made with enthusiasm. The streets were decorated within a day. People from even the remote villages started sending gifts to the princess. On the seventh day, everything was ready.

Mallika reached the venue, accompanied by her companions. Conches were blown announcing the auspicious occasion. Musical instruments were played and the sound reverberated all over the place. The ladies, who accompanied her, introduced to Mallika the kings who had come from various kingdoms. Mallika did not raise her hands to place the garland on any of them. If she did not choose any of those who had come for the swayamvara, it would be considered as an insult to those kings and would make war inevitable. Mallika was aware of that; she had heard stories of such instances. She also knew that even if Kalidasa came and she was able to wed him, such a calamity might happen. Kalidasa was not a king, he did not have an army to support him. Who will be there to fight for him? She could only comfort herself with the thought that Kalidasa would come and nothing untoward would happen. Nichula must have planned something and she felt assured that his plans had no flaws, she had confidence in his promises. Mallika prayed to Mahakaleshwara to show her Kalidasa seated in any corner, the last row or even among the audience. But she had no idea what magic Nichula was going to do to get Kalidasa in the hall. She just remembered what Nichula had said as she was returning that morning after worshipping Mahakaleshwara. 'Doesn't Mahakaleshwara live in Mount Kailas? At the same time, he is omnipresent. His all-powerful manifestation is here for the devotees to offer worship. No one worships Mahakaleshwara on seeing him directly,' Nichula had said.

Mallika had gone round the dais once with her companions. Her companions introduced each prince seated there, but Mallika did not choose any of them and passed the last distinguished guest. The kings, princes and other distinguished guests gathered there were surprised. Didn't Mallika like any of them? Or will she go round the dais once again? That could be done. She may want to see all those who had come for the swayamvara and then choose the most suitable person. Vikramaditya too waited anxiously. What would Mallika do? As she looked around her eyes fell on an image that had been placed there as a part of the decoration. And Nichula was seated a little away among the members of the assembly, looking at her.

Now Mallika understood what Nichula had planned. It was clear that Nichula would not be able to bring Kalidasa there. Even if he could come to Ujjaini, only kings and princes would be allowed to sit on the dais. But nobody would object to keeping an idol of Kalidasa, who was a well-known poet, there. Those who saw it would only see it as another idol among so many used to decorate the hall. Nobody had even noticed it; otherwise someone might have questioned the resemblance of a decorative piece to a member of the assembly.

Without any hesitation, Mallika put the garland around the idol. Everyone gathered there was stunned. Nichula had succeeded in what he had planned. Somebody shouted that the princess had chosen Kalidasa as her husband. The auspicious sound of the musical instruments was heard. No one could point out that Mallika had not chosen any of the invited dignitaries who had come for the swayamvara and therefore it could not be considered legal. Even if someone had wanted to point it out, the auspicious sound of the musical instruments had declared the completion of the swayamvara.

When they saw that Mallika had put the garland on an idol, everyone looked at it carefully. They noticed that it resembled the famous poet Kalidasa. That meant that Princess Mallika had chosen the poet Kalidasa as her husband. They shouted the names of the two, offering them their blessings.

Nichula noticed that Vikramaditya was looking at him. But there was a meaningful calm on his face; he was not angry.

'So you managed it!' the king's expression seemed to say. No one got a chance to express their displeasure. Vikramaditya was ready to accept the decision taken by his sister. He did not even glance at those who were trying to raise objections. He saw many of them get agitated, but he just ignored them.

The attendants understood the expression on the king's face. Silence was commanded. The king spoke, 'My dear friends, Princess Mallika has taken a decision that none of us had expected. It was not the power of a ruler or physical strength or beauty that attracted her. We all are aware of her interest in art and literature. Since she has decided that Kalidasa, the great poet, is the best partner for life for her, we cannot oppose it. We had decided that only princes would be invited to the swayamvara. So we did not allow anyone else to participate in it. But Mallika has accepted the dictates of her mind and not our wishes. So we will bring Kalidasa here from Ramagiri as early as possible and their marriage will be conducted on an auspicious day.'

Voices were heard shouting victory for Kalidasa. Nichula smiled in satisfaction as his plan had bore fruit. He was sure that the observant eyes of Vikramaditya must have seen the idol of Kalidasa there and must have understood what was going to happen.

Many of the members of the assembly could not accept this. But they knew that any protest they raised will be of no use as the king had already declared his decision.

Royal emissaries and soldiers were sent to Ramagiri. All arrangements were made to bring Kalidasa to Ujjaini with royal honour. Mallika started waiting anxiously for him to return. Vidyothama and her own companions congratulated Mallika on her bold initiative. Vikramaditya could only jokingly complain that she had defeated him.

As Kalidasa entered Ujjaini after being away for long, he received a hearty reception. Till then Kalidasa had only been the poet of Malava. But now he had become a member of the royal family. Even before this, he had all the royal comforts available to him but they were only what were due to a member of the royal assembly and the most important poet in the country. But now he had been elevated to a higher position. He was showered with love as a poet as well as a member of the royal family.

After Kalidasa had reached Ujjaini, Nichula explained all that had happened. But clouds of apprehension seemed to gather in Kalidasa's mind. Kalidasa realized that the picture of the evil planet, Rahu, approaching to consume the full moon, was gaining strength in his mind. The moon would not be able to escape from the evil planet by hiding behind dark clouds or by keeping the stars as guards around her. Some lines that had come up in his mind long ago, resurfaced... *'jhaṭiti praviśa gēhē mā bahistiṣṭha kāntē...'* (Enter the house immediately, don't stay outside, dear.)

Kalidasa sat lost in thought. Nichula was surprised—he noticed that Kalidasa seemed to be in despair at a time when he should be elated. Nichula tried to find out what was troubling his friend's mind but failed to get anything from him. But Kalidasa indicated that he was not happy at the decisions taken by Mallika and Vikramaditya as he had a premonition that the vagaries of fate were not going to play in accordance with their decision.

Kalidasa prayed ardently in the temples of Mahakaleshwara as well as Vindhyavasini Mahakaleshwari. His mind kept reminding him that nothing could stop what fate had in store for him. The key to real knowledge was not logic or strength; what the mind utters is the supreme truth. Everyone may not be able to read and understand the dictates of the mind easily. The mind helps not just in knowing oneself but also in knowing the truth of time, and to Kalidasa, his mind was not telling him anything desirable.

Kalidasa hinted to Vikramaditya his fears, 'Maharaj! Fate may not agree with what we think, wish for or desire. The yardstick of a man's mental strength should be the willingness to accept the dictates of fate.'

Vikramaditya looked at Kalidasa, unable to understand what he was saying. 'What do you wish to say, Kalidasa? Please be more specific,' he requested his friend many a time. But Kalidasa could not make it clear. The truth was that even the power that controlled one's fate would not be able to reveal clearly what was going to happen. The decisions of fate remain with fate alone.

Days passed and the arrangements for the wedding were going on in full swing. And then life in Ujjaini suddenly seemed to come to a standstill one day as the news broke that Princess Mallika had died. Their beloved princess was no more! None could believe it... They hoped for it to be untrue. The people refused to believe what they heard. But gradually they had to accept the unbelievable truth.

Mallika had gone to the terrace of the palace to gather flowers in the morning. As she was plucking flowers from a champaka branch that had grown onto the terrace, a flower came with the wind and she leaned forward to catch it. Her feet slipped and Mallika fell from the terrace. The maids and companions raised an alarm and people gathered. The palace physicians were summoned immediately but death does not wait for anybody. She did not even get a chance to bid goodbye to anyone. Mallika waited for none—not for her brother Vikramaditya, nor for her beloved Kalidasa.

Kalidasa stood looking at the inert Mallika, who looked like a flower that had been plucked. Death seemed to have approached her as a flower, or was the flower the harbinger of death? Is it possible that a beautiful, fragrant flower could be the cause of death? Yes! Fate had to end the flower-like life with a flower! The flakes of snow kill the lotus! Time and fate decide what is in store for one! When the time for death approaches, even amrut, the nectar of life, can act as the deadliest poison!

Kalidasa had not gotten a chance to talk to Mallika after he had returned from Ramagiri. He had been brought directly to the assembly hall. Their eyes had met during the discussions on the greatness of *Meghadutam*. There was a look of bashfulness on her which had never been there before. Before this, when she used to meet him, she had an expression of awe and reverence for the poet in him. She had never hesitated to express her own views on the poems and plays. She displayed a different expression on those occasions. But during this last meeting at the assembly, she had stood before him for a while and then had gone off with a bashful look.

Now what did her face reflect? How could she go away without even bidding farewell to him? What rose in his mind was the picture of Mallika, gazing at him intently, even forgetting to put the flower in the basket, when they had met for the first time in the garden. Drops of perspiration had not left her face, death did not have the patience to wait even for a moment.

'*Look! Your curly hair is still playing in the wind! Will I ever see a smile blossoming on your lips? Are you trying to tell me something? Wouldn't the holy, medicinal plants of the Himalayas be available in the deep, dark hollow of death? Can't you consume at least one of those radiant plants? Who is there to collect them for Mallika? Can I go with her?*' Kalidasa felt that his mind was approaching a state of madness. Would he lose control over himself?

Mallika was leaving him. Had she reached the forest of the radiant, holy plants that give life? The radiance was transforming itself into fire. The flames were climbing onto the sweet, soft, beautiful body. No... No... It is only a dream. Kalidasa tried to control his mind.

'*What will I do with the flowers of the Ashoka that cover the* tree like a flame? For whom should I gather them now? Who will be with me to sit on the floral bed made by the various flowering trees to recite the lines from Rithusamhram and Meghadutam? Will these lips ever move to recite my compositions? Wouldn't this Ujjaini lose its glory now?' Thoughts still conquered his mind.

'Who will now feed the birds that have made their nests on the branches of the champaka tree on the banks of the Kshipra? Who will be there now, to talk with the little birds, the doves, the peacocks and the swans that swam majestically in the lakes? Who will now rest on the bed of flowers in my bower, dressed in cloth as white as the lotus, with the designs of red flowers decorating it? Am I condemned to carry this picture of everlasting sleep in my eyes, when I had wished to keep looking at that lovely sight of peaceful sleep throughout the night, without closing my eyes even for a moment? How will I now see the little blackbirds fluttering on your face as the light of the rising sun touched you? Have they flown away, Mallika? Please open your eyes, Mallika... Please... Mallika... Mallika.'

Nichula could only embrace his friend in trying to comfort him. Gradually Kalidasa seemed to gain control of his mind.

Kalidasa realized that he had not been able to gauge the enormity of the danger that he had foreseen. Deep within his mind, he had a hazy idea that it was time that was going to batter him cruelly but he had never thought that it would lead to such a culmination. Life always put forth the most unexpected things. But Kalidasa wondered why his mind had been warning him of an eclipse. He realized with a shudder how his mind had been warning him of an impending disaster that would shatter the rhythm of his life.

Nichula had no words of comfort to offer Kalidasa. None could bear Vikramaditya's heart-rending sobs. After they had lost their parents early in life, he had brought up his little sister showering all his love and affection on her. He had dreamt of a happy future for her, full of the fragrance of poetry that she loved so much. The cry of the brother at the loss of his sister was enough to make even the granite walls of the palace weep in sorrow.

Many of the people were aware that Vikramaditya had secretly approved of the choice that Mallika, who was dear to all of them, had made at the swayamvara. He had closed his eyes to the plan that Nichula had made, knowing that it was against the interests of the state, only because he cared so much for his sister's happiness. But fate had decreed otherwise. Vidyothama also could not bear the loss of her little sister. As the last rites were conducted, the sorrow of whole of Malava reverberated. Fire started to consume that beautiful body, aided by the presence of fragrant pieces of sandalwood and cedar; returning that inert body to the five elements.

Many in the royal assembly had been against Mallika and Kalidasa's marriage but they all loved the princess in spite of everything. Even those who were against Kalidasa grieved at this loss. None could hold back the tears.

For a moment Kalidasa considered putting an end to this life which had to come to an end someday. But he remembered that it was not what Rishi Shalibhadra had taught him. The great yogis who had talked with him as they traversed the heights of the Himalayas, had also spoken otherwise. None had the right to challenge the dictates of nature. One had to accept whatever fate had in store for them and traverse the path that lay before them.

Kalidasa's face that had till then radiated the grandeur of an ascetic, was now clouded by sorrow. Those who approached him had to turn away with tears on seeing his expression. No one had any words of solace to offer him. Those who had read *Meghadutam* now realized that it was Kalidasa's message to Mallika, and it revealed to them the depth of the love that he felt for her. That realization remained as a painful wound in their hearts.

Kalidasa bid farewell to his beloved, sitting near the funeral pyre that reduced her body to the elements. Death is an eternal truth. Once the rope of time falls on one's neck, there is no escape.

10

Mallika was the essence of all that was precious in life. She was like a daughter to Vikramaditya and Vidyothama. She never gave them a chance to think that they were childless. Her death put an unbearable burden of sorrow on both of them. The loss of his sister made Vikramaditya closer to Kalidasa. The absolute silence that Kalidasa held gave some courage to the king. Vikramaditya felt that there was another man who grieved the death of Mallika more than he did and it was his duty to offer some consolation to that man.

If he had objected to the choice that Mallika had made at the swayamvara and forced her into a marriage against her wishes, he would have had to bear the feeling of guilt that it was mental agony that he caused her that led to her death. Though he had conducted the swayamvara without giving Kalidasa a chance to participate in it, Vikramaditya had not denied her the freedom to choose the man she wanted. The swayamvara took place in the absence of Kalidasa. Kalidasa was not a prince, looking through the eyes of a king, Kalidasa was nothing but a poet. In spite of all these drawbacks, Vikramaditya had given his consent to the marriage. The tragedy occurred while the preparations for the wedding were going on. Seeing her intense interest in literature and arts, he used to think of her as the poetry of Ujjaini. She had merged herself, like the wind or the fragrance of a flower, with the poet Kalidasa who had come to Ujjaini. Still, she was gone, she could forget her brother... but how could she leave Kalidasa? Vikramaditya tried to convince himself that he had done nothing against Kalidasa or Mallika.

Kalidasa did not attend the assembly. Nichula tried his best to bring Kalidasa back to ordinary life. But Kalidasa preferred solitude. Nichula did not want to leave his friend alone like that, but he was helpless. He could only hope that Shambhu would be able to get some control over his mind.

Then one day, at the insistence of Nichula, Kalidasa went to meet Vikramaditya. The palace seemed to be empty without Mallika. He could see Vidyothama and Mallika's maids perplexed on meeting him without Mallika by their side. Though many days had passed, the palace still looked like a house of death.

Vikramaditya requested Kalidasa to attend the gurukula and the assembly regularly. Kalidasa agreed, but Vikramaditya knew that his replies had not come from the heart. Vikramaditya could not think of ordering him to do as he commanded.

As they were returning from the palace, Kalidasa thought of the sorrow that the king and Vidyothama had suffered because of not having a child. Man may amass wealth and power but the control that thoughts of his own children and family had on him could never be erased. If a king had no child, it would affect not only his family but also the people who lived under his rule. This is not a new phenomenon. The famous Surya dynasty had once faced such a predicament. That powerful dynasty had reached a situation where there was no one to succeed to the throne.

Kalidasa had heard the old men praise some of the old rulers of Ujjaini. During their talk they used to describe the story of Maharaja Udayana and Vasavadatta while praising the glory of the Surya dynasty. Vikramaditya also prided himself as a member of the Surya dynasty. Many of the kings in the ancient land of Bharatavarsha prided themselves as belonging to the dynasty which had great monarchs like Sree Ramachandra, Raghu and Dilipa. Their stories dominated the folk songs of this land.

As he returned to his house, Kalidasa felt that he should put the history of the Surya dynasty in a poetic form. He made enquiries at various hermitages and talked with many teachers. He read copies of the old works that were available in the library at the gurukula in Ujjaini. At times he even doubted whether he would be able to create a good work on the background of such a great dynasty. It was evident that the story of a dynasty will include many glorious incidents as well as some that brought shame.

Kalidasa wandered along the shores of the Kshipra and Gambhira. He spent hours gazing at the flow of the water, seated on the lonely rocks on the shores. Sometimes he disappeared from Ujjaini for days together. He climbed the steep slopes of the Vindhya mountain ranges. Kalidasa wandered about in the forests on the banks of the Charmanavati, unmindful of the wild beasts that roamed about there. Kalidasa was learning to live a disinterested life, with no attachment to anything. The wild animals led their life while he led his. If he became food for one of them, the world would lose nothing. But he was surprised to see that these animals saw him neither as an enemy nor as something that would satisfy his hunger when he approached them with no fear and no attachment.

As he was wandering aimlessly thus, the fate of Maharaja Aja, mourning the death of his wife Indumati and that of Sree Ramachandra, who had lost his wife Sita, entered his thoughts. They belonged to the same famous royal dynasty. Sree Ramachandra was famed as the best among the kings of the royal clan of Raghu. Kalidasa felt that he should try to create a poem describing the life of the great rulers beginning with Dilipa, the embodiment of sacrifice and morality and lead to Agnivarna, who, even before he had an heir to the throne, threw away his life by overindulging in sensual pleasures.

In the royal palace at Kosala, the chief of the hermitage

of Vasishta was advising the king on what to do for begetting a child. He would begin with Dilipa. The background for his poem slowly took shape in Kalidasa's mind.

Kalidasa held consultations with Nichula and met the teachers of the gurukula and got their advice. He was aware that he was planning a long poem with the history of a famous dynasty as the backdrop. It was evident that a lot of preparation will be needed.

In a sublime journey through the entire universe, Sree Parameshwara and Sree Parvathi Devi were depicted as the father and mother of the cosmos, the supreme originators of creation. The ultimate basis of the evolution of this cosmos was the origin of sound and its permanence. Parvati and Parameshwara as the word and its meaning... Kalidasa's pen created the first stanza of the great work that he was planning. It was the prayer...

> vāgarthāviva saṃpṛktau vāgartha pratipattayē
> jagataḥ pitarau vandē pārvatī paramēśvarau.
>
> (*Raghuvamsam*, Stanza 1, I)
>
> (I pray to Parvathi and Parameshwara, the mother and father of this cosmos, complementing each other like the word and its meaning, for their blessings to have words and meanings flourish in me.)

He was planning to narrate the story of the great Surya dynasty. Into the dynasty of Manu was born Dilipa. He grew up to be a man of valour and brilliance. Dilipa ruled the land with courage and goodwill; he was like a father to his people. He was married to Sudakshina, the princess of Magadha. His desire for a child remained unfulfilled for a long time. He entrusted his ministers with the rule of the land and went to the hermitage of Vasishtda, the preceptor of his dynasty, with his wife. The royal couple was welcomed affectionately by Vasishta and his consort Arundati Devi and the reason for their sorrow was soon realized by the rishi. It was revealed that once when Dilipa was returning from heaven, he failed to pay his respects to Surabhi, the holy cow of the Gods. So he was instructed to tend to Surabhi's daughter, Nandini, and get her blessings. Kalidasa spent six days, writing this as the first chapter of his work.

Vikramaditya was happy to know about this. It was the story of his dynasty that Kalidasa was writing. Vikramaditya expressed his happiness in the assembly even though Kalidasa was not present there.

Dilipa allowed Nandini to graze at will in the forest for 21 days. The next day Nandini walked into a crevice near the Ganga, full of lush green grass. Dilipa was for a moment lost in the beauty of the surroundings and it was the heart-rending cry of Nandini that brought him back. A lion was attacking Nandini. Dilipa immediately aimed the arrow to kill the lion but was surprised to hear the beast talk to him in a human voice. He had been deputed by Lord Parameshwara to protect the devadar tree, very dear to Goddess Parvati. The lion could eat only the animals that came there and so he requested Dilipa not to stop him from eating the cow. Dilipa immediately offered his own body in exchange for Nandini. As Dilipa waited with closed eyes for the lion to pounce on him, he felt a shower of flowers and Nandini revealed the truth that she was testing him. Nandini gave him her blessings and Sudakshina, who was given Nandini's milk to drink, became pregnant. This formed the second chapter of Kalidasa's *Raghuvamsam*.

Kalidasa often remembered the fate of Vikramaditya and Vidyothama. They too were waiting to be blessed with a child. Malava had no prince to succeed to its throne till now. What penance would they undertake for a child? They did not have someone like Rishi Vasishta to advise them nor would they get a Nandini to look after. They could not expect to fulfil their wish through someone's blessings.

Kalidasa remained immersed in his work.

He was starting the third chapter.

A child was born, who had already been destined to be the most powerful king of the Surya dynasty. The child was named Raghu. Dilipa found eminent teachers to coach him. The father himself took up the duty of teaching the boy the art of warfare. When he felt that Raghu had become strong enough to be considered unconquerable, Dilipa decided to conduct the Ashwamedha and deputed Raghu to follow the horse. Ninety-nine yajnas, sacrifices in connection with the Ashwamedha, were completed; but Indra, who was jealous of the power of Dilipa, stole the horse for the last sacrifice. Raghu fought to get the horse from Indra. Indra was pleased with Raghu's prowess and blessed Dilipa with all virtue even without completing the last sacrifice. Dilipa soon left for the forest with his wife, leaving Raghu with the responsibility of ruling the land.

Kalidasa read through what he had written. He was happy to see that he had been able to describe the beauty of nature along with the depiction of the qualities of Dilipa and Raghu. He was happy with the progress that he was making in the new work.

After his father Maharaja Dilipa retired to the forest to spend the last years of his life, Raghu, the new king, started his rule with the intention of building a strong country. Once he was confident that his administration had been well established, he started on a tour of conquest to bring all the land from the Himalayas to the ocean under his control. His entire digvijaya yatra through Bharatavarsha found a place in Kalidasa's verse.

It was easy for Kalidasa to describe the path of conquest that Raghu had taken as they were all places that he had seen for himself, his pen effortlessly created the lines of the poem.

There he described how a son was born to Raghu with the blessings of Rishi Koutsa.

Aja, the son of Raghu, went to Vidarbha to take part in the swayamvara. Then he moved on to the swayamvara of Indumati, the daughter of King Bhoja. As he came to write this, Kalidasa felt a tide of emotions rise in his mind, as thoughts of Mallika enveloped his mind. As he wrote about Indumati, it was the figure of Mallika that came out. Vetravati took the princess to the different princes who were present there and introduced each of them to her.

Even after being chosen by Indumati at the swayamvara, Aja had to win another battle before reaching Kosala with his bride. Though Raghu had chosen the life of a hermit in the forest, he had been persuaded by Aja to stay near the city in a hermitage built for him. Very soon he attained everlasting sleep.

As Kalidasa was thinking of what more to write, he realized that King Aja had also been treated cruelly by fate. They had a son born to them who was named Dasaratha. But Indumati had left the world soon after. My Mallika...! A sob rose in Kalidasa's heart. As he was describing the intense pain suffered by Aja after the death of Indumati, Kalidasa was in fact putting into words the pain that he had suffered. He reminded himself that in real life, even suffering and sorrow bear similarities with similar experiences of others. Aja mourned the death of Indumati for almost eight years and then he too gave up his life after entrusting the rule of the land with his son Dasaratha.

As he went on writing the couplets one after the other, it became clear to Kalidasa that no death can be termed untimely. There had to be a logical reason for all the decisions taken by fate. There is a predestined period for each created being to remain on this earth and special reasons for a life to be in the form of a human being. Life on earth may be filled with happiness but many a deva, a celestial being, had been born on earth as a human being as the result of a curse. Hence there was the assumption that life of a human being is a cursed existence. He felt that whether it was Mallika or Indumati, it was better to console oneself with the belief that they had left the earth, once the period in which they had to bear the consequences of the curse had expired. It was better to think that they had been expiated from their curse.

As he started on the story of Dasaratha, Kalidasa realized that it was an entirely different type of life. Dilipa, Raghu and Aja had been monogamous and they were like a father to their people. Dasaratha, on the other hand, remained a good ruler for some years, but then started indulging in intoxicating drinks and women. He gave up the practice of killing wild animals when they posed a threat to the people and started killing all animals for sport. He married many times, became too indulgent in sexual pleasures. As he was immersed in the pleasure of hunting, he killed a boy from a hermitage mistaking him to be an elephant. He was cursed to die with the sorrow of separation from his son.

As he came to the end of Dasaratha's story, Kalidasa had decided what name to give his new work—this was the story of the dynasty of Raghu, so *Raghuvamsam* would be a suitable name. Now he had to include the story of Sreerama. He was known as Raghuvamsashiromani, the best among the descendants of Raghu, and also known as Raghava. The details of his life from birth, marriage with Sita, the altercation with Parasurama, the stay in the forest and Ravana's abduction of Sita were famous as part of the great epic Ramayana.

Kalidasa found no difficulty in going on with his writing till he had finished the story of King Agnivarna. Kalidasa realized that at some places, his narration was fast like the Kshipra and at other places, slow and majestic like the Gambhira. But he was confident that it would not affect the beauty of his poetry.

Nichula would come now and then and that would break the solitude. It sometimes hindered his writing but it was a relief for the writer. Nichula's visits prevented him from sitting in the same spot, going on with his writings for hours together and from forgetting to eat while he was thus engaged. The king had employed servants to see that Kalidasa was well looked after, but they could not do anything to interrupt his writing and they could not engage in small talk with him. Only Nichula, Guru Devasraya and the king had the freedom to do that.

There were some others who had become friendly with Kalidasa; like the common people of the village who were a little educated and the students of the gurukula. They too called on Kalidasa at times and enquired after his welfare. The people had noticed that Kalidasa would stop writing in the evening and he would be seated on the flat rock looking at the Kshipra. They knew that it was the best time to talk to him.

From those who came to see him at that time, the news of the new creation spread far and wide. Many waited eagerly for it to be finished.

11

Raghuvamsam was complete. It had already become so famous that all the kings, who had at least some interest in art and literature, started sending their envoys to Ujjaini to get a copy of the work.

It was this fame that created enemies for Kalidasa and made them lose sleep over it. They tried their best by pointing out lines that described the beauty of women from *Ritusamharam* and *Meghadutam*, but they did not do as much harm as they had hoped for. They tried to raise a hue and cry against *Sringaratilakam* but as it was not considered for study in the gurukulas or hermitages, it had become popular in the houses of prostitutes and among the libertines. Apart from them, it was the experts in poetics who read that work. It was not officially introduced into the hermitages and the gurukulas and to the students at these places.

The writing of *Sringaratilakam* happened purely by chance. The poet was sorting and arranging some of the writing leaves in his bundle when he came across some of the lines that he had written earlier. They were not part of the poems that he had given the maharaja, so he kept them aside. As he went through them, he felt like adding a few more to it. Romantic love was the subject of those lines. But he saw that even those lines had poetic beauty. So he made it into a work named *Sringaratilakam*. The poet knew that *Sringaratilakam* had no connection with the poems and plays that he had written. He did not feel that he should deny that such lines came from the feelings that he had in his heart. But this gave rise to the accusation that Kalidasa's works were more famous in the houses of prostitutes and among the lecherous.

Just like the accusations that were raised against him, the fame that *Raghuvamsam* gained did not affect Kalidasa. Enjoying literature had become a part of his being and his attention had turned towards writing. He never expected to gather fame or money through this but he was pleased to see people enjoying what he had written. His happiness was based on the fact that what he was writing was what the people wanted and they enjoyed it.

Vikramaditya was not stingy with his praise of Kalidasa in the assembly. The king felt that *Raghuvamsam* brought glory to him, as he was also born to the Surya dynasty. Though it was not his story, it was that of his predecessors. The story of the greatest among those who ruled under the Surya dynasty, like Dilipa, Raghu, Aja and Sree Ramachandra.

Vikramaditya convened a meeting of all the citizens of Ujjaini to felicitate Kalidasa. He gave instructions to send copies of *Raghuvamsam* to scholars around the world.

Meanwhile, those who were jealous of the fame that Kalidasa was getting were not idle and their attacks became well planned. Ghatakarpara went to the library and inserted some leaves into the bundle that contained the lines of *Raghuvamsam*. He felt that they should be enough to bring infamy to Kalidasa. Ghatakarpara was sure that Kalidasa would not bother to go through what he had written when copies were made and so the lines that he had added would destroy Kalidasa's name and fame.

The lovers of literature had already enjoyed *Malavikagnimitram*, *Pururavorvasheeyam*, in addition to *Ritusamharam* and *Meghadutam*. For them it was exciting to read another work by Kalidasa. They were thrilled to learn that it was the story of the Surya dynasty that they were going to get.

It was a massive assembly. Learned men had come from far and near. They did not mince words in praising Kalidasa.

King Vikramaditya announced that he was conferring the title of Kavikulaguru, the preceptor of all poets, on Kalidasa. Vikramaditya took the gem-encrusted crown from the pedestal and decorated Kalidasa's head.

Drumbeats filled the sky as the announcement was made. The claps and cheers of people reverberated throughout Ujjaini. It was the most fitting approval that the learned men and the ordinary people could give to the announcement made by the king.

Shankuka raised some criticism while felicitating Kalidasa at the meeting. He voiced his opinion that Kalidasa's ability to find poetical solutions to riddles was not the mark of a real poet. He even speculated whether Kalidasa would be able to complete a riddle that was given to him at the meeting.

Kalidasa did not feel that he needed to respond to such meaningless talk. He had been subjected to such words from some people since a long time. He had not created poems for fame or for wealth. Those who were interested in it could enjoy them; those who wanted to explain it further could do so and those who wanted to criticize them were welcome to do that too. But it was true that he felt happy on hearing that his poems were being enjoyed by many.

Quite unexpectedly, King Vikramaditya made an announcement. 'Kalidasa, who came to this assembly with a solution for one of the riddles that I had put forward, has now become the most honoured poet in Ujjaini. Now I would like to instruct him to come up with a solution to a riddle that I present now. The last line must be "*gulu guggulu guggulu.*" We expect some simple but enjoyable lines from you.'

Kalidasa gazed at Vikramaditya as if he could not believe what he had heard. For a moment he wondered if the king wanted to put him in a quandary by placing such a riddle before the whole assembly.

Kalidasa sat lost in thought for a few moments. As he saw Shankuka looking at him with a triumphant look on his face, Kalidasa understood that it was a trick that Shankuka had hatched to put Kalidasa to shame in the assembly. Kalidasa could not believe that the king had fallen for it.

Everybody encouraged Kalidasa to take up the challenge; he could not escape from it.

Kalidasa meditated, thinking about Goddess Kali. His poetic ability was nothing but the blessing of the Goddess. Guru Shalibhadra had told him that the Goddess would come to his rescue at any difficult juncture.

As Kalidasa sat lost in thought with closed eyes, the sight of the flowing river and the jambu fruits falling into the water came to his mind. He recollected a scene that he had witnessed while walking along the bank of the Gambhira. There were a few children wondering how they could get the fruits from a branch that was leaning into the river. They were afraid of climbing the branch that was above the water. The children approached Shankuka who was coming from the opposite direction and requested him to pluck the fruits for them.

'You want me to climb that tree?' he asked.

'Hey! The gurukula does not offer any lessons in climbing trees. So the guru would not know how to climb a tree,' said one of the boys.

Shankuka felt that the children were challenging him. He must have felt that he should show Kalidasa, who had also reached there, that he could even climb trees if he wanted to. He took off the cloth that covered his upper body and tied it around his waist and got ready. Pushing aside one of the boys who was trying to climb up the tree, Shankuka started climbing. As he was moving towards the branch that bore the fruits, a monkey jumped onto that branch. The monkey might not have liked a man trying to take the fruits that the monkeys generally enjoyed. The branch moved violently as the monkey landed on it and all the ripe fruits fell into the water. Shankuka stretched his hand to pluck the one fruit that still remained on the branch but the monkey took it and jumped onto another branch. The monkey sat there biting the fruit and spitting it into the water. Shankuka realized that he had made a fool of himself. The children forgot their disappointment at not getting the fruits and laughed aloud on seeing Shankuka's predicament. Shankuka got down from the tree and walked off muttering to himself.

This picture passed through his mind and Kalidasa got an answer to the puzzle. He put the picture into words and arranged them into lines. He stood up immediately and recited the lines he had made:

'jambuphalāni pakvāni
patanti vimalē jalē
kapi kampita śākhābhyām
gulu guggulu guggulu!'

(From the myths on Kalidasa)

(As a branch of the jambu tree is shaken by the monkey, the ripe fruits fall into the sparkling water with the sound 'gulu guggulu guggulu')

The hall reverberated with the applause raised by the members of the assembly. Drops of sweat appeared on Shankuka's face. He felt that Kalidasa had made him look like a fool.

The learned men who had come from different parts of Malava as well as from other parts congratulated Kalidasa on his genius. But the feeling that Kalidasa had insulted him in open assembly penetrated Shankuka's mind like a thorn. He decided that he should somehow destroy Kalidasa. That thought kept a strong hold on Shankuka's mind, like an octopus.

As Shankuka was returning after the meeting, some boys repeated the lines that Kalidasa had recited; this added fuel to the fire of anger in his mind.

That evening, Ghatakarpara and Devavarma, a scholar from Mahakosala, sought permission to meet the king. They came to see him as the king was walking in the garden in the evening.

'Ghatakarpara submits his greetings to the Maharaja,' Ghatakarpara said. He introduced Devavarma. 'Maharaj, this is Devavarma, a learned scholar from Mahakosala.'

The king invited them to sit on the marble platform in the garden. The king sat down and the two men followed him after greeting him once again with respect.

'What is the matter, Ghatakarpara?' the king enquired. 'Have you come to introduce him?'

'Devavarma wanted to meet you and bring some matters to your notice,' Ghatakarpara said.

Vikramaditya looked at Devevarma. 'I am happy to have got the opportunity to meet you. It is well known that meeting and communicating with learned men, acts like the flow of the water of learning into the great ocean of knowledge, like the holy rivers Ganga and Sindhu,' he said.

'Maharaj! Devavarma is the poet laureate of Mahakosala and he has written explanations of many great works. There are also many great poetic compositions that he has written,' Ghatakarpara continued.

'I remember seeing some of his works in the library here. Ghatakarpara, make arrangements to get the rest of them also,' Vikramaditya instructed Ghatakarpara.

'He has something special that he wants to bring to your notice, Maharaj,' Ghatakarpara said.

'What is it?' the king asked.

'Maharaj! A lot was said today in the meeting about the poetic quality and greatness of the epic poem, *Raghuvamsam*,' Devavarma began.

'Yes. I too was sure that it is a great work. But today, when those who spoke about it pointed out the different aspects of the work, I was surprised that I had failed to notice so much that Kalidasa has incorporated in the work,' Vikramaditya said with excitement.

'That is true, Maharaj... But...' Ghatakarpara and Devavarma looked at each other.

'Why do you hesitate? Do you think it is not so?' asked the king.

'No, Your Majesty! Both of us have nothing to say against the poetic quality of the work. But we wanted to bring to your notice some other things that were mentioned in it,' Devavarma said.

Vikramaditya looked at them anxiously, 'What do you mean by that?'

'Your Majesty! The poet has described the greatness and fame of the Surya dynasty in the work but he has culminated it with a suggestion that the dynasty is now in a pitiable situation,' Ghatakarpara said.

'We are not sure whether you paid attention to it, Maharaj!' Devavarma said as if continuing with what Ghatakarpara had said. 'The writer has ended the poem in such a way that it brings infamy to the dynasty.'

'You may be right in saying that it did not come to my attention. Tell me, what defect do you see in it?' Vikramaditya enquired.

'Maharaj, the description of Lava and Kusha taking up the administration of the empire after Sree Ramachandra attains heaven and of Maharaja Kusha coming back to Ayodhya from Kushaavati from where he had been ruling, has all been done very well. Kalidasa has then described the rule of Atidhi, the son of Maharaja Kusha, of his son Nishadha and 20 other kings of the Surya dynasty. He has chosen to portray Agnivarna as the last king of the dynasty. There he mentions how, after taking up the kingship from Maharaja Sudarshana, Agnivarna entrusted the ministers with the administration and spent his time with women of his choice. Your Majesty! There is no doubt that the last chapter is a disgrace to the Surya dynasty, also known as Ikshvaku dynasty. The disgrace that has been brought to the clan of Raghu affects you and my own king who rules Kosala. There are many other kings who belong to the Surya dynasty, ruling over many parts of this land. Kalidasa has brought disgrace to all of them through this work. He has mentioned that Agnivarna lost his life before he could have a son to succeed him. That is disgraceful, Maharaj! Some of the lines in that part cannot be recited even to you, who is well versed in the art of poetics.'

Anxiety clouded Vikramaditya's mind for a moment. Whatever had been heard about Agnivarna was not good. But it did not seem right that such matters should be portrayed in a literary work as such.

'Who is there?' Vikramaditya called and immediately one of the servants appeared there. 'Bring me a copy of the *Raghuvamsam*,' he ordered.

A copy was in his hands within minutes. As he glanced through the last canto, Vikramaditya felt that he could not raise his head because of shame. Did he feel enraged or sad? He had treated Kalidasa as his own brother. He had never doubted the greatness of his work. As some others had pointed out, he too felt that there was a slight tendency towards erotic descriptions but he had supported him, seeing it as the writer's poetic license. He had realized that all the men who pointed out these lines as immoral had been enjoying reciting them in secret. But when he was writing the story of the Surya dynasty, to which the king was proud to belong, it was unseemly to end it in such a disgracing manner.

Vikramaditya sent for Kalidasa then and there. 'Bring him here immediately. Don't come back without Kalidasa,' was the order given to the servants.

By this time many others had also come to meet the king. Ghatakarpara did not waste any time in informing them about what had happened. Many of them also started finding fault with Kalidasa. Some of them, who had remained silent when others raised objections about the propriety of what Kalidasa had written, now voiced their opinion. And those who had always supported Kalidasa now had to remain silent.

The discussion was shifted from the garden to the assembly. The dispute was assuming an official status. Hearing this, the ministers and other officials also arrived—the royal assembly of Ujjaini held an emergency meeting.

Kalidasa was there soon. Even as he entered, voices were raised against him. But Vikramaditya raised his hands commanding silence before it became an uproar.

'Please be seated...' said Amarasimha to all.

Many wondered what had happened that necessitated the assembly to meet immediately. Those who knew the reason soon divided themselves into two groups. Some of them expressed their view that when a work was based on history, such historical matter would naturally find a place in it; there was nothing wrong with it. But many who were in the habit of supporting whatever the king said, waited to find out what view Vikramaditya would take.

The assembly became quiet as the king started speaking.

'The assembly has been convened hastily as a matter connected to the royal dynasty has to be discussed,' Vikramaditya paused for a moment before continuing. 'It can be said that not only we in Malava but people all over Bharatavarsha are proud of the works of Kalidasa. We had convened a special meeting this morning to discuss the greatness of his work and had conferred the title of the preceptor of poets on him.'

Those who had come to disgrace Kalidasa were apprehensive on hearing these words. Was the king showering praise on Kalidasa again?

Vikramaditya continued: 'But we too have some opinion about the last canto of *Raghuvamsam*. The duty of the poet should be to praise the dynasty of the king. The glory of the Surya dynasty or the dynasty of Raghu is reflected throughout the poem, but there is no doubt that the last canto brings disgrace to the dynasty of Raghu. This royal assembly wishes to hear what Kalidasa has to say about this,' Vikramaditya turned towards Kalidasa with these words.

The king gave a clear indication that no one else need say anything. The king wanted Kalidasa to speak.

Kalidasa was shocked. What was the king saying? That the duty of the poet is to praise the dynasty of the king? Kalidasa searched his own mind for a few seconds. *'Was the glorification of the Ikshwaku dynasty my aim in writing Raghuvamsam? No,'* his mind answered. He wanted to write the history of that dynasty. When he began writing, he saw it as a dynasty that had gained glory; but as he went deeper into the history of the dynasty, some facts that were not complimentary to the dynasty came up.

Many matters prompted him to begin writing. It may be a momentary emotion towards certain things that leads to the creation of a line, a couplet, a poem or even a great literary work. Ultimately it is the result of a momentary inspiration. He decided to write *Raghuvamsam* with no special aim. He had felt a desire to write about the glory of that dynasty. But praising a royal dynasty was not his duty. It was true that the story had taken an entirely different direction towards the end.

The greatness of the brilliant rulers had been clearly brought out in the work. He had done nothing wrong in writing about Dasharatha or Agnimitra. How could he write about the grandeur of one who lacked all good qualities?

'Kalidasa, why are you silent? This royal assembly is waiting anxiously for your reply,' said Amarasimha.

Kalidasa rose from his seat. 'Salutations to the royal assembly,' he started and got straight to the point. 'Let me make one thing clear, the poetic duty is not to write stories of the greatness of the rulers. I write what I consider suitable. It may or may not be appreciated by the readers. They may like it or dislike it. There will certainly be the desire to create enjoyment for the readers. But if someone does not like what I have written, I can only say that he need not read it. In *Raghuvamsam*, it was not my intention to write the story of the Surya dynasty. My aim was to create a work with the historic background of that dynasty that would be enjoyed by the readers. I do not think that it is my duty to mask historical facts and write only that which adds to the glory of the royal dynasty. And it is my belief that no writer has such a responsibility. I have my right on my words, as long as they do not erode the rights of others.'

The assembly was shocked. None had ever used such strong words with King Vikramaditya either in the assembly or outside. Everyone had seen the king as God-incarnate. Now Kalidasa was opposing the king's words directly in the royal assembly. Nichula also felt that it was recklessness beyond imagination.

The assembly silently watched the king's face reflect the anger in his mind. Still, he seemed to be controlling himself.

'I have listened to all that you have said. I do not desire a discussion on this matter. I have only one thing to say. Kalidasa must rewrite the last canto of *Raghuvamsam*. There should be nothing that brings disgrace to the royal dynasty. This assembly has nothing against the literary quality of the work or against your ability, but the last canto is a disgrace to the Surya dynasty. So such a work should not be made available, not just in Ujjaini and Malava, but in any part of the Bharatavarsha.'

It was a decision that pleased those who had been waiting to malign Kalidasa. They were pleased to see the king speaking against Kalidasa's work and making him rewrite it as a punishment. They clapped their hands loudly, indicating their happiness at the king's decision.

Kalidasa sat immobile. Was this the King Vikramaditya who, he had believed, would stand firm for truth, justice and virtue? He now prefers to turn himself away from the truth. Kalidasa was sure that he had not written anything false about Dasaratha or Agnivarna. It was a true picture of the men that he had portrayed in the poem. They were all events that would never be erased from history. How could he write about it in any other way?

Kalidasa rose from his seat, bowed before the king and walked out of the assembly. Nichula as well as Amarasimha, the minister, wanted to call him back. But somebody made a statement, 'Your Majesty! Kalidasa has accepted to comply with your command. He would need just one night to rewrite the canto.'

Nichula was not sure about it. Did he walk out accepting the orders of the king or did he walk out in protest against such orders? The Kalidasa that Nichula knew would never agree to rewriting the canto. Kalidasa also knew that a royal approval and recommendation would help in increasing the fame of a literary creation. But Kalidasa's individuality had not deteriorated to such an extent that he would be ready to change the contents of his composition to please the king. If his work could get royal approval only if he rewrote it, he will decide to forgo such recognition.

'Stop the work of making copies of *Raghuvamsam* till

Kalidasa brings the new version of the last canto,' Vikramaditya ordered.

Anger and sorrow were battering his mind. Many greeted Kalidasa, but he saw nobody. They were surprised to see the royal poet and an intimate friend of the king walking alone on the streets of Ujjaini.

Vikramaditya and Kalidasa were never just the king and his subject. They were friends. He had been accepted as the king's brother-in-law. Was there a shift in the relationship all of a sudden? Kalidasa had no doubt that he had portrayed Agnivarna's life truthfully. If he were to rewrite it, it would be equal to writing falsehood. More than that, his works were not made to anyone's orders. They come from his mind. Matters that touch the main plot, as if by force of truth, alone become a part of the story. It was impossible for him to think of making any change to please anyone. Much that one has not witnessed will become a part of the work. That happens at the command of the mind. It is the mind's assurance of the truth of the matter that becomes the soul of that creation. But no work is a medium for searching historical truth. What he had written was a poem; it was meant to be read and enjoyed. Kalidasa took a firm decision.

Even if one wanted to search for historical truths, what relevance was there in trying to sanctify one's lineage on the basis of the fame and achievements of one's ancestors? If the king wanted to become celebrated like Dilipa, Raghu, Aja or Rama, should it be on the strength of the legends associated with them? He had given due space to historical facts in his work. What had been left out had still found a place in it, in the lines that were formed out of the poetic license that he enjoyed. He had made use of this freedom available to a poet only in such matters. But he would never be able to disregard historical facts in order to gain royal approval. Nor would he pawn his freedom of creation to please the king. He never wrote anything to be sold in the market. As long as his words did not break the limits of anyone's authority, none had the right to dictate their likes and dislikes to him. For the first time, Kalidasa felt contempt for Vikramaditya.

As one who had a deep interest in literary creations, the king should not have tried to interfere with his writings. He should not have imagined that the royal poet was under royal command. As a citizen of Ujjaini, he may be obligated to follow all royal decisions, but as a poet he should have the freedom to write what he wanted. Genius alone is the basis for poetic creation, and genius did not sprout at anyone's command or desire. Poetic genius did not obey orders; it had to come from an indefinable emotion in the poet's consciousness. No, the poet in him would never accept this royal command.

Kalidasa tried to control himself as he reached his house. Just as the king had the freedom to express his opinion, he had the freedom to refuse to do what was impossible. If criticism is raised, he is ready to listen to it, but he would never compromise his individuality because of critical comments.

As per usual he sat on the banks of the Kshipra. He saw the fish swimming in the water and the birds snatching them up. If the fish are to live they should be able to escape from the birds, but if the birds are to live they should be able to catch the fish—nature has created them thus. Fish that are clever enough would keep themselves safe from the birds, but there may be fish that do not mind being food for the birds. In short, the world itself is full of unique, unbelievable happenings.

Soon Nichula came to him.

'What have you decided, Shambhu?' Nichula asked as he sat near him on the rock.

'What is there to decide? That is a work that I have completed. Now my pen will not move for that. The king and the assembly can take whatever decisions they want,' Kalidasa replied.

'But the king has issued orders that the work of making new copies of the poem must be stopped till you give a revised version of the last canto,' Nichula pointed out.

'I never asked for any copies to be made and distributed. I have a copy with me. Those who like my work can come here and make copies from it, if they want. Many copies have already been made and they have reached far and wide. If a literary work appeals to the readers, they will get copies of it someday. No royal command can prevent a good work from reaching the readers. No ban can shut out a work that has genuine literary value. And if nobody wants to read what I have written, I don't mind that either. I will just accept such a rejection as an indication that it did not have any artistic value,' Kalidasa made it clear that he was ready to stand firm on his decision.

'I was sure that Shambhu would not do it. No writer with any self-respect would ever bow to the wishes and pleasures of others. If anyone did so, he would be selling his ability for monetary gains; making his genius a slave to power,' Nichula indicated that he supported his friend's decision.

As the sun was about to set, Nichula left the place.

Kalidasa reached the assembly the next morning as if nothing unusual had happened. Only routine matters were discussed; it seemed that the king was consciously avoiding any other discussion. But after the assembly, he invited Kalidasa to the place where personal discussions were generally held.

'What have you decided, Kalidasa? It is a royal command and you have to obey it,' Vikramaditya said.

Nichula intervened before Kalidasa could say anything.

'Your Highness, the death of Princess Mallika had brought untold sorrow to Kalidasa. Creating *Raghuvamsam* helped him get through that sorrow. I have seen how affected he was while writing about the sorrow of Maharaja Aja because of the death of his wife. I have seen him weep while writing some parts of it.'

'I know that. Only I know the intensity of the pain that I suffered at the death of my little sister. But I realize that Kalidasa's sorrow was even greater than mine. They were mentally united. I know that Kalidasa lost a part of his soul when Mallika left this world,' there was a tremor in Vikramaditya's words as he spoke.

Nichula continued. 'Maharaj! I feel *Raghuvamsam* is indeed a part of Kalidasa's soul. He is not ready to make any changes to it as per orders. Please do not force him to do it.'

Vikramaditya remained silent for a while. He could understand Kalidasa's mind. At last, he asked, 'Kalidasa, what do you think is the remedy for this? I can understand the poetic eminence of *Raghuvamsam*, but if it continues to contain matters that bring disgrace to my ancestors, I will be in trouble as the king. I am ready to accept whatever you have written. But I have to act to silence those who raise criticism against your work. My dilemma is in deciding what to do. Wouldn't it be humiliating for me when people say that I remained silent even while my ancestors were being disgraced?'

Kalidasa thought about the king's words for long. He did not want to put the king in any difficult situation. He was sure that *Raghuvamsam* would gain a lot of popularity because of this controversy associated with it. So there was only one solution, something that would suit the writer, the king and the work. He said, 'Maharaj! Punish the writer if necessary. Put him in prison for not obeying the orders of the king.'

Both the king and Nichula were shocked to hear this.

'What do you mean, Kalidasa?' asked Vikramaditya.

'Maharaj! I will lose nothing by this. People will give you more respect as a king. Many in the assembly will praise you for taking this decision. No one will support me if I refuse to obey a royal command. The message will be clear— "one who disobeys a royal command will be punished, whoever he may be".'

'That may be so. But why should Kalidasa be jailed?' asked Nichula.

'Even if Maharaj bans my work in Ujjaini, many people here will feel irritated on seeing me. So you may have to dismiss me from the assembly or deport me from here. Why should you wait for more protests and then take such actions, Maharaj? Putting me in prison immediately would be better and I can continue to stay in Ujjaini. Your Majesty, those who complain about my work are more against me personally than my writings. Even if you ban *Meghadutam* or *Raghuvamsam*, they will not be satisfied. They want to destroy me on the basis of this accusation. I am their enemy, Maharaj, and not *Raghuvamsam* or any other work of mine. They will be happy only on seeing me punished,' Kalidasa said.

'That is true, Your Majesty. They may bear the popularity of *Raghuvamsam* as a poetic creation but they will not be able to see Kalidasa being acknowledged. Kalidasa has already received fame and recognition which has been denied to many old poets and those who consider themselves to be experts in art and literature. Maharaj! There are many who study Sanskrit now in order to enjoy the writings of Kalidasa. There may be no one who does not sing at least a few lines from Kalidasa's works in Ujjaini today. The learned men of the royal assembly chose to ignore the beautiful lines in Kalidasa's poems. They thought that if they did not say anything either for or against those works, no one will show any interest in them. But much against their expectations, his works got a lot of popularity mainly because of your interest in them and also that of many who love good writing. The other writers of Ujjaini have paled in comparison to Kalidasa. They want to destroy Kalidasa. If Kalidasa walks about freely, they may even plot to murder him. That is dangerous, Your Majesty!'

As he listened to the words of Nichula, Vikramaditya understood that he too supported what Kalidasa was suggesting. 'I feel that what Nichula is saying is true. But who has so much enmity towards Kalidasa?' he asked.

'Maharaj! Just think about this. Who lost the position as the most important poet of the royal assembly after Kalidasa came here? Who lost their importance here? Who are the people who have told you things against Kalidasa during this time? Shankuka, Ghatakarpara, Hemabhadra, the chief priest at the Mahakaleshwara temple—these are the people who have lined up against Kalidasa,' Nichula explained.

Vikramaditya silently listened to Nichula's words. What Nichula was saying was true. But he would have to think carefully before deciding to take any action against them. Shankuka was in charge of the gurukula. If Hemabhadra wanted, he would be able to turn the people of Malava against the king. If these two men stood together, the peace that now existed in Malava would be destroyed. Vikramaditya knew that he could control such unruly behaviour using the army, but he knew that it would bring only dishonour to him if he tried to use power to control the situation instead of logically answering their accusations. Kalidasa would never be ready for a discussion, except to stand by what he had written. He does not consider it a poet's duty to do anything beyond expressing what is on his mind without any ill will. Neither Vikramaditya nor any of the others who loved Kalidasa have been able to justify the poet satisfactorily. Vikramaditya sat lost in such thoughts for a long time.

At last when he raised his head, Nichula said, 'Maharaj! When Kalidasa is deprived of the freedom to wander about at will, he will have a chance to remain in one place. That may pave the way for a new work... A great work that will silence all his critics... Let Kalidasa be careful not to include anything that would lead to another controversy. It is difficult for him either to change or remove what he has already written.'

'Yes, Maharaj, what Nichula has said is true. Issue orders for my imprisonment tomorrow itself and ban *Raghuvamsam*,' Kalidasa said with a smile.

Vikramaditya was surprised. He was seeing a man request his own imprisonment, for the first time.

'I will be in my house. Send the soldiers tomorrow in the morning. Let your decision be announced before that. The people will be happy to hear it,' said Kalidasa.

Vikramaditya stood looking at Nichula and Kalidasa as they walked away. If Mallika had been alive, Kalidasa would have been a member of this palace. Would the same sequence of events have happened then? How will Mallika's soul bear the sight of her beloved being arrested and led to the prison?

Before long, the announcement was made in the streets and market places of Ujjaini. 'Maharaja Vikramaditya has ordered the arrest of Kalidasa for disgracing the great Surya dynasty in his work and refusing to obey the king's orders to change what he has written.'

Those who listened to the announcement were surprised. He was the most respected poet of Ujjaini—one who was considered the preceptor of all poets—now he is going to be a prisoner in Ujjaini!

There was no need for an explanation to be issued from the palace for Kalidasa's imprisonment. Shankuka and his coterie saw to it that all the accusations they had raised against Kalidasa had reached all ears.

The common people talked with one another. Kalidasa had disgraced the Surya dynasty in his work! Pictured the ancestors of the king as lechers! Opinions differed, some supported the poet, others were against him. Those who had not seen or read *Raghuvamsam* started searching for a copy. Most were surprised that the poet had refused to obey the orders of the king!

12

Kalidasa was ready at sunbreak to go the prison. For whom was he accepting such suffering...? For some who pretended to be wise and were jealous of him? Questions kept on surfacing in Kalidasa's mind.

The soldiers arrived. They tied up the poet's hands and led him away. Most of the citizens could not bear the sight of their dear poet being led like a prisoner, but some rejoiced at the success of their vile plans.

Kalidasa looked around. Some of the trees had started shedding their leaves. There were a few flowers still on the leafless branches.

The trees, plants and the animals quickly become aware of the change of seasons. That may be the reason why man wants to be close to nature. When the people who want to lead a life of worldly pleasures, come to live together, cities are born. But those who are more spiritually inclined wish to be closer to the wild nature and withdraw into the hermitages in the forests; Kalidasa let his mind follow such thoughts...

The fact that he had been made a prisoner and was being taken there did not trouble him. He did not feel that he was being dragged by the soldiers. He did not feel humiliated. He walked along as if he were being taken somewhere ceremoniously. Nichula followed him along with those who had joined the group.

By the time they reached the palace gates, a huge crowd had gathered. Some were angry that Kalidasa had not obeyed the king but many felt that the king was being unfair to the poet.

But those who wanted to remove Kalidasa from the scene were delighted; they felt that Kalidasa was going to a place where he deserved to be. Now he would remain in prison for many years for bringing dishonour to the royal dynasty, for refusing to rectify what he has done.

Vikramaditya saw this from the palace terrace. Amarasimha was with him. Kalidasa had been tied up. Seeing the king on the terrace, the men shouted their greetings. Some were heard shouting that Kalidasa was being punished to satisfy the ego of some men.

Hearing the shouts, Maharani Vidyothama also came out to the terrace. Vikramaditya did not go down.

'Put Kalidasa in prison until further orders,' Vikramaditya gave his command in one short sentence. Vidyothama stood transfixed with shock. She had heard of this from the king, but this sight was more than she could bear. Kalidasa who had come before her as a wise prince and later as a foolish woodcutter had risen to be the greatest poet not only in Ujjaini but in the whole of Bharatavarsha. He had now been arrested and imprisoned for an indefinite period! Will she be able to do anything about it?

As he saw Vikramaditya and Vidyothama, Kalidasa's eyes longed for the sight of Mallika. The memory of his first meeting with Vidyothama passed through his mind. For a second, he felt Mallika was also there, bidding him farewell with a smile.

As soon as he had delivered his orders, Vikramaditya left the terrace. Minister Amarasimha accompanied him. Vidyothama remained there for a moment before going inside. Nichula came near Kalidasa, greeted him and wished that this would help him create another masterpiece. The soldiers moved to the building on the northern side of the palace where a room had been made ready for Kalidasa.

Soon the king and the minister reached near the prison. Nichula greeted both of them. For the first time, Vikramaditya felt a pain in his heart for a man he had sent to prison. He turned to Nichula, 'Nichula, what did Kalidasa say? Did you talk with him in the morning?'

'Yes, Your Majesty. Kalidasa is not regretful about what has happened. He has no complaints against your orders,' Nichula answered.

The minister remained silent. Both the king and his minister felt that what they had done was wrong. They kept asking themselves whom they were trying to please by sending Kalidasa to the prison.

At last, the king spoke as if justifying what they had done. 'I could not think of any other solution. Complaints had been raised about many other works of Kalidasa before this. I could justify Kalidasa's work then. But I couldn't do anything about *Raghuvamsam*.'

'Please do not feel bad about this, Your Majesty! Kalidasa has no regrets or complaints about the punishment given to him. He sees it as a chance to rest, to be at peace with himself,' Amarasimha said.

'Those who were eager to criticize Kalidasa and those who supported them are now happy. They think it's a great achievement. I could see their jubilation when the announcement was made last evening, they were celebrating their victory as Kalidasa was brought here as a prisoner,' Nichula observed.

'Amarasimha, make sure that Kalidasa does not feel that he is in prison. He must be provided with everything. Get him whatever books he wants to read. There should be no dearth of writing leaves. Give him a room with windows opening to the garden. Don't prevent Nichula or any of his friends from visiting Kalidasa,' Vikramaditya made sure that Kalidasa does not face any further inconvenience.

Though the king had ordered his imprisonment, Kalidasa realized, as he entered the room, that he was being given royal comforts. The room was equipped with all that he would need. Through the windows at the back, he could have a view of a lake full of red and white lotus flowers with the swans moving about gracefully in it. Many flowering trees added to the beauty of the scene. He could see the river Gambhira flowing beyond that. The chair had been arranged in such a way that he could see the garden from there. Many books were kept there. The oil and the lamps were kept ready. Kalidasa stood for a while, looking at the river. White clouds were passing by in the sky. The wind that came over the waters of the river was cool. Kalidasa realized that Vikramaditya had made sure that he would be comfortable in prison.

Kalidasa brought his mind to the world of writing. How did it matter where he was? His mind was with him. He had enough writing leaves and pens for doing his work. He could write without any disturbance. For the first few days, Kalidasa was immersed in the books that he had been provided with. When there was nothing more to engage his attention in reading, he allowed his mind to wander free in the world of imagination. He sat in meditation for long, praying to Mahakaleshwara and Mahakali.

His mind wandered through the ancient works. He wanted to write a play, more enjoyable than *Malavikagnimitram* and *Pururavorvasheeyam*. He wanted to wipe out the difficulty that the king had to face because of him. He realized that many had a grievance against the king as they felt that he was treating Kalidasa well even when he had portrayed his dynasty in a bad light. A better work would be the only compensation for that. He was ready to try.

There were many who were happy that Kalidasa had been imprisoned. They believed that *Raghuvamsam* would not get much popularity as it had no royal backing—fools who did not realize the power of poetry!

Nichula visited him frequently and thus he knew what was happening outside. Many thought that Kalidasa could now be forgotten. They dreamed that the king would not have any friendship with him and so no one would bother to read his works. He heard that Shankuka and his men had held a drinking bout on the night that Kalidasa had been imprisoned. Some of the men there also recited the lines from *Sringaratilakam*! So even they enjoyed Kalidasa's lines! Nichula had told him that they were spreading rumours about Kalidasa, that he spent his time with prostitutes and was a womanizer. Any one could say anything about a man. The king could stop the people from gathering at one place or from holding processions and demonstrations. He could oust a man from his country or imprison him, but he could never imprison anyone's tongue. None could ever impose any control on thoughts!

Let it be so! Let their desires be satisfied. He had to write something that would silence these people; he had to do it for the king. A play would reach the people better than a poem. And the thought of writing in this lonely place was itself most satisfying.

As he let his mind wander through the ancient narratives, one small story caught his attention. Dushyanta was a king of the Puru dynasty. Shakuntala was the foster daughter of Rishi Kanwa, growing up in his hermitage. When Rishi Vishwamitra was about to reach the position of Indra through his penance, Indra sent Menaka to earth in order to tempt Vishwamitra. Menaka became the wife of Vishwamitra. Shakuntala was the daughter born to them, but Menaka left the baby girl on the banks of the river Malini. The girl was looked after by the Shakunta birds and later Maharshi Kanwa took her to the hermitage and became her foster father. King Dushyanta saw Shakuntala when he came hunting in the forest and begged her to be his wife. Shakuntala made him promise that her son would be the king and agreed to marry him according to the Gandharva system. Dushyanta left for the palace with the promise that he would come back soon to take her to the palace. Meanwhile, Shakuntala became pregnant. Kanwa, on coming to know about it, blessed her. But Dushyanta did not come back. The child was born in the hermitage. The child named Sarvadamana, grew up playing with lion cubs and riding on the back of bears and lions.

As it was improper to keep a married daughter in the father's house for long, Rishi Kanwa sent Shakuntala and her son to Hastinapura. But Dushyanta failed to recognize her. When Dushyanta accused her of lying, Shakuntala retorted that their son would grow without his father. At that juncture, a voice from the sky informed Dushyanta that the boy was his son and told him not to disown Shakuntala. Dushyanta accepted them. He justified his behavior by saying that if he accepted her without any question it would tarnish his image as a king.

Kalidasa thought about the story. He knew that he would be able to create a beautiful play from this plot.

The writing leaves and pens were ready. The play started with a prayer to the Almighty who existed in eight different forms. The dramatist in him felt that he should bring the sootradhara, the one who introduced the characters and controlled the progress of the play and the actors together at the beginning. He could make them reveal the fact that it was a new play by Kalidasa. He wanted to indicate the time when the play was taking place and wrote a couplet about the summer season.

subhagasalilāvagāhaḥ
pāṭalasaṃsarggasurabhivanavātāḥ
pracchāyasulabhanidrā divasāḥ pariṇāmaramaṇīyāḥ

(*Abhijnanashakuntalam*, Act 1, Line 3)

(Those beautiful days, when a dip in the river provides pleasure and a soothing sleep embraces as one rests in the shadow of a tree, enjoying the breeze carrying the sweet smell of flowers, are about to come.)

The first act was devoted to Dushyanta reaching the hermitage, following a deer during a hunt. The residents of the hermitage stopped him from killing the deer. There Dushyanta met Shakuntala and fell in love with her. He introduced a romantic scene of how a big black beetle came near Shakuntala's face which made her cry out for help. Dushyanta came forward to help her. As he created such dramatic scenes in the play, the original story seemed to come alive. The circumstances that made Shakuntala grow up in the hermitage as the daughter of Rishi Kanwa was also added.

In the second act, Kalidasa created a situation because of which those who had accompanied Dushyanta from his palace were forced to leave him. This was done to prevent anyone from the palace from being a witness to the Gandharva wedding of Dushyanta and Shakuntala.

The third act revealed how Dushyanta tried to find out what was in Shakuntala's mind. He made Dushyanta overhear what Shakuntala was telling her maids and that made him realize that she was in love with him. Kalidasa pictured Shakuntala writing a letter on a lotus leaf with her nails, expressing her love. Her maids went away under various pretexts. It was at this moment that Dushyanta suggested getting married under the Gandharva custom.

As Kalidasa was describing the beauty of Shakuntala as seen through Dushyanta's eyes, he wondered whether people would raise their voice against it. Hence he presented it in verse, using very few words. Kalidasa contemplated describing their dalliance in love and marriage, but he was sure that it would again lead to controversies about his writing. A play was not like a poem; what the dramatist wrote will have to be acted out on stage. What is difficult to be acted out on the stage can later be indicated as having taken place. He felt that it was unnecessary to write everything in a play.

Kalidasa had to think carefully before writing the next act and made some changes to the story.

Kalidasa portrayed Shakuntala, lost in thought about Dushyanta, failing to realize the arrival of Sage Durvasa. The enraged Durvasa cursed her that the person about whom she was thinking of would forget her. Kalidasa then created another scene in which Shakuntala's companions prayed to Durvasa and got the remedy to escape from the curse. The sage pronounced that if she showed some object that the person was familiar with, he would remember her. But as he was writing this scene, he felt that it was not necessary to present it on stage; it need only be mentioned. Thus he made the companions decide that Shakuntala need not know about the curse.

When Rishi Kanwa reached the ashram, he came to know what had happened. He decided to send Shakuntala to the palace. The fourth act showed the preparations for Shakuntala's journey to the king's palace and how she bade goodbye to the hermitage.

The fifth act was Shakuntala's arrival before Dushyanta. Kalidasa felt that the story should not have an ending like that of Mahabhrata. So he created a scene where Shakuntala realized that she had lost the ring and tried to describe their meeting. But Dushyanta did not remember anything. The people who had accompanied Shakuntala left her at the palace and went back. He ended the fifth act with the priest informing Dushyanta that a celestial lady appeared before them and took Shakuntala away with her.

Vikramaditya and Nichula visited Kalidasa many times

during these days. They were both relieved to see Kalidasa very happy and immersed in writing.

Kalidasa was aware of the passage of time and the change of seasons. Though he was a prisoner, Vikramaditya was ready to allow Kalidasa whatever freedom he wanted. He was allowed to go into the garden and enjoy the beauty of the river and the forest beyond that.

Kalidasa did not consider any of these as a difficulty. When he was engaged in writing, the food that was served remained untouched for hours. Many a time the servants had to remind him about eating or drinking something.

Kalidasa decided to devote the sixth act to creating a situation by which Dushyanta would remember Shakuntala. The ring that Dushyanta had given Shakuntala was found by a fisherman in a fish that he had caught. When he tried to sell the ring, the soldiers arrested him and brought him before the king. Then Kalidasa brought in a celestial woman who had come from Shakuntala to know how Dushyanta fared. When Dushyanta got back his memory he was in sorrow and repented the way he had rejected Shakuntala. Kalidasa then added the story of a merchant who died without an heir in order to reveal how Dushyanta longed for a son. The king ordered that a search should be started to decide if any of the wives of the merchant were pregnant and the son who was born to that woman must be made the heir to the wealth of the merchant. Dushyanta was devastated by the thought of who would inherit his throne and wealth. Now Kalidasa felt that he should create a situation to take Dushyanta to the celestial world and make him meet Shakuntala there. There must be an occasion for Dushyanta's visit to the world of the gods. In ancient legends, the devas used to seek the help of the powerful kings of the earth when there was a war with the asuras. So he created a scene where Indra's chariot arrived to take Dushyanta to help the devas in the war, at the end of the sixth act.

While returning to the earth after helping the devas in the war, Dushyanta visited the hermitage of Sage Kashyapa. As he waited for the sage he was attracted by a boy playing with lion cubs. On observing the boy, the king noticed the signs of an emperor on his body. The hermits requested Dushyanta to help them persuade the boy to leave the lion cubs. Coming to know that the boy was born to the Puru dynasty, the king asked him his father's name. The boy told him that he was not ready to utter the name of the father as he had abandoned his mother. Hearing this Dushyanta realized that the boy was his own son. Here Kalidasa added another story to prove that Dushyanta was the father. The boy was wearing a sacred thread on his hand. If it came loose and was touched by anyone other than the father of the boy, the thread would turn into a serpent and bite that person. Situations were created to bring Shakuntala there and they recognized each other. The three of them were shown as returning to earth with the blessings of Prajapati Kashyapa.

Kalidasa was able to create an attractive plot by introducing Matali, the charioteer of Indra and the hermits at appropriate places. He went through the text many times making changes and introducing couplets wherever he felt they would add to the attraction of the play. The work was named *Abhijnanashakuntalam*.

Kalidasa looked at the bundle of leaves with satisfaction. This was the longest of all the plays that he had written. He could add many dramatic moments in the course of the events. Did he write remembering the warning that Nichula had given that there should be nothing controversial in the play? Or did his imagination lead him naturally? He was not sure. Did he allow his thoughts and imagination to be regulated by the suggestions put forth by his dear friends? Did he compromise his freedom as a poet in doing so? Was there anything for his critics to say that he curtailed his descriptions of the romantic scenes fearing punishment while in prison? All these thoughts passed through his mind as he sat before his work.

He went through what he had written again and again. No, he had not left anything out. As he had kept some events off the stage and revealed them only by other means, he had been able to add to the dramatic quality of the play. He felt that it was by suggestions more than full revelation that he would be able to capture the attention of the audience. Now it was for the audience to decide. A lot of work would have to be done to present this on stage. The king was sure to enjoy what he had written. So he planned to present it to the king as quickly as possible.

Kalidasa tried to see his work presented on stage in his mind's eye. He was sure that it would be successfully presented. He felt happy and satisfied.

That day, the three of them, Nichula, Vikramaditya and Amarasimha came together to see Kalidasa. When the soldiers informed the king that Kalidasa wished to see him, Vikramaditya had not thought that it would be to announce that the work had been completed.

The soldiers opened the door and Vikramaditya, Amarasimha and Nichula entered. Kalidasa gave the king the bundle of leaves covered with a silken cloth.

'Maharaj!' he said, 'I have completed a new play named *Abhijnanashakuntalam*. Please make arrangements to have this presented on stage on a suitable occasion.'

'Let this play be presented as early as possible. There is no need to wait for a festive occasion for that.' Turning to Amarasimha the king gave his instruction, 'Make arrangements to get copies of this work made.'

Nichula intervened immediately. 'Maharaj, please get those who are to make copies come here for the work. Don't allow the copies to be made public now. As the copies are made, please be kind enough to read them first before it reaches anybody else.'

Nichula had his own doubts whether some of the lines in the copy of *Meghadutam* were actually written by Kalidasa. Most of the lines that Shankuka and the others pointed out as being vulgar in *Meghadutam* were not found in the copy that Kalidasa had given him. Hence he felt that they should be more careful with this work.

Vikramaditya did not ask Nichula why he had made such a suggestion. He agreed to it after thinking about it for a few seconds.

'Make all arrangements for the performance on stage along with the work of making copies. Give instructions to the master of dramatics to choose the actors and actresses. As each act is completed, let it be sent to him. We will free Kalidasa from prison immediately. I am sure that all the accusations against him will cease to exist with this work,' said Vikramaditya enthusiastically.

Nichula had something more to say. 'Maharaj! I feel Kalidasa would not mind being here till the copies are made and you have read the whole work. Let it be done under his supervision.'

Nichula was apprehensive about what Kalidasa might have written. If some trouble came up now, the king would not be able to do anything. The friendship and affection that he now had with the poet would then vanish. Kalidasa would not have written to please anybody's whims and fancies.

'Will it be difficult for you, Kalidasa?' the king asked accepting this suggestion.

'No, Your Majesty! I too feel so. For me this prison and my house are the same,' Kalidasa had understood what was on Nichula's mind.

Nichula spent the next few days with Kalidasa. Nichula also

made a copy of the play. Though there were romantic scenes, nothing objectionable could be found in it. Nichula was sure that this was better than all the other works that Kalidasa had written. There was no doubt that Kalidasa would ascend the mount of fame with this.

A few days later Vikramaditya was walking to the palace with Kalidasa. As they walked, Kalidasa looked around the garden. He remembered that he had started work on *Abhijnanashakuntalam* in the summer. Now summer, as well as the rainy season, autumn and winter had passed by. The beauty of spring had dimmed as summer was about to come again. Ujjaini was at its most beautiful state during spring. Was it because he was seeing Ujjaini after a long time? Though the flowers were not seen in plenty, there were a few trees still bidding goodbye to spring with their flowers. This was a good time to have the play presented on stage.

When it was time for the assembly to meet, Amarasimha, Nichula and Kalidasa went there. Many were surprised to see Kalidasa who had been in prison, at the assembly. Many approached him and talked to him. Some asked among themselves why the king had freed Kalidasa from prison. Their plots against Kalidasa had succeeded; but now he was back again.

They started planning new strategies to destroy Kalidasa.

13

Kalidasa was released from prison, which was so only in name. He did not feel any difference. The Ujjaini that he knew was the same. He had spent some days composing; Kalidasa could easily forget that he had ever been in prison.

Kalidasa was pleased to see *Abhijnanashakuntalam* enacted on stage. His solitude in prison did not go in vain. He was able to write a good play. Kalidasa felt complete satisfaction as he listened to the applause and cheering of the audience during the presentation of the play on stage. The king was also enjoying each scene.

But at the end of the play when Kalidasa saw the king's face, he was shocked. Instead of joy, there was a shadow of sorrow on his face. Maharani Vidyothama also left the place with a similar expression on her face. Kalidasa couldn't understand why the play had not appealed to the king.

Many came up to the dramatist to congratulate him. They called the play the best they had witnessed. But his joy was short-lived. He was disturbed by the look of sorrow on the face of the king. He had to find out why the king had not enjoyed the play. He wondered if he had written the play for the king's pleasure alone, but he also knew that it was not as the king but as a friend that he wanted Vikramaditya to congratulate him. More than any gifts that the king may bestow on him, it was his acceptance as a friend that mattered to Kalidasa.

The stage and the hall were emptying. Kalidasa stood unable to decide what to do. Nichula approached him.

'Let us go,' he said.

Kalidasa looked at Nichula and asked, 'Nichula, what has happened? Maharaja Vikramaditya left for the palace without uttering a word about the play. Maharani Vidyothama also did not say anything. Wasn't the play enjoyable?'

'There is no doubt that the play was enjoyable and many from the audience came here to congratulate you. They seemed to be thrilled on seeing the various scenes,' said Nichula.

'Then why didn't the Maharaja and the Maharani say anything? Why did they not like it?' there was a sense of dejection in Kalidasa's voice.

'I don't know, my friend, I can't even imagine it. Is the king not well? Maybe it is because of that, that they both left immediately after the play?' Nichula tried to guess the reason for the king's unusual behaviour.

'But I do not think it is because the play is bad,' he added.

'Why don't we go and meet the king?' Kalidasa asked Nichula also to go with him.

~

It was a journey with no specific place in view that brought Kalidasa to Devagiri beyond the river Charmanavati. He stayed there in the temple of Kartikeya for a few days. His mind went to the mountainous abode of Gouri-Shankara-Shiva with the crescent moon adorning his hair, Kalakala with the serpent round his neck and matted hair, trident in one hand and the deer in the other, the mace in the third and showing the sign of blessing with the fourth. Sree Parvati Devi, who had courted Pashupati after undertaking penance in the bone-chilling cold of the Himalayas as well as in the burning heat of fire. Sharavanabhava, the son of the Lord and the Devi—she had entrusted the life growing in her from the power of Shiva with the fire as she could not bear the heavy weight. Agni, the fire, deposited it in the Ganga and it was the Sharavana birds that looked after it. He had heard all these stories from the rishis on the Himalayas, about the new power that comes into being by the union of prakruti, nature and purusha, pure consciousness. And Kumara was born for the destruction of evil forces. Kumara was also known as Sharavanabhava, Skanda, Kartikeya. The story describes how Kumara became the commander-in-chief of the army of the Gods.

To the north was the abode of the Gods, the Himalayas, fit to be seen as the lord of all mountain ranges. A treasure trove of all invaluable things, a storehouse of wonders. In Kalidasa's mind, the height of the Himalayan peaks appeared like a scale to measure the earth and this idea took the form of a couplet.

astyuttarasyāṃ diśi dēvatātmā
himālayō nāma nagādhirājaḥ
pūrvāparau tōyanidhiṃ vigāhya
sthitaḥ pṛthivyā iva mānadaṇḍaḥ

(*Kumarasambhavam*, Act 1, Stanza 1)

(There is, in the northern quarter, the soul of the deities, the lord of mountains, by name Himalayas, who stands like the measuring rod of the earth, spanning the eastern and western oceans.)

The memories of Ujjaini gradually receded from Kalidasa's mind and the sights of the Himalayas came back with added colour. Vikramaditya and *Abhijnanashakuntalam* no longer dominated his thoughts. His mind was lost in the beauty of the Himalayas.

The poetic genius was finding a place in the writing leaves in the form of a new creation. The unparalleled, resplendent beauty of the snow-covered Himalayas was reflected in letters, the manifestation of the universal soul. He could experience the cool drops of the Ganga that were sprayed wide when the river that bears the nectar fell on the rocks on her way to the valley. Before the magnificence of the Himalayas, all other mountain ranges like the Vindhyas were nothing. The Ganga, also known as Jahnavi, was an ornament for the pure beauty of the Himalayas. Jahnavi got that name when the waters took away the hermitage of Rishi Jahnu who drank up the whole river in anger. Later, at the request of the Gods, he allowed the waters to come out through his ears and this river became a blessing for the continent. The Himalayas bore the footprints of those rishis who have ended their worldly existence by walking to its immense ranges. Kalidasa's mind travelled with the clouds that sailed by, touching the tips of the peaks.

Kalidasa remembered the words of Rishi Shalibhadra. Dakshayani was reborn as the daughter of Himavan and Mena. The picture of Sati immolating herself in the sacrificial fire after her father's rejection fell as lightning on her heart, rose clearly in Kalidasa's mind. Then Shivatandava shook the Himalayan ranges! Shakti had been separated from Shiva. But how long could it be so? The world would come to an end if it continued. It was the need of time that Shiva and Shakti remain together. But everything had to bide its time. All animate beings are the slaves of time.

Sati was re-born as the daughter of Himavan. She was named Parvati. Kalidasa could feel the figure of Mallika dressed as Parvati or Parvati assuming the beauty of Mallika. Kalidasa could actually picture the red lotus-like feet stepping on the white snow with the tinkling of anklets, a girl who told stories to the waves on the Mandakini and played with dolls.

Kalidasa felt that he had once again reached the Himalayan ranges and could feel himself travelling back by eons. Kalidasa used the heavenly language at its best to write the lines to describe the little girl playing in the courtyard of the palace on the slopes of the Himalayas, growing into a beautiful young woman.

~

Vikramaditya was worried after not seeing Kalidasa anywhere in Ujjaini. He even feared that Kalidasa might have left Ujjaini. But he had never gone anywhere without bidding goodbye to the king.

Vikramaditya remembered that there had been some unpleasantness when they had parted the last time. Vikramaditya could not forget the scene in the *Abhijnanashakuntalam* after Dushyanta got back his memory and remembered Shakuntala, where the question of who should inherit the wealth of a merchant who had died in a shipwreck was brought up. The decision was that the son born to the wife who was now pregnant would inherit the property. It made Dushyanta think longingly about his own son. That scene reminded Vikramaditya and Vidyothama that they too did not have a son. The pain intensified on seeing the joy that Dushyanta experienced on recognizing his son. So, both of them returned to the palace immediately after the play. Vikramaditya wondered whether his reaction was unnecessarily sharp when Kalidasa had come to see him after that. When he asked Kalidasa whether he wanted to intensify that pain in their hearts, his voice had risen. When his own deficiency intensified his sorrow, he felt angry at everybody. Was he angry with himself or with the Creator? But Kalidasa who had come to enquire whether he had left immediately because he was unwell, had to bear the brunt of his anger. After that Kalidasa had not come to the assembly. Vikramaditya realized that his reaction had been too sharp. His sorrow might be justified but he did not know with whom he was angry.

As days passed Vikramaditya came to realize that there was

no need to blame Kalidasa. His mind kept on reminding him that he had been unfair towards Kalidasa. Vikramaditya felt that Mallika also was accusing him of that. She must be angry with him. As he thought of his dear Mallika and of Kalidasa, he could not control his sorrow. He could hear her question, 'Brother, where is my Kalidas?' Now the sorrow at the loss of Mallika and the sense of dejection at being without a child was more than he could bear. The sobs that escaped from him unknowingly seemed to reverberate in the palace.

Kalidasa had written the story of Dushyanta. He would never have imagined that the sorrow felt by Dushyanta would become Vikramaditya's sorrow.

When Vikramaditya mentioned Kalidasa's absence in the assembly there were some unwelcome comments.

Somasekhara, a member of the assembly who used to be silent said, 'Where can he go? He must be in the house of some prostitute, drinking and writing descriptions of the physical beauty of the women there while enjoying sensual pleasures.'

Vikramaditya was irritated to hear this. 'What are you saying, Somasekhara? Are you spreading infamy about a great poet?' Vikramaditya realized that his courtiers would never understand his sorrow.

Shankuka supported what Somasekhara said. 'Your Highness! There must be some truth in what Somasekhara says. I don't think I need to repeat the old stories. There have been eminent poets before this here. None of them have based their description of beauty on the prostitutes. When you look at the way Kalidasa describes the physical beauty of women, anyone will feel that there is some truth in what Somasekhara has said.'

'I have already talked about this in this assembly. Still I wish to remind you of it again. Kalidasa describes the physical beauty of the women of that class as he feels that it is these women who would be happy to see themselves being described. They take great care to keep their body beautiful and are eager to show it to others. A housewife would not consider displaying her physical beauty. They do not like their beauty being described or enjoyed by others. They keep themselves beautiful only for their husbands. So no one need complain about Kalidasa describing the prostitutes,' Vikramaditya explained.

Vikramaditya felt repentant that his anguish was revealing itself in front of a bunch of insensitive and cruel men.

'Still, Maharaj! If anyone suspects that the description of the women's body that Kalidasa makes, shows his attraction towards prostitutes, can they be blamed for it? Your Majesty has seen how badly he has described the life of King Agnivarna in *Raghuvamsam* and even some vile comments about Dasrath,' Somasekhara continued his argument against Kalidasa.

'You cannot say that a poet writes because of his attraction towards the subject. Writing poetry is an art. The artist's mind thinks in an artistic way. Attraction or repulsion is not the basis of his creation. Minds devoid of any artistic taste may be able to describe things that attract or repulse them. But there will be no artistic beauty in it,' Nichula expressed his opinion.

Vikramaditya was aware that it was Kalidasa's absence that encouraged everyone to speak against him. No one knew where Kalidasa had gone. If there was one person who was close to Kalidasa it was Nichula. So he might know.

When the assembly dispersed, Vikramaditya called Nichula but he too knew nothing about the poet. Kalidasa had not said goodbye to him either.

Vikramaditya sent soldiers to Vidisha and Champa to look for Kalidasa. They went to Ramagiri also but it was all in vain.

Many seasons passed by and there was no news about Kalidasa. Then Nichula approached Vikramaditya. He expressed his concern about his friend to the king. 'I suspect that he might have gone to Devagiri. He did not tell me so. But for a few days before his departure, he seemed to be disturbed. The thought that his play had caused sorrow to you and the maharani affected him deeply. He had never imagined it to have such an outcome.'

'After Mallika left us Kalidasa lost all interest in worldly life. In Champa he used to live with a rishi. Hence, for him, the sorrow that one feels at not being blessed with a son may be just a scene to be portrayed in a poem or a play. I have been noticing the sorrow that Vidyothama has been experiencing for long. *Abhijnanashakuntalam* only helped to multiply that sorrow a hundredfold,' Vikramaditya said.

'He was devastated that he had written something that caused you personal sorrow. Kalidasa has always loved you like his own brother. He was sad that his work had caused pain to you and the maharani,' Nichula explained. 'He used to lie on the rocks near the Kshipra for long hours. He wouldn't get up when I called him. I tried to comfort him but it was all in vain. He went on repeating that a play that he thought was the best that he had written had brought sorrow to you and the queen,' Nichula added.

'He once had talked about how worshipping Karthikeya at Devagiri would provide some comfort for the mind. That is why I feel that he might have gone to Devagiri. It has been a long time since he disappeared from Ujjaini. We have searched for him everywhere except in Devagiri,' Nichula said.

'Go to Devagiri, Nichula. We cannot forget Kalidasa. We should not have caused him such distress. But I could not control myself. He represents the poetic consciousness of Ujjaini. Ujjaini without Kalidasa is as lifeless as this palace without Mallika. Many others write poems. But none of them can cause the emotion that his lines create. Kalidasa's pen has been blessed by Goddess Saraswati. Tell him how sorry I am if you find him there,' Vikramaditya told Nichula.

Anxiety filled Nichula's mind as he travelled to Devagiri.

Nichula crossed mountains and forests, taking many days, to reach Devagiri. Nichula found Kalidasa in a cave in a lonely place, immersed in writing. Nichula sat there for a long time and Kalidasa saw him only when he turned to get a pot of water to drink.

Kalidasa immediately put the pot down. 'Come, Nichula,' he welcomed his friend with pleasure.

The bright smile that he saw on Kalidasa's face comforted Nichula. Kalidasa had regained his composure. The bundle of writing leaves indicated that he was at work. There would soon be a new poem or a play. Nichula sat near his friend.

Kalidasa had become lean and his beard reached below his stomach. There was a glow in his eyes similar to what you find in the yogis. But there was still a shadow of sorrow on his face.

Kalidasa looked at Nichula as if asking him a question.

Nichula said, 'How long have you been away from Ujjaini? You left without telling anybody. You should have thought of the king who has given you the place of a brother-in-law even after he lost his dear sister. The king is sorry about his behaviour that day. He told me to tell you that, Shambhu.'

Kalidasa sat silent. Nichula could see the pain in his mind as his eyes became moist.

'Did you come here alone, Shambhu?' Nichula asked.

'I had not decided to come here when I started from there. Though I had suggested worshipping here, I never thought of starting immediately. I wanted to walk for some distance. When I put the bundle on my shoulders, there was no thought of going on a journey. I wandered about here and there for some time. There was no chance to tell anyone... It was not intentional,' Kalidasa said.

'What have you been doing here? It looks as if you have been engaged in writing,' Nichula observed.

'Yes, I have written a bit. It is not completed; I have only begun.'

'What is the topic?' Nichula took the leaves in his hands.

As he read what Kalidasa had written, Nichula could not control his joy. The beauty of the Himalayas! Even at first reading, it seemed to make him feel that he was seeing the Himalayan ranges in reality. Then there was the birth of Parvati, her growth, her beauty as she attained youth. The lines seemed to have absorbed the beauty of the Himalayas... Language rich with poetic mastery!

'Great! Very beautiful! This surpasses all the other works that you have completed,' Nichula observed happily.

Kalidasa listened to Nichula's words with no emotion. Nichula had broken his solitude but he did not see Nichula as an intruder. For many days now, his mind was on polishing each word to perfection. He had not written much but he was happy with whatever he had written.

'Now?' Nichula asked.

'I am not planning to return to Ujjaini immediately. My mind is eager to write so much. I can feel the pressure from within to continue with the writing. I can't leave without finishing what I have started.'

'Do you want me to leave?'

'Not today. You can go tomorrow,' Kalidasa said. 'You must tell King Vikramaditya that I am sorry that I left without informing him. Tell him that I will be there as early as possible.'

'Can I say that when you come there, you will present to him a beautiful poem?' Nichula had understood what Kalidasa was planning.

'Yes, you may say so,' Kalidasa agreed. 'Have you come to Devagiri before this?'

'No, this is the first time.'

'Did you worship Karthikeya before coming to see me?' Kalidasa wanted Nichula to worship Karthikeya at Devagiri.

'Yes, I went to the temple and worshipped the Lord but my mind was searching for you, Shambhu. So I want to go there again. Lord Velayudha blessed me so I don't have to go back disappointed,' Nichula said while bowing before the Lord in his mind.

'What about Ujjaini? I hope the king and the queen are doing well?' Kalidasa asked.

'Your absence has been causing some distress to the Maharaja. The Maharani is doing her best to comfort him but he regarded you as a close friend. Both of them are being treated by experts in Ayurveda to enable them to have a child. Everyone hopes that the treatment will be fruitful.'

'Yes... There will be a positive result soon. Time seems to suggest that,' Kalidasa replied.

Then Nichula spoke, 'More accusations have been raised against you in the assembly. It was then that the king decided not to wait for you to come back and asked the soldiers to go in search,' he said.

Kalidasa was anxious. 'What complaint can be made against me now? Nothing has to be done about *Raghuvamsam*. The king had declared that it will not have royal support. I have not interfered in state matters or the governance of the gurukula or in the publicity of *Raghuvamsam*. *Abhijnanashakuntalam* is like an arrow that has left the string. Now it can't be stopped. There is only one remedy. The king should have a child...' Kalidasa said.

'The same old matter...When the king remarked that there was no news about you, many unwelcome comments came up. Somasekhara commented that you must be spending your time with some harlot, drinking and indulging in a detailed description of her physical beauty,' Nichula said, 'Shankuka observed that the description of the prostitutes that appears in your works is an indication of your attachment to such women.'

'They have the right to express their opinion. I don't think there is any need to correct that. I do not need any letters of praise or recommendation from them,' said Kalidasa without any change in his expression.

'But the maharaja rejected their opinion completely and praised your poetic genius. The king is unhappy only about the description of Agnivarna in the *Raghuvamsam* and a little bit about Dasaratha,' said Nichula.

'That reveals his ability to enjoy what is beautiful. A poem is to be enjoyed. It is not a criterion for deciding the nature of the poet's lifestyle. Let those who can understand that do so. Those who cannot understand that...let them see everything as per their ability and mentality,' remarked Kalidasa with a smile.

Kalidasa went into the cave and lighted the lamp. The whole cave lit up immediately.

Nichula examined the cave. It was quite vast. The wind did not disturb the flame. The writing leaves were kept on one side. Near that were a few rocks that seemed to suggest that it was the place where Kalidasa sat while engaged in writing. Both of them sat there.

The next morning as he was about to leave after worshipping Karthikeya, Nichula asked, 'What should I tell the maharaja?'

'Tell him what you saw here. You may tell him that I will soon be back with my new work of poetry,' Kalidasa was confident that he would be able to complete the writing very soon.

Nichula returned to Ujjaini and Kalidasa to his cave.

14

Kalidasa went through what he had written describing the extraordinary beauty of each limb of Parvati in her youth. It was an exact description. It was the beauty of nature as a Goddess that filled his mind at that time. The darting eyes, the face that lights up with a beautiful smile, the feet that resemble a fresh bud—a detailed description of every part, from the top of the head to the toes. When he had completed the description of Parvati in the snowy Himalayan background, the picture of Mahadeva, immersed in penance on top of the Kailas came to Kalidasa's mind. It must have been the will of the Creator that prompted Himavan to depute his daughter to serve Mahadeva. That must also have made the creator send Narada, whom the Creator considered as his own son, to inform Himavan that Mahadeva was destined to wed Parvati.

Was it proper for Parvati to try to wake up Mahadeva when he was immersed in penance? Karthikeya had to be born to become the commander-in-chief of the devas and destroy Tarakasura. The devas wanted Tarakasura to be destroyed. The Creator was repentant about allowing Tarakasura to grow like a poisonous tree capable of destroying the whole world. He couldn't destroy what he had brought up. The Creator could not be the destroyer. Mahadeva was the destroyer. Only the power that came out of Mahadeva would be able to destroy Tarakasura. As Kalidasa finished describing the scene where Brahma reveals all this to the devas who had come to him to complain about the atrocities committed by Tarakasura, the sun was about to set.

Kalidasa sat looking at the horizon, observing the beauty of the red of the setting sun colouring the west. The change of colour of the snowy clouds with the bright rays passing through at times was thrilling to watch. He remembered seeing the rays of the sun reflecting off of the snow-clad mountains of the Himalayas. Maheshwara sat in penance on the snow-covered peak and Sree Parvati was showering flowers at his feet. Even while he was in the rocky cave at Devagiri, Kalidasa felt as if he was watching Shiva and Parvati in the background of the enchanting beauty of the Himalayas.

Flowering trees stood around the place; the lake was full of lotuses in bloom. The sweet smell of these flowers penetrated the atmosphere. The cooing of the cuckoos reverberated from the snow on the mountains. The slow wind that came through the peaks made the music of the celestial beings.

The beetles moved from flower to flower; birds rubbed their beaks in a romantic mood; the cranes swam majestically in the lake and beyond all this, Kailas stood covered in snow. Hara sat in penance there and flakes of snow flew about around him.

Then entered Parvati, adorning herself with ruby-like Asoka flowers and the golden laburnum, dressed in the bright red of the rising sun. As Maheshwara awoke from meditation and Parvati offered the flowers in reverence, some of those that had adorned her hair and ears also fell onto the heap. Maheshwara raised his hands to bless Uma.

At that instant, a floral arrow came towards Maheshwara and the third eye of Rudra sought out the one who had sent that arrow. Kamadeva, who had come at the request of Indra to send the arrow to attract Mahadeva to Parvati, was reduced to ashes. As Kalidasa tried to picture the burning face of Parameshwara who jumped up in anger, the poet seemed to experience the anger in person. As he looked around to ascertain if he had really heard the thunder pealing, Kalidasa noticed that darkness had fallen. Mahadeva, Parvati and the Himalayas had vanished. The dark sky was cleft by the streaks of lightning, accompanied by the peals of thunder.

Immediately, he lit a lamp and took up the leaves and the pen. As he sat down to write, he did not have to think about anything. What he had seen in the mind's eye transformed itself into words, lines and couplets on the leaves.

Days passed by. As he was arranging the leaves on which he had written, keeping them in different bundles, he had the feeling of complete satisfaction. He could describe in fascinating words the lamentation of Rati Devi at the death of Kamadeva and how the Gods comforted her with the assurance that Kamadeva would come back to life with the union of Shiva and Parvati. Even after writing the lines, he could not forget the description of Parvati's penance and Shiva appearing before her in the guise of a Brahmachari to speak badly about himself.

As he took up a fresh bundle of leaves to write, he realized that it was the last bundle and that it would be used up in one day. What would he do then? He had not expected his work to be so vast. Nor had he taken care to see how many leaves he had in store.

Kalidasa felt angry with himself for his carelessness. He got up and walked to the temple. The temple attendant Sandeepa must be somewhere there. He met Sandeepa near the temple. He knew of a village in the valley where they could get the writing leaves. Though there were no schools nearby, it was on the route that the merchants took. Sandeepa knew someone who made the leaves to be sent with the merchants and promised to get what Kalidasa wanted.

The very next day Sandeepa sent him a small bundle. He was about to describe the marriage of Shiva and Parvati. He had a clear idea of what he had to write. So he started writing in the light of the lamp. As he took up the new bundle, Kalidasa felt that the way it had been arranged in the bundle was familiar to him. This was not like the bundles that he had been using till then. Then why did he feel familiar with this new bundle? The thread used for tying the bundle was made from the leaves of the pandanus. Even the twists on the thread seemed strangely familiar. With a tremor in his heart, he realized that it was similar to what his father used to make. He could see the mark of his father's handiwork in it. Did it mean that his father, Bhanumitra, was alive? Or was it only that someone was making these just as his father used to make them?

Kalidasa sat lost in thought. Nichula also believed that Kalidasa's parents had lost their lives in the forest fire, he couldn't have been mistaken. This must have been made by someone else. The same person who had taught his father the art of making the writing leaves must have taught this person also. So it must be a natural similarity.

Though he tried to tell his mind that it was just his flight of fancy, Kalidasa found himself eagerly waiting for the sun to rise. He could not write anything more. His pen did not touch even a single leaf as his mind travelled back to his childhood days.

Even when he was a small boy, he was not in the habit of sleeping late and he would be up with his father in the morning. One day he heard his father say, 'I have to give the writing leaves to the gurukula within a day or two. Much has to be done.' His father had brought the leaves from the forest. His mother had helped him in cutting the leaves and keeping them to dry. His father had been bending the edges slightly and cutting them to the required size. Now the leaves had to be kept immersed in the juice taken from some leaves and then dried again. The leaves from which the juice had to be extracted were brought the previous day. A couple of days before that, the basin in which the leaves had to be kept was made and plastered with cow dung. Once that had dried, the job left for the day was that of extracting the juice from the leaves.

He could hear his mother sweeping the courtyard. As his father got up and went outside, he too joined him. The sun had not yet risen high when he walked to the pond to brush his teeth with a stick of neem.

The birds had started chirping on the trees. Some had already gone in search of food.

By the time he came back his mother had started removing the leaves from the branches. He fed the doves and a couple of parrots that had come to the courtyard.

He helped his father in separating the leaves. Some fruits were crushed along with the leaves and the juice was extracted. The leaves were spread in the earthen basin and the extract was poured over them.

In the evening the leaves were taken out from the basin. The next morning holes were made in them at the required places and they were kept to dry in a shady place.

The small planks to be kept above and below each bundle were made from bamboo sticks and immersed in the extract. The thread to tie the bundles was made from the leaves of the pandanus by removing the fleshy part and twisting the filaments together. The thread was strengthened by dipping it in the leaf extract and glue before drying.

Two more days were spent drying the leaves. Guru Devasraya came to see the work and it was then that the guru had asked his father to send him to the gurukula. Thus, he had started his education.

Kalidasa's mind came back to the present. He could still remember how his father had arranged the leaves with the planks at the top and the bottom and tied them up with the thread they had made. He had never seen the writing leaves tied up that way anywhere else. During his travels, when he was reading some works, he had imagined that it was written on the leaves that his father had made. But it was only now that he could see a new set of leaves that bore the mark of his father's handiwork. He couldn't sit anymore, as the hope that his father was alive, entered his mind. He had wandered all over Malava in search of his parents. He had gone to see all those who made writing leaves in Ujjaini but none of them were his father.

He was at the temple immediately. Sandeepa had not reached the temple and Kalidasa went to his house. As Sandeepa was about to get out of the house, Kalidasa walked up to him.

Sandeepa was surprised to see Kalidasa there at that time. Why had he, who spent all his time in the cave, engaged in writing, come to his house?

'Guro, what happened? Why have you come here? We could have met at the temple,' Sandeepa said.

'Sandeepa, from where did you get the writing leaves that you gave me yesterday? Who made them?'

'Why, Guro? Were they not good?' asked Sandeepa with anxiety.

'Yes, they were good. But I want to see the man now itself, who made them. Who is he?' Kalidasa asked.

'We will go and meet him, Guro. His name is Bhanumitra. He stays in the village near here.' Kalidasa listened with bated breath to what Sandeepa was saying. He could not control his own legs as they took long, quick steps.

Sandeepa found it difficult to keep up with Kalidasa. He could not understand why Kalidasa was going to meet Bhanumitra in such excitement. Sandeepa was sure that the writing leaves that he had given Kalidasa were made from good leaves and they had been properly treated. So what could have happened?

Leaving the forest area, Kalidasa walked through the village. There were small houses close to one another. There were one or two markets too. Sandeepa could not walk in front to show him the way as Kalidasa rushed ahead asking him for directions every now and then. Finally, he reached the house.

It was a very small house, thatched with palm leaves. A few flowering plants grew in the courtyard. Strange emotions filled Kalidasa's mind. The place seemed to be familiar. He remembered that he used to stay in such a house when he was a child. On one side of the courtyard was the trough plastered with cow dung for immersing the leaves in the leaf extract. The writing leaves had been left to dry in the shade.

A man came out of the house. Kalidasa had no doubt about his identity. His father! His father who, he had feared, had died in the forest fire! He had searched for him all over Malava. But his search had not led him here, so far away from his previous home near the forest in Malava. The passage of almost 20 years had brought much change in his father. But Kalidasa had no difficulty in recognizing him.

As Bhanumitra knew Sandeepa, he talked with him.

'Why, Sandeepa, you had come yesterday also. I had given you all the leaves I had. Who is this man with you?' Bhanumitra asked saluting Kalidasa.

Kalidasa went forward and touched his feet, looking at him anxiously to see if his father would recognize him.

Then he saw his mother coming from behind the house. He rushed towards her and touched her feet also.

Bhanumitra again asked Sandeepa, 'Who is this?'

'Kalidasa. The great poet of Ujjaini, of Malava,' Sandeepa replied.

Vedavati looked at Kalidasa as if she could not believe her eyes. Who was this man who was bowing before them? He looked like an ascetic with the long hair and beard.

Kalidasa smiled at his mother. He was anxious to know whether she would recognize him. As she looked closely into the eyes of the man who stood before her, she felt that young Bhanumitra was standing before her. She couldn't believe her eyes. Could it be Shambhu? She could not even imagine that Shambhu, who had been caught in the forest fire, would come back to her. And Sandeepa had said that he was Kalidasa.

Kalidasa could not control himself any longer. 'Amma, I am your son, Shambhu,' he said.

'Shambhu!' Vedavati embraced Kalidasa. It was almost a wail. Tears fell from her eyes in abundance. Kalidasa felt that to be the most blessed moment in his life.

Bhanumitra looked at him as if he could not believe what was happening. Yes, the same eyes! He could recognize that face. He too could not control himself. 'Shambhu!' he cried as he embraced his son.

Sandeepa realized what was happening. Kalidasa who had come from Ujjaini had succeeded in finding his parents after so many years.

After sharing the joy of this reunion, Sandeepa went back. The joy of the parents at getting their son back after such long years was immeasurable. Kalidasa described how he had escaped from the fire. They had not known anything about the fame gained by Shambhu who had become Kalidasa. But finding that their son was the great poet in the royal assembly of King Vikramaditya, they were overjoyed. All the villagers gathered there to share their joy. Their joy became the joy of the village.

Kalidasa told them how he had come to Devagiri and started composing his new work. He wanted to go back and complete his work. So he returned to his cave after a couple of days, knowing that they could meet whenever they wanted.

The southern wind that blew that evening was unusual and he was looking at the flock of storks that were flying against the wind when he looked into the valley. Someone could be seen walking towards his cave. Usually no one came to see him there. Sandeepa would come through the path behind the rock when he came from the temple with food and water for him. His father came every day but he only came in the morning. Kalidasa stood up to see who was coming to see him.

Yes, it was Nichula. Kalidasa was elated. When Nichula left him, Kalidasa had told him to come after two seasons. Now, why was he coming earlier? Had something special happened at Ujjaini?

Kalidasa went down and welcomed Nichula joyfully. They both came into the cave and sat on the rock. Nichula kept his bundle down.

'What is the news from Ujjaini? Are the maharaja and the maharani doing well?' Kalidasa asked.

'I have come with happy news. The maharani has become pregnant, putting an end to their sorrow. Both of them wanted me to bring this news to you. You need not feel any more that *Abhijnanashakuntalam* intensified their sorrow. "When one's sorrow is removed, there is a special affinity towards what had originally caused that sorrow"—that is what the maharaja said,' Nichula said.

'Oh! I am so delighted to hear this! It is indeed happy news. It is wonderful that they are going to have an heir to the throne,' said Kalidasa. 'What other news, Nichula? Hope the Minister Amarasimha, Shankuka and Kshapanaka and the others are all doing well? Are they still trying to raise new accusations against me or have any of them been able to write anything significant?' Kalidasa enquired.

'They seem to have forgotten Kalidasa now. There has been no mention of you in the assembly. Maharaja knows that though there are many others who enjoy your writing and support your stand on the freedom of the author, it is only with me that you have any personal friendship. He has asked me many times about you. When I was planning to come to Devagiri he even told me that he would make all the arrangements for my journey,' Nichula said.

After a pause, Nichula again asked, 'How far along are you with the new work? Have you run out of writing leaves? I have brought enough of them for you to write another major work,' said Nichula pointing to the bundle that he had brought.

'Yes, I have written much and I am happy about what I have done. Then, there is another thing, Nichula,' Nichula noticed the extreme happiness on Kalidasa's face. Without wasting any more time Kalidasa said, 'My parents are alive, Nichula.'

'What?!' Nichula jumped up from his seat. 'Did you see them, Shambhu? Where are they now?'

Kalidasa described how he had found his parents. Nichula was eager to see them but they decided to wait till the next morning.

Both of them got up. Kalidasa walked back towards the cave but Nichula stood there looking at the western sky. The beauty of the setting sun held his eyes. He had seen sunsets in Ujjaini also. But this seemed to be a different picture. Hadn't he seen this when he was here before?

Kalidasa too turned back. They left for the cave only after the sun had set completely and darkness had spread.

'I am anxious to know about your work, Shambhu,' Nichula said.

'Stay here for a few days, if you are not in a hurry to go back, Nichula. As I write, you can make copies. After the work is complete, we should present the king with one copy. If the king decides to make more copies for the learned men of his land, one copy can be given for that. We will keep the third copy with us,' said Kalidasa.

'That is good. I will certainly do it and I will get a chance to read it as it is written,' Nichula agreed with Kalidasa's suggestion. If, as in the previous works, it was found that some parts are objectionably erotic, he could at least suggest that it would be better to change it.

Whatever fruits and roots had been kept for Kalidasa was shared with Nichula. They sat talking till the moon in the glory of the eighth night was up in the sky.

Nichula was eager to go to meet Kalidasa's parents early the next morning. They started for the village before Bhanumitra came to Kalidasa's cave as usual. They met Bhanumitra on the way and the three of them proceeded to his house. Kalidasa had mentioned that he had met Nichula in Ujjaini and so Bhanumitra had no difficulty in recognizing him. His mother, Vedavati also guessed that it must be Nichula who was coming with them. They spent the whole day there and returned to the cave only in the evening.

The next morning, as Kalidasa took up the leaves and started his work, Nichula also started his work.

He had described up to Shiva appearing before Parvati. Now he had to proceed with their marriage. Kalidasa's pen flew over the leaves. Himavan did not go to request Hara to marry his daughter. Similarly, Mahadeva also felt that it would not be proper for him to approach Himavan to ask for his daughter in marriage.

It would not be proper to make Parvati submit herself to Shiva. So Kalidasa made a companion of Parvati approach Shiva. Shiva, in his turn, meditated on the Saptarishis and through them made his request reach Himavan. As he started describing the Saptarishis, he took care to write about the position of the celestial Ganga in the universe and the position of the seven rishis and Arundhati there. He composed the lines to shed light on the real nature of the power of Shiva—the cause for creation, preservation and destruction. As he wrote the scene where the Saptarishis were coming back after meeting Himavan and talking about the marriage, Mahadeva was made to bid them goodbye with the words that he would meet them on the shores of the Mahakoshi. At that point, his mind went back to the visit to the Himalayas that he had made years ago. At that time the rishis had shown him the spot where Mahadeva was believed to have waited for the Saptarishis. He had even made an attempt in his mind to see the whole land from there to the ocean in the south. Afterwards, he had travelled up to the holy feet of Devi Kanyakumari. Kalidasa's mind took another tour of the whole land of Bharat.

Next, he presented the beauty of the city of Himavan as seen by the rishis when they reached Oshadhiprastha. Couplets were written to glorify Himavan, the Saptarishis and Shankara. As he wrote about the beauty of the golden city of the Gandharvas, Alakapuri and how the Gandharvas described the glory of their city to Shiva and Parvati, Kalidasa's mind wandered to the time he was writing *Meghadutam*. While writing that he had imagined himself to be a Gandharva at Alakapuri.

Days passed with Kalidasa engaged in creation and Nichula making copies. As he wrote about the union of Shiva and Parvati and the birth of Sharavanabhava, he took care to give due importance to the birth of Karthikeya. He went through the different acts again and again to make sure that the various aspects of the union of Prakruti and Purusha—nature and pure consciousness—as well as the glory of the creation of this universe were clearly presented.

Kalidasa found himself in an entirely different world of emotions when he was writing about the effulgence that arose from the union of Prakruti and Purusha being given to Agni, the fire, and later to Ganga and how the son of Shiva and Parvati was brought up by the Sharavana birds in the Ganga.

The young Karthikeya grew up to be capable of handling all weapons. He went to the world of the Gods at the request of Indra. He assumed the position of commander-in-chief of the celestial forces with the blessings of Kashyapa Prajapati and Aditi and got ready to confront Tarakasura.

As he gave a detailed description of the war and how Kumara used his power to behead the Asura, Kalidasa felt confident that he had given a good description of how the object for which the devas wanted Karthikeya to be born had been achieved. On many an occasion he felt that his work was too bulky, but he did not want to cut any part as he was sure of the poetic beauty of each line.

After he had completed the work, he sat for long looking at it. Eighteen cantos! All made up of couplets that were one better than the other and giving it all that is needed to call it a great poetic creation. The birth of Kumara and the fulfilment of his duty were the matters taken up for treatment in the work. Kalidasa took a leaf and wrote—*Kumarasambhavam*.

Nichula who was immersed in making copies of what Kalidasa had written raised his head and looked at him. Shambhu's face showed his satisfaction. Nichula felt that Kalidasa had completed his work, that relief was clearly reflected on his face. Nichula had noticed that once he started writing, Kalidasa would be at it for hours together. Sometimes he would sit for hours in meditation like a yogi.

While making the copies, if he had any doubts about some lines or scenes, he had to wait for hours to ask Kalidasa about it. Nichula was careful to see that when Shambhu was engaged in writing, there should be nothing to disturb his concentration. There were some scenes which, Nichula felt, would give his detractors a chance to raise accusations against him. But Kalidasa was a poet who had full confidence in what he had written. He explained to Nichula how some of the couplets had a deeper meaning according to *Yogashastra*, which was different from the superficial meaning that the ordinary people assigned to it. He was of the opinion that if some people saw descriptions of beauty as vulgar and obscene, they would consider the whole work to be so. The mentality of the viewer was the criterion to decide if something was vulgar and obscene or not.

Nichula listened with rapt attention as Kalidasa described the yogic meaning of the relationship between Shiva and Parvati. When he listened to his words, he realized how true it was.

Months had passed since Nichula had left Ujjaini. The king must have been blessed with a child by now. He and the maharani would be waiting to share the good news with Kalidasa. They must be worried about Nichula also failing to return to Ujjaini. Now Nichula knew that Kalidasa had completed his work. So it would be possible to return soon.

'Have you completed it?' Nichula asked.

'Yes, it is complete. Let us go and worship Karthikeya,' Kalidasa replied.

'Let's go,' Nichula got up.

As he stood with folded hands before Karthikeya, Kalidasa's mind was filled with the satisfaction that he had completed the work.

It had been almost eighteen months since he came to Devagiri. Now he could go back. Kalidasa bid goodbye to the priest at the temple and to Sandeepa who had been helping him in different ways all these days.

The next morning, when his father came, Kalidasa informed him that he was planning to go to Ujjaini. They were happy to go to Ujjaini with Shambhu. Nichula completed the work of making copies of *Kumarasambhavam* that day itself. The next morning Kalidasa's parents came to Devagiri, ready for the journey.

Kalidasa and Nichula were also ready for the journey with the writing leaves carefully bundled up.

They were leaving Devagiri; with prayers to Skanda in their hearts, they bid goodbye.

They travelled for days, taking rest here and there. On reaching Ujjaini, they left Kalidasa's parents in his house and went straight to the palace to meet Vikramaditya. When the king reached the assembly, Kalidasa handed over the bundle of leaves covered with a silken cloth.

'Maharaj! This is *Kumarasambhavam*. It is the story of how Dakshayani, who was the wife of Mahadeva Shiva, was reborn as the daughter of Himavan and got Shiva himself as her husband through severe penance. The story of Karthikeya who was born as the son of Shiva and Parvati for destroying Tarakasura is written as a long poem, "Mahakaavya". Please keep this copy in your personal collection,' Kalidasa said.

'I am so happy, Kalidasa. I was unhappy that you were not here. But now you have come with good news,' Vikramaditya expressed his delight.

'Maharaj! Congratulations to you and the maharani for the birth of your son. May the boy raise the glory of Malava with his valour and good behaviour. May he be the jewel among kings in this holy land. Will I be able to see the prince?' Kalidasa expressed his delight at the blessing that the royal couple had got.

'Of course, Kalidasa! You come too, Nichula,' Vikramaditya invited Kalidasa and Nichula to see the child.

Nichula informed the king about finding Kalidasa's parents. The king expressed his happiness at the news and enquired after them.

15

*P*raise and felicitations were heaped on Kalidasa for *Kumarasambhavam*. The readers saw the intensity of Sree Parvati's penance and the power of Kumara Karthikeya in the most exalted poetry. Others saw the purity and beauty of poetry in the work.

In the assembly while felicitating Kalidasa, Jinadeva said, 'This work is a glowing example of the love that the poet has for Maharaja Vikramaditya as well as his patriotism. I can't even imagine how proud a father would be to have such a work written about his son.'

The audience did not understand what he was speaking about.

'Kalidasa is trying to place this dynasty at the peak of its glory through many, many centuries. Your Majesty, Kalidasa has written this in praise of our dear prince Kumaraditya.'

There was a thunderous applause but Kalidasa was shocked. Jinadeva was saying something that had never entered his mind. He had not thought of Kumaraditya while writing this. Only Karthikeya had existed in his mind throughout the writing.

Vikramaditya and the rest of the assembly listened in surprise as Jinadeva continued. 'Maharaj, our prince was born at the time when Kalidasa was writing this, an heir to the throne of Malava. Kalidasa has given the most suitable name also for it—*Kumarasambhavam*.'

The assembly applauded again. Some of them felt jealousy burning in their hearts to see Kalidasa once again reaching heights of fame. All others will be nothing but worms in the world of poetry now. Who will read their work?

Kalidasa and Nichula glanced at each other. When Kalidasa was getting ready to get up and speak Nichula cautioned him with his eyes.

After the assembly had dispersed and when he could talk to Kalidasa alone, Nichula said, 'Let them analyse your work as they please. Once you have completed writing, the book belongs to the readers. The writer has no right over it. If you try to explain how your work should be approached and how it should be enjoyed, it will be like trying to influence the reader's right to enjoy a creative work.'

'But, Nichula, how can I accept this view that this work, which even I felt to be superior to all the others, is something that I have written to praise the prince?' Kalidasa asked in a distressed voice.

'No Shambhu, now you have no right over it. As you are the poet who created it, the readers have a right over you. They can praise and congratulate you. If any one feels like criticizing you in the name of this creation, he can do that also.'

'Do you mean to say that I have to suffer all this?' Kalidasa demanded.

'You will not have to do it. Those who can enjoy your poems at the highest level will answer to the critics for you,' Nichula comforted him.

'Yes, what you say is true, Nichula. If I start answering people, I may not get time to write anything else,' Kalidasa observed.

'Take what Jinadeva said as praise for your work. At least in the eyes of the maharaja and those who do not have the capacity to enjoy your work in the proper sense, Jinadeva was only praising your work. Those who see *Kumarasambhavam* in the real light will know and enjoy it as it should be seen. Its greatness will be revealed in that light,' Nichula said.

Kalidasa felt somewhat pacified. Still he was sorry to see this work, which he considered to be superior to *Raghuvamsam* and *Abhijnanashakuntalam*, being denigrated to a work written to praise the king and the prince.

But matters took a turn which Nichula, Kalidasa or his supporters could have never imagined. *Kumarasambhavam* was becoming the new weapon for those who could not bear to have Kalidasa in Ujjaini.

It was Shankuka who brought the matter before Vikramaditya.

'Maharaj!' he said, 'Kalidasa is being praised and honoured for the beauty of his work and copies of his work are being made available everywhere.'

'Yes, he is a blessing for Ujjaini,' the king replied.

'But, Your Majesty, as it has been pointed out in the case of former works by Kalidasa, in this also he has used vulgar language. There are many lines that cannot be recited in public. The poetic license is not meant for him to describe anything and everything. While his lines please the readers, they should also conform to social norms,' Shankuka expressed his opinion.

Vikramaditya thought of some lines in Kalidasa's works. He had not read *Kumarasambhavam* in detail. He had found whatever he had read to be great.

Shankuka placed a leaf in front of Vikramaditya.

sthitāḥ kṣaṇaṃ pakṣmasu tāḍitādharāḥ
payodharotsedha nipāta cūrṇitā
valīṣu tasyā skhalitā prapedire
cireṇanābhiṃ prathamoda bindavaḥ

(*Kumarasambhavam*, Canto 5, Line 24)

(The teardrop remained in the eyelids for a moment and then fell to the lips and shattered as it fell on the breasts and from the stomach reached the navel.)

'Maharaj! Is this how Devi Parvati is to be described while she is undertaking penance on the Himalayas? We must remember that these lines are describing the Goddess, wife of Mahakaleshwara,' Shankuka said with a show of indignation.

Lines appeared on Vikramaditya's forehead. And Shankuka realized that the arrow that he had released had touched the right spot.

'Maharaj, please be kind enough to read *Kumarasambhavam* once again. Then some rites of atonement for having read such lines about Devi Parvati must be performed at the temple of Mahakaleshwara. I too will pray that no harm should befall the royal family,' he added.

Vikramaditya didn't say anything. He had a clear view on the freedom of expression enjoyed by a poet. He also believed that it was wrong to instruct a poet on how to write and how to describe things and people in his work. Kalidasa was not willing to rewrite the last chapter of *Raghuvamsam* and he was ready to accept that. But as Shankuka has pointed out, how long could a king support works that do not conform to social norms?

By that time Somasekhara also joined them. He kept the writing leaves that he had brought before the king.

'What is this? Have you also written something?' Vikramaditya asked.

'No, Maharaj. I pray to the Creator not to bless me with the ability to write such lines. If I write like this, may my arms be cut off, my eyes blinded and my mind affected by madness. Your Majesty, this is *Kumarasambhavam*. I don't want this to be read by anybody in my family. Even if I take care to see that the children do not read it, I feel that it is not good to have this in a household. I do not have the strength to face the anger of Mahadeva and Sree Parvati. I do not know how to expiate the sin of having read this work,' Somasekhara spoke with a show of emotion.

Vikramaditya was in a quandary. If he commanded that this should be rewritten, it would be as useless as the orders he had issued in the case of *Raghuvamsam*. Kalidasa would not be ready to do it. We could only hope that he may be ready to make some changes as the lines were about Devi Parvati.

'I have heard both of you. I have not read the whole of *Kumarasambhavam*. So I have not considered it deeply. But I can understand the seriousness of what you are saying,' Vikramaditya said.

'You must take some action after consulting the ministers. If Mahakaleshwara opens His third eye, our Ujjaini will be reduced to ashes, Maharaj! You must save Ujjaini, Maharaj!' said Shankuka.

Vikramaditya was aware that what Shankuka was saying did not conform to the concept of the power of Mahakaleshwara. But he could not forget the fact that most people did not worship Shiva and Parvati with the deeper understanding of the principles regarding their power. The ordinary people were still rooted in the physical reality of life while worshipping Shiva and Parvati. So, as a ruler, he could not wipe away all such opinions as meaningless utterances.

Vikramaditya held discussions with the ministers and there was no consensus of opinion.

'We cannot ignore the greatness of Kalidasa as a poet. We cannot ignore the fame that he has achieved among the readers. So whatever decision we take must be done after considering these facts,' Amarasimha expressed himself clearly.

'Different people have had different opinions about what he had written in some of his previous works also. They felt that some of the descriptions were indecent. But in those works, it was only the prostitutes who were the subjects of such descriptions. But in this, it is Devi Parvati and Lord Shiva who are being described thus. This is not something that concerns only those who enjoy poems, this affects all the people,' Gunasoma said.

'What is the solution for this? I do not think it will be of any use if we ask Kalidasa to remove these lines or rewrite them. Apart from being the king and a member of the royal assembly, we are friends. I will try requesting him, it is useless to try to order him,' Vikramaditya said.

Amarasimha knew that this problem had to be solved somehow or the other. 'Maharaj, you request him, ask him to do it and then order him to do it. If he does not agree to do so, you will have to do something to pacify the critics. That is what I think.'

Vikramaditya looked at Amarasimha, unable to believe what he had heard. It is inappropriate to take disciplinary action against a poet on the basis of some unpleasant parts in his writing, especially in a country like Malava where the rulers gave all possible support to literary and artistic pursuits. Will he have to do it? Now no one will be satisfied by his imprisonment. Giving him the same punishment for the same offence once again will look ludicrous.

'Maharaj! Orders must be issued to confiscate all the copies of *Kumarasambhavam* and consign them to flames. Kalidasa must be asked to go away from Malava. If we do not do at least this, there will be disturbances here,' Amarasimha added.

'Yes, Maharaj, what the minister has suggested is the right course of action,' Gunasoma supported what Amarasimha said.

Vikramaditya had no options. He had to meet Kalidasa. He must warn him before taking any action. Kalidasa must keep himself away from Malava at least till this uproar against his work is over. It would be better for the safety of Kalidasa's life. Under the present circumstances, Vikramaditya would not be able to offer protection to his friend. If he tried to do it, his own safety may be jeopardized. The reports from Malava pointed to such a situation.

As Hemabhadra, the priest of Mahakaleshwara temple, started walking towards the palace, many people followed him. There were those who knew why he was going there and also those who knew nothing. They just believed that if the priest was so angry there must be sufficient reason for it.

Nichula was just getting out of the palace when he saw Hemabhadra and some intellectuals along with many people coming into the palace, talking loudly in great agitation. As the soldiers did not dare to stop the priest, they allowed them to go in.

Nichula stood on the side of the road, looking at them. Words like 'Kalidasa' and '*Kumarasambhavam*' were heard in the midst of the confusing noise and Nichula became anxious to know what it was about. Why had Kalidasa become a topic of discussion for these people? Had the complaints over *Kumarasambhavam* reached the temple also? With a shudder Nichula remembered—Hemabhadra was the priest at the temple of Mahakaleshwara. He will not see a poem as just a poem; he will not think about its poetic quality. He may describe the description of Goddess Parvati to be indecent... that was the type of thinking that was becoming prevalent in society. It was a plan to close one's eyes to the natural truths and find special meanings to the concept of modesty and propriety. They were trying to give new definitions to morality in the light of what they thought was virtue and thereby an attempt was being made to establish the power of the so-called intellectual class over the ordinary people. This will only lead to the destruction of our culture... But who will reveal these hidden truths?

At the same time when a poetic work becomes popular, it will have to face the criticism that comes from the limited intelligence of the ordinary readers. It was only the learned and wise men who used to read books earlier. But Kalidasa's works have become popular. The ordinary readers cannot understand the artistic beauty of his works. That is why these people now involve themselves in the controversies raised by those who claim to be learned and wise. Nichula did not know what he could do in this matter.

Nichula followed them. They reached the assembly hall. Usually when somebody came to the hall, the king would come there to listen to what they had to say. The people had the right to meet the king, whether it was to make a complaint, express their opinion or to present the king with something they had brought.

Nichula remained there, keeping himself away from the crowd. The soldiers had gone to inform the king about the arrival of these people. Fear gripped Nichula's heart as he heard snatches of conversation where people demanded that Kalidasa must be made to leave the country, or be imprisoned or even that his hands be cut off. This was not something that would die down after a while, as Kalidasa and Nichula had imagined. People were angry. Those who had read the poem and those who had not were equally involved in it. The common people were getting a negative message. It had the support of the chief priest of the temple of Mahakaleshwara. There may be others who want to undermine the throne of Malava behind the priest who had an interest in it. This was a dangerous matter.

Vikramaditya took his seat at the public assembly soon. All those who were assembled there bowed their head before the king and shouted, 'Long live Maharaja Vikramaditya!' Hemabhadra came forward and bowed his head once again before addressing the king. 'Maharaj! I had earlier pointed out to you the indecent descriptions that are rampant in Kalidasa's writings. It was such immoral and indecorous actions that led to the untimely death of Mallika. A thunderbolt seems to have fallen on Malava with the arrival of Kalidasa. Now Kalidasa has committed an even greater sin. I don't have the words to describe it, My Lord! But as the priest of the temple of Mahakaleshwara I cannot endure this.'

Vikramaditya raised his hands to stop him. 'I understand what you're saying. I have already held a discussion about this with our ministers. We will take a decision soon.'

'Maharaj! The devotees of Mahakaleshwara are all angry and agitated,' Hemabhadra added.

Before Vikramaditya could say anything, the men started shouting: 'Put Kalidasa in prison! Cut off Kalidasa's hands for sacrilege.'

Vikramaditya again raised his hand to stop the shouting. 'We will take a decision soon.' The king then got up indicating that all should disperse. The priest and his followers left the assembly. Nichula could hear them say, 'Even the Maharaja is convinced...' 'That man will be taught a lesson...'

As he was about to walk back to the inner chambers of the palace, Vikramaditya saw Nichula standing there. He paused and Nichula approached him with reverence.

'Nichula, didn't you see and hear everything? What is this? How can we solve it?' he asked.

Nichula did not know how to respond. He could see the king's helplessness. Even a despot cannot do anything against the wishes of the people... Nichula knew that. And Vikramaditya, who gave utmost importance to the welfare of his people, would never be able to ignore their voice. The king of Malava would never be able to approve of any literary composition that was rejected by the people. What Vikramaditya, the lover of literature could do was not the same as what Vikramaditya, the ruler could do.

'Maharaj! I will talk to Kalidasa. I can understand what is going on in your mind. I will try to convince Kalidasa. He will come to see you. He will have something to tell you... Please make your royal edict after that,' Nichula requested the king.

'Go now itself Nichula and bring Kalidasa to me,' Viramaditya commanded.

As Nichula was walking towards Kalidasa's house, many different thoughts passed through his mind. No one could question Kalidasa's freedom as a poet in matters of composition. But when the imagination of the poet spread its wings in a manner that is against the beliefs of the people, trouble will spring forth against it. When the priestly class decides to classify what is virtue and what is vile, what is moral and what is immoral and what will invite the wrath of the gods on the land and its people, the ordinary citizens will get agitated. How can one convince them about the poetic license and freedom of expression that the poet has a right to enjoy? Who will be ready to believe that the power called God will never, unlike the king or the priest, wreck His anger on the people? It is true that the freedom of imagination enjoyed by the poet should not infringe upon the freedom of belief of the people. The question here was whether Kalidasa had made such an intrusion. Who would decide that? The king? The priest? The assembly of learned men? The royal assembly?

If it was proved that Kalidasa had done that, what is the solution? Force him to change what he has written? Destroy what has been written? Punish him for what he has written? Things have reached such a state that if the chief priest declared that Kalidasa deserved to be punished and this was the type of punishment that Mahakaleshwara desired to give him, people would believe him.

Nichula was trying to find answers to his own questions. Questions arose in different forms in his mind and the answers also were of different hues. No one could decide who was right and who was wrong.

Kalidasa was not at his house. His parents were there but they did not know where he had gone. Nichula walked both sides, along the banks of the river, but he was not there. Who could he ask? There was no one nearby.

Nichula wondered how he would keep his word to the king that he would bring Kalidasa to him. Where was he?

When he was not at home, he was generally on the rock near the Kshipra. He loved to observe the fish and the swans that swam about in the water or lie on the rock and look at the birds that flew across the sky and explain the changes in seasons. He loved the line of birds that could be seen flying across the evening sky. But today, he was not there.

Nichula walked back disappointed. He would have to come in the morning and take Kalidasa to meet the king. He decided to go to the temple before returning home.

As he neared the temple, Nichula observed a crowd gathered there. As he went near to enquire, he realized that it was the same crowd that had come to meet the king a while ago, the priest was also there. They were standing around Kalidasa! Nichula made a way for himself and approached Kalidasa.

Kalidasa was sitting on the platform under a banyan tree. The priest was talking to Kalidasa in an angry voice.

'How could you write like this about Mahadeva and Sree Parvati? What sin of previous births brought you to Ujjaini? I cannot allow such a sinner to enter the temple...' the priest went on shouting at Kalidasa. But Kalidasa was sitting there without saying anything. As the priest became more and more agitated, other people also joined him in abusing the poet. It seemed possible that they would attack Kalidasa physically if something was not done immediately. Nichula felt relieved that he had come at the right time. He went near his friend and held him by the hand, 'Kalidasa, come with me,' he said.

The priest turned to Nichula. 'Where are you taking him?

Let him answer me first,' he said.

Nichula felt that the people would not allow them to go. So he said, 'It is an order from the king. He has asked me to bring Kalidasa to him.'

Someone had brought a copy of *Kumarasambhavam*. They put the copy in front of the temple. The priest shouted, 'We have to do something to expiate the sin that Kalidasa has committed. Sree Parameshwara, please accept our offer...' With these words, he took the fire that someone had brought and set the book on fire.

'Hey! What are you doing?!' Nichula and Kalidasa tried to stop him but before they could do anything, the priest and the men had surrounded the burning book reciting *'Aum Namahshivaya... Aum Namahshivaya...'*

Nichula felt that it was better to leave immediately with Kalidasa. The people were becoming more and more agitated and the priest was adding to their anger through his words. This fire may not die down.

Nichula pulled Kalidasa away as he was trying to prevent the burning of *Kumarasambhavam* and started walking towards the palace.

Once they were away from the crowd, Nichula said, 'Shambhu, the king has asked me to bring you to the palace immediately. I had gone to your house. How did you reach the temple?'

'I felt like worshipping Mahakaleshwara. When I reached there, the priest would not allow me to go in. There were also many people with him,' he said.

'They were coming back after making a complaint to the king. He has promised them to make enquiries and take appropriate action. Fortunately, I was there at that time,' Nichula told him.

'What action will the king take? Will my work cease to be

what it is, whatever action anyone may take against it? Or will he ask me to rewrite it, as in the case of *Raghuvamsam*?' asked Kalidasa, fully aware that he could not expect to get any reply from Nichula.

Nichula didn't utter a word. He too was not sure what would happen.

They reached the platform where discussions were generally held. Soon Vikramaditya also arrived.

The king sat down and asked them also to be seated.

Nichula explained what had happened at the temple gates. 'Maharaj! If things go on like this, the situation will only become worse. As the priest has involved himself in it, the devotees will all be angry. Those who have not read *Kumarasambhavam* and even those who are illiterate will turn against it.'

'How can we stop this, Kalidasa?' the king turned to him.

'What foolishness are they indulging in, Maharaj? Because of this, people would have come to know about *Kumarasambhavam* and they would be reading it now. They are actually giving more popularity to *Kumarasambhavm*,' said Kalidasa. 'And as its author I can only be happy about it...' he added.

'But as the king, that is not a solution for my problem. The assembly of the learned men has also raised its voice against *Kumarasambhavam*. I cannot avoid taking some action,' said Vikramaditya.

'Maharaj! I do not want to put you into any trouble. But as its author, I am happy at the publicity that my work is getting,' Kalidasa said again.

'But many of your lines seem to be denigrating Sree Mahadeva and Goddess Parvati as far as the common people are concerned.'

Kalidasa reacted to what Vikramaditya said, 'Maharaj! I cannot agree with that view. Have the common people read *Kumarasambhavam*, Your Majesty? No. Are they learned enough to read poems and plays? No. It is some of those who have read it that accuse it of containing immoral passages and ask them to raise their voice against it. Who has given the right to the priestly class to decide what is decent and indecent? Maharaj! Aren't those who give such ideas to the common people, the so-called pandits, the intellectuals the real wrong-doers? What is there in nature that is not *satyam, sivam, sundaram*—true, godly and beautiful? It is some men with selfish interest that incite the people to raise voice against *Kumarasambhavam*. The people who have really understood the artistic, poetic and yogic excellence are the ones who are behind this. I am not ready to believe that the chief priest of Mahakaleshwara is ignorant of all this.'

'The problem that we face is not whether the priest is aware of this or he understands this. We will not be able to make the people see the truth by talking to them. If some people come forward to stir up their emotions, it will be difficult to control them,' Nichula expressed his opinion.

The look on Kalidasa's face indicated that he did not agree with what Nichula had said but he remained silent.

'Well, you may go now. Let me think of what has to be done,' Vikramaditya bid them farewell. As he walked back to the inner quarters of the palace, he was lost in thought.

16

The next morning, it seemed to Vikramaditya that all the citizens of Malava had gathered in front of the palace. Even during the spring festival such a crowd did not gather. It was a repetition of what had taken place yesterday.

Nichula too saw the people gathering and came to find out what was happening. He found that they were raising their voice against *Kumarasambhavam*. Someone had once again stirred up the emotions of the people. Who was deliberately doing this? Who could make the people understand the real greatness of that work? Was this happening because the people of Malava were not proficient enough to enjoy the poetic excellence of the work?

Vikramaditya appeared on the terrace and greeted the people. Then he came down to the hall where discussions were to be held. Minister Amarasimha remained by his side.

It was Hemabhadra who came forward to speak. 'Maharaj! The people of Ujjaini cannot any longer suffer the vulgarity that Kalidasa has written in the work named *Kumarasambhavam*. Your Majesty must issue orders to send Kalidasa to the land of the dead. All the copies of *Kumarasambhavam* must be committed to flames. Mahakaleshwara has become angry, Maharaj!'

For the first time Vikramaditya felt angry with Kalidasa for placing him in such a dilemma. Vikramaditya would never be able to do anything to hurt Kalidasa. But he could find no way out of this. He looked at Amarasimha.

Jinadeva came forward, 'Maharaj! I apologise to you for

telling you that *Kumarasambhavam* is based on the birth of Kumaraditya. It was a mistake, Maharaj! I misunderstood it.'

'Why do you feel so now? It can be considered to be that way,' Vikramaditya asked.

'No, it must not be taken that way, Maharaj. I admit that Kalidasa might have thought about it that way. I do not deny that a poet has the right to describe beauty as he wants. But I feel that some of the lines cross the limits of decency,' Jinadeva said.

Nichula intervened, 'Who has set limits to the freedom of the poet to describe beauty? The beauty of a woman is the beauty of nature. Nature is depicted as mother...a Goddess. As long as one sees beauty as just beauty, it is attractive. Maharaj! The description of beauty is never a scale to decide the quality of a composition. Some lines in one or two couplets of a work should never be the criterion for deciding the quality of the work.'

'Kalidasa has shown the prince of Ujjaini becoming bold, courageous and valiant like the unconquerable Kumara Karthikeya, hasn't he? People of Malava can wish that our Kumaraditya would conquer the whole land extending from the Himalayas to the ocean and present exemplary and excellent governance. Why shouldn't we congratulate Kalidasa for writing such a poem?' asked Vikramaditya.

'Maharaj! All the citizens wish and pray for the prosperity of our prince. The ruler of Ujjaini is the guardian of the people, like a father, and the Maharani is like our mother... But...' Hemabhadra paused.

'Why did you stop? What do you want to say? asked Vikramaditya.

'Maharaj! If we were to think of the prince in the place of Karthikeya, you will be in the position of Sri Parameshwara and the maharani that of Goddess Parvati.'

'Yes...' Vikramaditya did not see anything wrong in that traditional concept.

'Maharaj! In the first canto of *Kumarasambhavam* the beauty of Goddess Parvati is described... If it is said that it is our maharani who is described thus, it will not be possible for the people to accept it. In the later cantos, the marriage between Shiva and Parvati as well as their indulgence in love is described, and none of us will be able to bear the thought that it is about you and the maharani,' Jinadeva said.

A shudder passed through Vikramaditya. If it is said that Kalidasa has modelled Parvati on Vidyothama, he would not be able to tolerate it. Vikramaditya felt all the sympathy and love that he had for Kalidasa evaporating at that moment. He used to say before this that Kalidasa was describing the prostitutes in his works and they liked their beauty being described. But now... When it seemed that Kalidasa had written about his wife in this vein, he wondered what his own reaction was... Was it shame? Or anger? When he thought of it as a description of Goddess Parvati, he could see it in a spiritual light. He felt that the poet had described the goddess of nature in a poetic manner, he felt that there was an otherworldly plane for it. But...

Jinadeva tried to see if the mental state of the king was being reflected on his face.

Then he glanced at Hemabhadra and nodded his head.

'Maharaj! Whether it is about Goddess Parvati who is considered as the mother of this world, or about our maharani whom we see as our mother, this is too much. Only a sinner would be able to describe the relationship between Shiva and Parvati in such an objectionable manner. None should dare to create such works after this. The fact that the poet's mind traverses such immoral paths points to the arrival of evil days for our land. I fear that some calamity is about to befall Malava, My Lord.'

Nichula could no longer remain silent. 'Maharaj! There is no need to see Kalidasa's work in this light. He has portrayed a high and shining concept of beauty in *Kumarasambhavam*. It is the people who are incapable of enjoying the beauty of this poetic masterpiece that raise objections against it.'

Vikramaditya looked at Nichula. Nichula could not gauge what those eyes showed. Was it anger, pain or grief? Helplessness was writ large on his body language. When he heard others say that it was his wife who had been thus described by Kalidasa, it was natural that he felt shame and anger. But he could not bear to hear people accusing Kalidasa, his dear friend, the beloved of his sister Mallika and one who was unparalleled in his ability to write poems and plays.

Some soldiers entered the hall and their leader said, 'Maharaj! There has been a fire at the Mahakaleshwara temple and some of the area has been completely destroyed.'

Hemabhadra, the chief priest spoke immediately, 'Maharaj! This is the beginning of some great calamity that is to befall our country. Mahakaleshwara is angry. We must not allow Kalidasa to remain in Malava for even a minute now. The ancient land of ours as a whole has become defiled because of this sinner.'

Vikramaditya was in a dilemma. He had to do something against Kalidasa.

Hemabhadra did not remain there any longer. 'Please allow me to leave, Maharaj,' he said, 'We do not know what has happened to our temple,' he said as he walked away.

Vikramaditya said, 'You may all go now. We will take a suitable decision soon.'

Hemabhadra hurried to the temple of Mahakaleshwara. The people followed him. They were waiting to go there as soon as they heard that there had been a fire in the temple.

Nichula realized that everything was going against Kalidasa all of a sudden. The fire of hatred, started by Shankuka and his men had now spread among the common people. Kalidasa is the beloved poet of the people and they would continue to consider him so. But someone had managed to make a move against Kalidasa in a deliberate manner by bringing the chief priest and some intellectuals to their side. They had already decided that they would rest only after Kalidasa was banished from Ujjaini. Now Kalidasa had given them an opportunity to achieve their aim. Nichula remembered the description of Goddess Parvati in *Kumarasambhavam*. Kalidasa had described the deeper meaning of the relationship between Shiva and Parvati to him. Nichula did not feel that there was anything in it to wound the feelings. But for those who were waiting for a cause to make trouble for the writer that was enough. They might have felt that what they had done already was not as effective as they wanted it to be. So they decided to make a renewed effort that day also.

When the people left, Vikramaditya turned to Amarasimha and Nichula. 'What has Kalidasa done now? There have been similar accusations about some of his writings before this. I had justified most of them and then even had him imprisoned. I had also stopped royal patronage for *Raghuvamsam*. Now what can I do about this?'

'Maharaj! Even from an udder that is full of milk, a mosquito will draw only blood. That is its nature. The chief priest seems to me like a mosquito or a leech, drinking the blood from the body of Ujjaini,' Amarasimha said.

'We can see it in that light. But as the priest of Mahakaleshwara, his words are the words of the Lord for the people. I fear matters are going to get worse,' Vikramaditya expressed his apprehension.

'Maharaj! There is nothing so bad in *Kumarasambhavam* as these people allege. I know it because I made the copies. I had discussed some parts with him then. You can see this for yourself when you read it,' Nichula said.

Vikramaditya told them what he thought of the work. 'I read some parts of it and thought that to be a beautiful poem. But it is true that some of the parts that Jinadeva pointed out are degrading. I do not feel like forgiving Kalidasa for those lines.'

'Yes, Maharaj. But this will not die down easily. I fear that more trouble will arise because of a part of the Mahakaleshwara temple having burned down,' said Amarasimha.

'We should not allow the peace and calm of the city to be affected. Take necessary steps to ensure that,' Vikramaditya gave instructions to his minister.

Nichula went home from there and went to Kalidasa's house only in the evening. He doubted whether Kalidasa would be at home. He found him lying on the flat rock on the banks of the Kshipra. It was clear to Nichula that none of the troubles that were brewing in the city about his writings was on Kalidasa's mind as he lay there looking at the birds and the clouds that floated across the sky. Now and then he threw some grains for the birds. The birds came near him without any fear.

Nichula sat under a champaka tree, watching Kalidasa. Nichula realized that he felt a special joy as he sat watching his friend just as Kalidasa seemed to get the same joy in watching the birds and the clouds. The works that came from his friend's pen were among the best in the world. And the writer had an almost ascetic frame of mind.

After some time Nichula went near Kalidasa.

'Nichula, look at the flamingos flying in a line. How can they keep the line and distance among themselves so perfectly? See, as they reach under the white clouds, they seem to become drawn into it,' Kalidasa went on pointing to the birds in the sky.

Nichula was surprised. Kalidasa did not seem to be bothered about the uproar against his work or the conspiracy being hatched against him. He did not seem to be affected by any of it. But now even the king was losing sleep over this man.

'Shambhu,' Nichula began. 'Right now there are some other very important matters that we have to consider.'

'What is it? Is it about the arrival of the dark clouds even before the rainy season? Or is it about the soldiers of Ujjaini marching to the western border? Is it about the Shakas gathering forces or about the kings of this ancient land destroying themselves by fighting against one another? Or is it about the march of the Greek forces?' Kalidasa enquired.

Nichula could not say anything. He sat looking at his friend. Was he making fun of him? Was he pretending to be ignorant even when he knew the truth?

'Shambhu, it is a serious matter. There have been a lot of accusations against *Kumarasambhavam*,' Nichula said.

'Yes, I heard about that too. I know that more people will read *Kumarasambhavam* because of all this publicity. I feel many are making copies of it,' Kalidasa replied.

'That may be so; many copies may be getting prepared. But the priest of the Mahakaleshwara temple, Shankuka, Jinadeva and many others have come together and are bent upon creating trouble over it. The priest, with a crowd of men following him, came to meet the king. They demand that your hands be cut off or you should be beheaded or banished from Ujjaini,' Nichula said.

'Let them demand what they want and let the king decide what is to be done. I have nothing to do about it. If one has been found to be a culprit, is his opinion taken before deciding on the punishment?' Kalidasa asked.

'But shouldn't you offer some explanation...or come to an agreement after a discussion with the priest and the other learned men...'

Kalidasa did not allow Nichula to complete what he had started to say.

'Nichula, did anybody invite me for that? Did anyone ask you to get an explanation from Kalidasa? Do you think this problem will be solved by such an explanation?' Kalidasa sat looking at Nichula for a while before continuing. 'Anyone can make any remark about my writing. No one needs any explanation from me. If there are things that they do not understand I can explain it to them. But that is not what is happening here now. They pretend not to have understood even when they have understood my writing very well. They misinterpret whatever I write and try to create trouble. Let them interpret it to their liking. Just as I have the freedom to write, they have the freedom to interpret. I have no complaints about it,' Kalidasa concluded.

'The maharaja is unhappy with the way things are going. You have described the youthful appearance of Queen Vidyothama and...' Nichula stopped and sat looking at Kalidasa for a while. 'Much more... That is what they have made Vikramaditya believe. I too haven't understood their real intention. But it has caused him pain and shame. At least to comfort him...' Nichula hoped that Kalidasa would be ready to make some changes in his work at least to give some relief to the king.

'At least the king should have better sense. I have always seen him as a connoisseur of the arts. But I am disappointed at the way he reacted. I have lost my faith in Ujjaini. Now I have no rights over *Kumarasambhavam*. It belongs to the people... to those who appreciate poetic creations. Let them explain it in whichever way they want and understand it in their own way,' Kalidasa said in a firm voice.

Nichula knew that nothing could be gained by talking about it. '*Whatever is to happen, will happen...*' he thought.

'It is getting dark... Let us go back, Shambhu,' Nichula said.

But Kalidasa wanted to lie there for some more time. 'I have nothing to do now. Let us lie here looking at the stars in the sky and the moon rising in the horizon. We can see the Milky Way and the Saptarishis. Let us see where Venus will be tonight... We can hear the music of Kshipra and listen to the chirping of the night birds.' Kalidasa was detached, disinterested in what was happening around him.

But Nichula was still worried. The priest will stir up the devotees and create havoc in Ujjaini. Shankuka and his friends will be trying to analyse the work in their own way before the illiterate as well as those who could read the work for themselves. Shambhu was not ready to do anything to stop that. Nichula felt that even the king will keep silent on this matter. He too had felt that the description of Parvati was really that of Vidyothama. How could anyone make him realize that it was not so? Was it possible that Vikramaditya could not see it as a description of the Goddess—the mother of the universe? While Kalidasa was contemplating the stars in the sky, Nichula was filled with apprehension. The question, 'what next?' troubled him.

At last he said, 'Shambhu, let me go home now. I will try to explain things as best as I can. You too go home as your parents must be waiting for you.'

'Tell them to go to bed, Nichula. Let me enjoy the beauty of nature here for some more time, watch the path of the stars that appear and disappear within seconds, observe the clouds sail by in the moonlight,' Kalidasa said. Nichula could not see the expression on his face in the darkness.

Nichula went to Kalidasa's house and talked with his parents. He informed them that Kalidasa would be late in coming back and requested them to go to bed. From there he proceeded to the temple of Mahakaleshwara. He wanted to try explaining things to Hemabhadra. He could try to make him understand the plane from which Kalidasa had written the poem.

But as he came near the temple, Nichula saw that things had not become normal there. Though it was late, the people had not dispersed. Lighted torches, not just one or two but hundreds, could be seen in the darkness. Where were they going with the torches? It was only during the war that such scenes could be seen. If they had to start for a battle at night, this was how the soldiers would move—with the people holding up torches to show them the way. What was causing such movement now? Nichula looked at the people with anxiety.

A flash of lightning seemed to strike Nichula as he realized that the people were talking about Kalidasa. They were moving towards Kalidasa's house. An agitated crowd would do anything without thinking. Kalidasa's life was in danger. There was no sign of any soldiers sent out to keep control over the people. Just one or two of them were standing there and even they were not trying to control the crowd.

Nichula started running towards the king's palace. He felt as if the distance was increasing, he could not reach there even after running hard for a long time. If he reached there, there would be soldiers at the palace gates. But there seemed to be none of them in the vicinity today. He could see no preparations for meeting an emergency and controlling the people. Could it be that no news of what was happening near the temple had reached the palace? People in such an excited mood may do harm. They had to be controlled.

Nichula reached the palace and rang the bell. He would speak to the king, make him understand the gravity of the situation. No harm should befall the great poet, the preceptor of all the poets of this ancient land, the great Kalidasa, on the soil of Malava. The people have to be controlled.

Vikramaditya appeared there soon. The servants had lit more lamps by then.

'Maharaj! People are moving towards Kalidasa's house with torches in hand, his life is in danger!' said Nichula anxiously.

As he looked closely at the king, Nichula felt that this was a man he had not seen before... anger had made his face seem unfamiliar.

'I know what is happening, Nichula. Don't say anything more about Kalidasa. He is a cursed man. I feel sorry, repentant, that I considered such a man as my friend for so long. I tried to justify his actions on many an occasion. I can't do that anymore,' said the king.

'Maharaj! This is not the time to think of what is right and wrong. His life is in danger... Please order the soldiers to go there, Your Majesty,' Nichula begged.

'Why? Whom should I save? Kalidasa? If I tried to save Kalidasa, even Lord Mahakaleshwara will not pardon me. You read what he has written, Nichula. Who could think of describing Lord Parameshwara and Sree Parvati in such a way? Didn't you read the eighth canto, Nichula?' Vikramaditya's voice was shaking with anger as he spoke.

Nichula was shocked. What was special about the eighth canto? That canto described Mahadeva Shiva along with Sree Parvati going to see Sree Hari, Brahmadeva and Himavan and the Gandharvas inviting them to enjoy the beauty of Alakapuri. There was nothing in it to make anyone so angry.

'Maharaj! What are you saying?' Nichula was aware that each passing moment was valuable for saving Kalidasa. 'Your Majesty! There is no time to waste discussing such things now. They will kill Kalidasa... The priest and Shankuka and his men have incited the people against Kalidasa... How can you think of what Kalidasa has described at such a time?'

'You have not read the eighth canto, Nichula... If you had you wouldn't raise such a doubt,' Vikramaditya said.

'Maharaj! I was there with Kalidasa when he was completing the work. I prepared the copy of his work. I did it with my own hands...' Nichula could not control his agitation as he spoke.

'Stop, Nichula. This evening, Shankuka and Jinadeva had

come to see me again. They put the eighth canto before me and pointed out lines from it and asked me to see what Kalidasa has written... I couldn't utter a word, Nichula. Now I can't speak even a word to justify Kalidasa.'

Doubt and fear were growing like a mountain in Nichula. 'Maharaj! Did they take back the copy that they had brought with them to show you?'

'No, they left it here, for me to read. They said it would help me know Kalidasa better.'

'Maharaj! Can I see those lines that they pointed out for you?' Nichula asked.

Vikramaditya left in a hurry. He did not wait to call the servants to get the leaves for him. Within minutes he was back with the leaves in hand.

Vikramaditya pointed out many lines in the eighth canto. Seeing them, Nichula could not control his shock and anger. Jumping up he shouted, 'They have cheated us, Maharaj!' The voice was loud enough to shake the palace walls.

Vikramaditya was surprised to see the change in Nichula's behaviour. Nichula continued, 'These are not lines written by Kalidasa. I too agree that there are lines which can be said to be objectionable in what Kalidasa writes. But these lines, lines that have no meaning, with no poetic quality or grace, these have not been written by Kalidasa, Maharaj. They have cheated us, Maharaj. Your Majesty, you can imagine what they must have wanted to achieve by introducing these lines to *Kumarasambhavam*. The protest by the people is the result of their machinations. If you want you may punish him. But don't allow their conspiracy to succeed.' Nichula felt that he could not breathe as he was talking with so much excitement.

Vikramaditya looked at Nichula for a long moment. 'Who would do this? This copy has been prepared for the palace library. Who would write this other than the author, Kalidasa himself?' he asked.

'No, Maharaj. Please believe me. Kalidasa has not written these lines. I have seen the work written in Kalidasa's own hand. I prepared the copies myself. These lines have not been written by Kalidasa in the original or by me while I was making copies,' there was a strength of conviction in Nichula's words.

'How could these lines come in this copy if they were not there in the original?' Vikramaditya demanded, still unable to believe what Nichula was saying.

'Maharaj, Kalidasa had given you a copy of the work, one which I had made. You may remember, he had submitted it to you, covered in silk,' Nichula said.

Vikramaditya thought for a while, 'Yes, he had given me a copy when he came back from Devagiri. I handed it over to Amarasimha with instructions to have copies made in the library.'

'Please be kind enough to get that copy and check this canto. The lines in the leaves that Jinadeva brought to you will not be there in that. I am sure about it. You will understand what has happened,' Nichula said with confidence.

Vikramaditya still couldn't believe it. How was this possible? But he was confident that he could believe Nichula. He would not lie. Vikramaditya got up in a hurry and shouted, 'Who is there?'

The servants came running. 'Ask the commander-in-chief, Chandrasena to come here immediately,' his voice reverberated in the palace.

The soldiers ran to Chandrasena's house. They must have conveyed to their chief the change in the king's countenance, he hurried in within minutes, dressed in civilian clothes.

'Victory to the Maharaj,' he greeted Vikramaditya.

'Send some soldiers to Kalidasa's house immediately. Bring Roopadatta, the writer in the royal library and Gomedaka, the copy-writer to the assembly tomorrow in the morning,' Vikramaditya ordered.

Nichula felt relieved. He could make the king see the truth. There was nothing to be worried about now. He would see the conspiracy.

Chandrasena left immediately. Waves of anxiety kept buffeting Vikramaditya's mind. He had got some information that some men were trying to turn the people's wrath against Kalidasa. He had to do something immediately. Discussions on what was right and what was wrong could wait. If what Nichula said was true, Kalidasa was innocent. He suspected that a serious conspiracy had been hatched against Kalidasa.

'Wait, Nichula. I am coming with you. We must see Kalidasa immediately. I can't wait for him to come here after sending a message to him,' saying this Vikramaditya went inside. Within a few minutes, he was back in royal clothes. The servants were ready and as they came out of the hall, soldiers had brought horses for them.

Kalidasa lay lost in the beauty of nature bathed in moonlight and of the Kshipra that looked like the daughter of the ocean of milk. Some night birds were flying across the sky. The clouds at times covered the moon and soon moved away. He did not hear the commotion till the crowd had reached near him. Then he saw that a large group of men bearing lighted torches were near his house. Kalidasa sat up. It was an unruly crowd, shouting loudly. Trampling the plants in the courtyard, they were now close to the house. Birds that had taken shelter in the trees that grew around his house flew up with disturbed cries. The red flowers and the flames from the torches seemed to be dancing in unison.

A crowd, ready to wreak havoc, was searching for him. He knew that he would not be able to meet this crowd all alone. He decided to wait for them to leave. He saw one of them push the door open and go in. He must be searching for him. So what Nichula had feared had come true. Kalidasa moved away from the light of the moon and stood in the shade of a tree. His father and mother were inside the house. But no one would harm them.

Then he was shocked to see the man who had entered the house come out...it was one of Shankuka's men. He was leading this attack. The priest of the temple of Mahakaleshwara was also with the crowd. He could see the light come from inside the house—that man had set his house on fire! His parents were inside that house...Kalidasa lunged forward.

Then there was a shout. 'There...he is there!' The people turned around. They started moving towards him. The shadow of the tree disappeared as the flames came nearer. With a shock he saw the fire reaching the roof of his house. They had torched his house at different points. His parents! He had found them after a long period of separation. Did he bring them to Ujjaini to have them killed by these devilish people? All his works, for which he had struggled day and night, were inside the house. If all those works were burned? Kalidasa tried to run towards his house, but he was already surrounded. He realized that his fate now lay in their hands. He looked at the house on fire and the men who surrounded him. His Ujjaini! Malava, which he considered his own! Was his Ujjaini cheating him? His Ujjaini where the soul of Mallika still hovered! No, it was not Ujjaini. It was a group of selfish men. Jealous men! No, his life could not be sacrificed before a group of vicious men. Kalidasa looked at the Kshipra. Kshipra seemed to beckon him... She was waiting for him... He thought he could see the face of Mallika in the clear moonlight over the river... Was Mallika calling him? No, his parents were inside the house; he had to save them. Kalidasa tried to push the men aside and run towards his house. But he couldn't move. Someone put the torch on his dress and it started burning. The men who had come forward pushed Kalidasa into the river with his clothes on fire. Kshipra welcomed him, the torches followed Kalidasa and put themselves out as they touched the water.

Fear gripped Nichula's mind as he saw flames rising from Kalidasa's house even before he had reached there. Torches could be seen moving here and there. 'O! Mahakaleshwara!' the cry rose from his throat. Speeding up the horses they reached the house. As the soldiers had reached before them, the crowd had been controlled and they were fleeing from there. On seeing the king they shouted, 'Long live King Vikramaditya; Victory to Mahakaleshwara.' None remained to take up the responsibility of the cruel atrocity that had been committed there. No one was ready to meet the king. That was proof enough to show that what had happened there should not have happened.

Vikramaditya did not pause to respond to the greetings. As they reached the house, Nichula felt that it was all over. The flames had consumed the house. Long ago Shambhu had escaped from the forest fire and left Malava. Did that fire wait patiently to catch him again on the soil of Malava? They had all believed that Shambhu's parents had been killed in the fire in the forest. Did Kalidasa find them and bring them to Ujjaini after so many years to offer them to the fire again? Nichula realized that they were late. What was he to do now? Kalidasa's parents were in the house. Was Kalidasa also there? What had they done to Kalidasa? When Nichula left him, Kalidasa was lying on the rock on the banks of the Kshipra, looking at the moon and the stars. Did he go home? If he was inside the house... Had he been consumed by the flames? Nichula felt that tragedy had struck Kalidasa.

He had to do something to save the parents. He remembered the many manuscripts which Kalidasa had kept in the house... some of the small writings had been finished but not submitted before the king and others were not complete. They would all be destroyed by the fire. Nichula looked at the house once again. He could get inside through the door. If fate willed it, he would be able to save the people inside. He could also bring the leaves on which Kalidasa had written his works. Nichula knew that he had to do it. Kalidasa's life was a penance. All that he gained through that penance was inside that house in the form of his writings. If he could not save the original of the *Kumarasambhavam*, he would not be able to prove Kalidasa's innocence before the king. He was not sure that they would be able to get the copy given to the king from the royal library. If it was known that the king was asking for it, Shankuka and his men would easily be able to remove it. Nichula rushed towards the house without waiting for permission from Vikramaditya who was standing there like the monument of despair.

'Nichula...!' cried the king, but he was gone before Vikramaditya could stop him. He had gone into the burning house. Did he know that Kalidasa was inside? Death seemed certain for anyone who entered that burning house. He looked at Chandrasena. 'Where is Kalidasa?' he asked.

'I don't know, Your Majesty, I don't know. Before I reached here, the people had set fire to the house. I didn't get a chance to see if he was inside. The crowd was too excited to be easily controlled. But if he was inside, he would have tried to escape. That great genius must have been consumed in the wild attack of fire...or he must have felt that the fire was better than the cruelty that Ujjaini had shown him and submitted himself to the fire, to be a part of the five elements of nature again. If Kalidasa was outside, we can be assured that Ujjaini has been saved from a great sin. But his parents must have been inside the house. We do not know if these people had tied Kalidasa up inside the house before setting it on fire. If that has happened, we will have to conclude that the great genius has been confined to fire by the sinners of Ujjaini. Ujjaini will be destined to bear the consequences of that sin forever. But if he has escaped...we can find him...wherever he may be...' Chandrasena said.

Within seconds Nichula came running out, with Kalidasa's mother in his hands. One of the soldiers ran forward to support her.

'Nichula...' Vikramaditya called again but he could not go near him. The king could not believe his eyes. Nichula had rushed in once again, not listening to the king. The roof of the house would fall any moment. Once again Nichula came running out, carrying the bundles of writing leaves, tied up in his upper cloth. And then the roof caved in. The king could only see Nichula's raised hands in the flames.

'Shambhu...' the cry penetrated the king's ears. The lament of the mother seemed to pierce his heart. The old face seemed to be burning in the light of the fire. As he stood looking at her, he saw the fire of wrath spread on her face.

Vikramaditya approached the mother. He confessed that he was responsible for the death of Kalidasa. If he had acted more promptly, this would not have happened.

But this repentance which came too late did nothing to cool the heat of the mother's anger. 'Did you kill my son? He held Malava above even his life. Ujjaini was his own soul. Let the dynasty of Vikramaditya, who threw my son to these devils, be destroyed forever! Let this Ujjaini that killed his father in this fire, be ruined! All these great structures of Ujjaini will be reduced to the earth. Wild hogs will roam about in this great city! River Kshipra will dry up! Let Ujjaini be reduced to a city without any life or prosperity!'

Vikramaditya fell at the feet of that mother, 'Please do not curse me, mother,' he begged. But the mother did not hear the king as she walked to her own death in the burning house before anybody could stop her.

'If I had reached here a bit earlier, all this would not have happened. I had got some information about it even before Nichula came. I had heard about Hemabhadra shouting to the people that Mahakaleshwara could be pacified only by sacrificing Kalidasa. But some unpleasant feelings towards Kalidasa had already taken root in my mind. The descriptions in Kumarasambhavam had made some deep wounds in my mind. A thought that the author of those lines should not be on the soil of Ujjaini any longer had been formed in my mind. I was ready to think that if the people punished Kalidasa, it could be seen as the wish of Mahakaleshwara. But I had forgotten that Kalidasa's parents were in the house. And I didn't think that the people would go to this extent. If what Nichula said is true, I am a sinner... I am responsible for the death of all these people. I have been defeated...' These thoughts passed through Vikramaditya's mind.

He had seen Kalidasa often on the rock on the banks of the Kshipra. Vikramaditya walked towards that spot with a secret hope that Kalidasa would be there lost in meditation, not aware of all that had happened around him. But the place was empty. He looked at the river... Was it Kalidasa's boat that was moving along the water? Would Kalidasa leave without telling him? Vikramaditya was not sure whether he had actually seen his friend in the light of the moon... Or had it only been a reflection of the hope in his heart? But it gave his heart some consolation that he had seen a shadow on the waves of the Kshipra. Still, his mind reminded him that Ujjaini would never be freed from the curse of the three people who had lost their lives in the fire.

~